LORNA MITCHELL

THE REVOLUTION OF SAINT JONE

The Women's Press

sf

First published by The Women's Press Limited 1988
A member of the Namara Group
34 Great Sutton Street, London EC1V 0DX

British Library Cataloguing in Publication Data available

ISBN 0–7043–4118–2

Typeset by MC Typeset, Chatham, Kent
Printed and bound in Great Britain by
Cox & Wyman Ltd, Reading

1

Jone Grifan, newly ordained priest of the Church of the Rational Cosmos, walked through her tutor's garden for the last time. She sat down for a moment by one of the Frangipani bushes at the side of the path. As she breathed in the perfume and felt the balm of warm air on her face, she could already picture herself in a frame of the future looking at Now as the past and longing to return. She wished she could stop the turning reel. If the past was already dead, couldn't she kill the future? The future was a year, and maybe more, in Skosha, one of the Yukeys, a small cluster of cold, damp little islands off the north-west coast of Yurope. The image of the cold and damp seeped into her mind and made her shiver. She moved on.

The tutor's palace was part of Mayry Theoversity, the second most important seat of Krischan indoctrination in Strylya. The year was 401 PA (Post-Armageddon) and Jone had only made this year's crop of ordinations by a hair's breadth, with a Sanctification Quotient of 120.003. That was why she was being sent to the Yukeys – the lower your SQ, the further away from civilisation you were sent.

Jone walked into the palace savouring every curved-space geometric shape. She hadn't often been in here during the last few months. She had been too busy organising protestant fasts and pilgrimages. That was the reason for her low SQ. She wasn't nervous about seeing her tutor, she knew he was tolerant of student protestantism, but she was regretful that she hadn't basked in his paternal ions more often.

The tutor welcomed her into his room with an offer of a psalm stimulation electrode from his very fashionable altar.

'There's a marvellous new anagram symphony just out from Wittgenstein Priory, want to try it?'

Jone shook her head. She knew the pleasure of psalm brain play would be no pleasure, not today. The tutor smiled with paternal sympathy, and moved on to the subject of her mission placing. He had a film chapter on Embra, the township she was going to, and suggested they watch it first.

The chapter was a typical bit of Mission Control propaganda. If Jone had been watching it as a student with her protestant chums they would have been pouring scorn on it. Now it was quite different. This was reality, and the sarcasm felt like dryness in her throat. 'Embra,' the voice said, 'has come a long way in forty years since it was brought into the Kingdom. The saints' and Blessed/ Venerable quarters are situated north of the river, and are now fully holomorphic.' The cameras swept over the area and Jone drew herself in tightly. Holomorphism (buildings designed in a variety of shapes by curved space geometry) tended to attract all the best mathematical talent in Strylya. In Embra it looked like either the best mathematical talent was expressed elsewhere, or it didn't have any. The shapes were so banal and unimaginative. Jone wasn't sure she wouldn't have preferred the traditional cube. It would have been more honest. If she hadn't been feeling so frightened and sad, she would have felt angry. And she would have been angry at the lack of weather-free domes too. What did the commentator mean, saying, 'Embra hadn't achieved high enough communal merit'? Surely it was a right, not a reward.

The cameras moved over to the south side of the river, to Plotin, the ethnic quarter. Rows upon rows of boxes fanning out in semi-circles round the large green patch: the grounds of Jondik Abbey. This was where Jone would be fulfilling her mission vocation, helping to Krischanise the young ethnics between the ages of twelve and seventeen, preparing them for their baptism as adult ethnic Krischans. Fear now quelled any thought of protest in Jone's mind. Fear at the thought of attempting to civilise ethnic youth. The cameras panned through the streets. They were clean and tidy enough, but the people looked like walking symbols of the Kayos, the time before the Coming of the Kingdom. A riot of dissonant-coloured clothing and hairy heads. Even baptised ethnics didn't have to shave their heads and they very conspicuously didn't. It made Jone feel queasy just looking at them in a chapter. How would she cope with it close up?

'Embra still has a long way to go to reach the level of true

Krischan civilisation, but with the dedication of the Abbey saints and community salvationists, it will one day soon play its full part in the creation of Almyty Gawd.' Jone groaned. However dismal and awful the subject of a mission chapter, it always ended up with this sentimental rubbish about Almyty Gawd: the great computer mind that was one day going to replace mere physical humanity. Very few saints actually believed it could be achieved, and a fair few were atheists. It was an empty piety that was trotted out by the Bishopry as a justification for everything they did or thought. And there was a perfect example: what could be more remote from Alymyty Gawd than this dismal little settlement?

When the chapter had finished the tutor smiled ruefully at Jone again. He really felt for her.

'I know it's going to be very difficult for you at first, but believe it or not, people do get used to it. If you can survive the first few months, you may find real fulfilment in it. You know, it's a statistical fact, not just my fantasy, that the rebels make the best missionaries in the end. I think it's their independence of thought and idealism. If you can hang on to your ideals in that sort of deprived environment, you will be able to change things.'

If she hadn't been ensconced in a floform in a superbly mathematical palace in sunny Strylya, Jone might have believed him.

When Jone stepped off the photoplane at Nace teleport it was as if the hollow shell of her student protestantism lay broken at her feet. The sky was clouded over and reminded her of a weather-free dome that had malfunctioned and stopped breathing. The ugly blobs of Nace's holomorphs made her nauseous, as if her face was being pushed in a bowl of white sucrose. She sat in the underground train in a kind of daze and by the time she had walked through the door to her mansion, she was ready to burst into tears. Normally she would have soul-controlled such an outbreak of sensual expression, but the sheer lonely desolation of her situation made her resentfully ignore her soul. Who cared how idistic her emotions were here? For a whole year at least, there would be no escape from this unmathematical hole and she seriously doubted if her soul had developed the wave-lengths to cope with all the dormant idistic negativity it would stir up in her.

After unpacking her surplices and robes she set about stacking her miserably small number of tapes into her altar and visional. Not just a sense of hollowness but an intense regret swept over her. All that time she had spent on crusades and pilgrimages she could have spent creating beautiful mathematical patterns to plug into, to help her escape from this horrible place. It wasn't that she now thought the ideals of protestants were wrong. On the contrary, Embra's deprivations confirmed the protestant view. But in Mayri Theoversity, with all its intellectual freedom, it had been so easy to indulge in the avocation, the hobby, of protestantism. And what had it achieved? Instead of changing the world, all Jone Grifan had ended up with was her own quota of deprivations.

On her first day at the Abbey Jone was relieved to find out that the catachumens (as the young ethnics preparing for baptism were called) weren't arriving till the next day. She was ushered into the saints' communion chapel (the comm, as the priests called it) as soon as she arrived. Its windows looked out on to the very low hills in the distance. The window was high enough to give a reasonable view of the sky and Jone was glad she had some basic cloud geometry. She would need to improve on it if she wanted to retain her mathematical sanity.

She found she had been put beside some of the other ministers in her denomination: Thyatira. The woman next to her introduced herself as Fess Orlam. She looked to be in her mid-forties, thin, with dark brown eyes, elegant body movements and a conspiratorial smile. Jone warmed to her at once, and answered her questions openly. Fess assured her she would get used to the drabness of Embra, and that there were compensations. If Jone was a keen scenery computer, the surrounding countryside was a delight.

'How do you think you'll handle the cats?' she asked Jone.

'Cats?'

'Sorry, that's what the catachumens call themselves and so do we.'

Jone shrugged. She had truly no idea.

'Well, don't worry. We'll give you all the help we can. They will respond to someone with fresh ideas, and someone who cares for them. But you have to have the discipline too. Start by being very firm and then get to know them as individuals.'

'Excuse me butting in,' said a tall burly man sitting opposite Fess, 'but I heard that bit about starting off firm. Believe me, that's absolutely essential. Take my advice, use your rack, right at the beginning. A quick burst of maximum to a ringleader sinner and you'll have no more trouble from then on. Believe me, it works. You'll hardly ever have to use it again but it acts as an ultimate deterrent. Ever seen people training horses on the Vulgate Bible? It works exactly the same way. Remember you are working with zoologically raised people here. That's not so far from animal conditioning is it?'

He slumped back in his floform and the man next to him immediately engaged him in another conversation. Jone swallowed hard, relieved to be saved from a response. Just at a point when she was beginning to hope things would not be so bad, that hope had been instantly drained off. The rack! Up till now Jone had only associated pain stimulators with Sinner Atonement Colonies. Her only sight of them had been in adventure chapters on the Vulgate Bible. At theoversity she had been told that very few institutions in the colonies still used them. Why, oh why, did she have to land in one of those very few?

Fess could read Jone's reaction. She gave her a sympathetic, wry smile.

'Didn't you know we used the rack here? Quite a few ministers don't use it, but they tend to be very experienced and have a lot of confidence. For a novice it's probably the best thing – if you use it the way Jak Leeam suggests.' She pursed her lips and paused for a moment. 'Please do think hard about that one. It might be one of the compromises you'll have to make. Well, at least you'll have time to think about it, since you won't be indoctrinating on your own for the first few weeks. You'll know what they're like by then. I suppose it is a bit like taming wild animals, but wild animals have their good points too.'

As she finished her sentence, she glimpsed the comm door opening. She turned her head to look. 'Oh, oh, here comes our Father. Have you met him?'

'Yes, he wasn't very nice to me.'

'Don't worry, he's not very nice to many people. He's retiring soon. I think there'll be a lot of changes for the good around here when he does.'

No one else in the room paid any attention to the entrance of the Abbot and the Dean; they carried on with their animated discussions about their vacations. Already after half an hour in the comm they were looking as if they'd been in the same position for

5

years. Much to Jone's puzzlement, since nobody seemed to be watching him, the noise began to abate when the Dean rose to speak. When silence did descend he didn't have a lot to say. First he welcomed the novices and then he handed out the term's programs.

'No problems with these, much the same as last term. The main change is more intensive group therapy with those approaching baptism. Also, rearranged timetables to allow more use of the sacred games machines. It says a lot for the dedication of our ministers that we have twenty more catachumens ready for sacred games. So without further ado, I'll hand you over to Abbot NkDod.'

Jone started when she heard the Skoshan prefix. In Strylya, designations of ethnic origin were regarded officially as racist and never used. It didn't do anything to curb saintly snobbery in social intercourse, but it did stop discrimination in filing systems. But perhaps she shouldn't leap to hasty conclusions. Maybe it was a badge of honour here, that you had made it against the odds.

Abbot NkDod arose, like a giant statue being hauled upright. The face pale and deeply lined, the body lean but strong, he looked hewn from Skosha's granite. He leaned slightly backward and clutched his surplice in front of him. His voice had a rock-like edge:

'If you switch on your hand bibles you will see I have inserted my commandments. These are the foundations of the Krischan way of life in this Abbey. I'm not here to tell you how to supervise the catachumens at play and at prayer, etc. You should have your own ideas on that – though I'm sure I could still teach some of you a few tricks that never fail. However, my main concern is that you should administer these commandments. I drew them up some years ago and I can assure you they have been by far the best method of introducing these people to Krischan morality. Mission Control gives us such vague guidance, being so far away. They think a few words of kindness are enough. But these rules of mine are very practical. Insist on them with the catachumens at all times and you are well on your way to winning them for the Church. I will go through them so you can understand them fully.'

He paused and scanned his audience for the first time, picking out the faces with eyes like hooks. A smile had not yet appeared on his face and made no sign of ever doing so.

'Before I start, a word to our novices. You must be very clear how different the ethnics are from you. First, they have been

6

brought into the world by zoological reproduction. They are brought up in separate gender clans, either by their ovagenitor and her siblings, and then later, if they're male, by their spermogenitor. None of them has been born into the luxury of a Nursery with all its material facilities and its nurses and guardians precisely selected by the most sophisticated theological criteria. In short, they're heathens. And to assume they have achieved anything but the minimum veneer of Krischanism is a stupid and terrible mistake. If you imagine they're your equals, you'll get nowhere with them. They will never be your equals, most of them will never get beyond 90 Grace Quotient. That's why they need these commandments. That's the only morality they're capable of understanding. Very well, I'll begin.'

And so, just as he said he would, he went through the commandments, reading them out slowly and emphatically, with added bits of explanation after each one.

Emotions welled up in Jone so much that she could feel the dial on her soul-control quivering in the red. She released a minute amount of relaxant to her finger nerve-ends, then got to work guiding the dial back into the analytic wave-lengths of the black. First, there was astonishment and anger that the Abbot should be treating his priests as if they were children, reading out to them rules they could perfectly well understand. Then there was fear at the thought of having to impose these commandments on the ethnics, presumably against their will. Did they really need all these rules prohibiting non-medical physical contact, spelling out hygiene requirements, restraining their movements, and so on? These were all norms of conduct that a saint never thought about consciously and it made the image of the ethnics as 'wild animals' begin to seem realistic. But her strongest feeling in need of purgation was humiliation. That was her reaction to his forbidding wearing pagan colours, using ethnic language and playing music. The very things that Jone had ardently advocated must be not suppressed but transformed during her mission training at Mayri Theoversity. She remembered the reassurances and encouragement of her tutor. The Abbot was absolutely right. Mission Control was very far away. The memory of her urbane tutor in his highly original-shaped private chapel was like an absurd dream in contrast to this grim, relentless sermonizer in this grim, relentlessly boring rectangle of a room.

When the Abbot finished, the Dean spoke about what they were doing for the rest of the day and that was the introductory meeting over. The pair swiftly departed. As soon as they went out, the older members of the priesthood, who had appeared to be in a state of suspended animation during this introductory meeting, squirmed to life again.

'Every term, he does this, every term –'

'He stands there and lectures us as if we were the cats –'

'As if we didn't know the rules better than he does. We're the ones who have to put them into practice everyday while he sits there in his command base tuned into his altar all day.'

It was as if they were coughing to clear phlegm from their throats. After a few minutes of grumble they settled back comfortably into the topic that really mattered: the vacations.

Jone beat a hasty retreat to the ashram, which proved to be the most pleasant space she had come across so far. It was decorated solely with one or two metrifacts, obviously executed by abbey catachumens – unpretentious but creative. Jone was able to reach a state of Samadhi by her sixth yoga position. Thus refreshed, she made her way to the denomination chaplain's playroom, where the denomination gathering was to be held.

Play was the heart of the Krischanisation of the young. All over the Krischan empire young people sat before their gawds, their computers, playing 'Apocalypse', at mundane, spiritual, sacred or celestial levels. 'Apocalypse' owed its origins to the ancient game of chess, but instead of the hand moving pieces over a chequered board there was a bank of dials and keys manipulating lights on a display screen, in a great variety of movements, shapes and speeds. The player played against the gawd, programmed at the required level. The purpose of 'Apocalypse' was to purify the brain of idism, that is, of irrational passion, through the exercise of logic, concentration and intuition grounded in rational disciplined thinking. Jone was well aware of the fundamental protestant criticism of 'Apocalypse'. It was all very fine in itself, but did it really purify the brain? Didn't the luxury of the saints' environment count for far more? All this she had to put behind her. She would be spending most of the year ahead indoctrinating, or attempting to indoctrinate 'Apocalypse', whether she liked it or not.

The moment she stepped inside the playroom the good effect of the yoga evaporated. It was the smell that hit first: human body odour, faint, but quite clear. Why were the cats not given uniforms?

Then the sight of the games machines: old, worn, scratched, bits broken off. Why were they not regularly replaced? And of course, no metrifact decorations or floforms. She slumped down on one of the seats near the chaplain's console, and guessed at the answers.

Her thoughts were disturbed by movement behind her. Another minister, a man, walked in. He smiled and sat down, not quite next to her. He had a muscular, physical presence which made her instinctively nervous, and when he announced himself as Mik ArBrenan, it reinforced her inhibition. Ar, like Nk, denoted ethnic origin, in his case from the even less developed island of Ern. The heavy way he moved his body and the shy way he avoided looking straight in her eyes when he spoke betrayed the self-conscious masculinity of a zoological upbringing.

'Having problems adjusting to the environment?' he said. 'I know how you feel. Even though I was brought up in an even less civilised place than this, I found it hard coming back after theoversity. You can take to the lap of luxury very quickly.'

Jone, too inhibited to talk about herself, asked about the state of the machines.

'It wouldn't make any difference if they were replaced more often, they'd just mess them up again.'

'Are they really that destructive?'

'I don't believe they are really, the truth is they're bored. "Apocalypse" is completely irrelevant to most of them. I mean, it's pointless, you can't purify the brain unless that brain has had positive attitude conditioning as well, and you can't get that unless they see that the Krischan way of life is positive for them. And I can't say I blame them for not seeing it here.'

Though outwardly still inhibited by his manner, inside Jone warmed to him as she had to Fess. There was protestantism outside of Mayri, after all. Her reply almost burst out of her with relief.

'There doesn't seem to be anything positive here, just these sordid rooms, and – NkDod's set of don'ts.'

'Yes, well, NkDod. Don't get me started on that subject – I'll tell you something, it's him that makes the place sordid, not the building. As a matter of fact, I was brought up and indoctrinated in places far worse than this, but it didn't matter. That's because we had a marvellous indoctrinator. He took us out and showed us what Armageddon did, what it was like before it, got us landscape computing right from the start. That's how we came to believe in

Krischanism, because we loved him and he loved us and inspired us with his love of Krischanism.'

For the first time Mik looked for more than a second into her eyes. 'Sorry, I mustn't start sermonising. You'll get enough of that from NkDod and our Chaplain.'

Jone was beginning to wish she wasn't inhibited by his zoological masculinity, for she felt that here was a human landscape worth computing. The more she was impressed by what he said, the less she was able to think of a reply, and the entrance of the rest of the denomination ministers was as much of a relief as a disappointment.

With a welcoming smile at Jone, Fess placed herself between Jone and Mik and introduced her to Blane Milar, who sat down on the other side of Mik. A few years older than Fess, Jone thought, full-faced and a little on the stout side, she had the confident and kindly air of an experienced maternaliser. She turned to Jone and smiled.

'What do you think of the Abbot's commandments? You're probably thinking, how do you get to inspire them to play well if you have to spend all your time stopping them doing what they want?'

'Now don't twist things, Blane!' It was the Thyatira Chaplain NkCroom himself who burst in, taking the centre of the stage behind his console. 'Control of idism comes before everything. You know NkDod and I have had our disagreements, but I'm in complete agreement with him on that score. They've got to have a moral code holding them in check. They've got to start off learning the habit of obedience and you know I'm talking from my own experience.'

He nodded his head towards Jone, from which she understood he was about to address her. An older generation zoologically raised, she thought, who finds it even more difficult to look a woman straight in the eye.

'I'm a Plotinian you see, still live here as a matter of fact. I love these people, I'm part of them, that's why I know what they need – I needed it too. I needed my idism held in check before I found any spirituality. There is only one way of holding idism down and its not by dropping people into some hedonarea with 24-hour visionals, like some moderns at Mission Control seem to think, and it isn't done by fixing souls on to them that sedate the limbic system. It's done by forming the habit of obedience, right here,' he tapped his forehead furiously, 'in the cortex. No one has found any other way, no one.'

NkCroom spoke as if he had to thrust each sentence out of himself against some internal resistance. Jone wondered if he was still keeping his idism 'in check', and if so, was the method really so effective?

Fess came in, sounding maternally concerned to help NkCroom in his struggle. 'But Robby, you know it isn't just forcing them to obey as the Abbot thinks. You admit yourself there's got to be love in it, and we know you have plenty of that.'

Mik didn't want to discuss commandments. 'How about a flick through the bright ideas store?' he suggested. This acted like a switch to start Chaplain NkCroom musing. As he spoke, he leaned his head to one side, furrowed his brow and stroked it with his fingers.

'There's a lot that's worth watching on the Vulgate Bible, you know, especially the evangelists. This series on the martyrs of Gandol, have you been watching it?' He directed the question at the opposite wall and didn't wait for a reply. 'That prophet, Vysali, I really identify with her. This business of being on the edge of spiritual death, all the time, spiritual blackouts you might say. Oh, I know what she was talking about. It's, it's a state of utter hopelessness, a loss of faith in the whole process towards building Almyti Gawd. Don't you have an inkling of it sometimes – when you see all this stuff on the Vulgate, all the outbreaks of heresy and satanism everywhere? Don't you find it difficult to believe sometimes that we'll ever all get to be one in the final great mind?'

No one ventured an opinion and he rambled on down the meandering pathway of his dark states of mind, and into the cellars of his family history. Blane and Fess interposed the odd ironic teasing comment and Mik smiled benevolently as if he were nostalgically remembering his old indoctrinator. The forefront of Jone's consciousness was fascinated by this window into the colonial Krischan mind, but the deeper background was anxiety about the next day and this was no help at all.

Towards the end of the session NkCroom's wrist-bible buzzed and he left abruptly, leaving the 'admin' to the rest of them. Blane turned to Jone. 'He's a marvellous preacher, but a hopeless chaplain. But don't worry, we're here, if problems come up.' Jone was grateful, but thought, 'If!'

Back in her domicile that night she put the people who had entered her experience in boxes on a mental shelf. Fess and Blane: marvellous maternalisers but hardly religious fellow travellers. Mik: a religious fellow traveller, perhaps, but coming from a very foreign place. And NkCroom and NkDod, though very different people, in the same box, utterly alien monuments of a passing colonial class. When she went to face the 'wild animals' tomorrow, she would still be very much on her own.

2

Jone's first sight of the catachumens was through the comm window. They were gathering in the courtyard, waiting to be allowed in. And a chilling sight it was: the walking breathing opposites of the Abbot's commandment. The initial assault on the senses was the crude single colours, predominantly red on the females, green on the males. And then the hair; like piles of cut grass and luridly coloured too. For the first time Jone really appreciated the saint's shaven head; the hair was a mathematical abomination. She looked at the clothing in more detail. It was sewn cloth. Didn't they use their mannapoints for surplices? Then again why should they if they didn't want to? Her conditioned revulsion was fighting against her own ideals. Her thoughts were interrupted by Dean Paul, hovering behind her. He had come to give her tapes of her assigned maternal charges. 'Luner and Geever,' he said, beaming first at Jone, then at Blane, who was sitting beside her. 'That'll be a challenge for Reverend Grifan, eh Blane? Perhaps you could give her some sage advice.' And off he went.

Jone turned on the tape: two scowling hairy-topped faces of adolescent girls. She took a deep breath. Blane smiled at her, thoughtfully, compassionately.

'Well, I think they're all challenges in different ways. But Luner and Geever, well, they made themselves a few enemies among the ministry last term, but you know, there's a lot that's likeable about them, easier to get at as a maternaliser than in the playroom. I suppose its Luner who's the problem, Geever's her sidekick. But I think people have been unfair to her. She's had a hard time. Well you know, with the ovagenitor being the infantile need servicer it can be so precarious. You see, she left. Left the clan, went off to Lundin when Luner was small. It had a devastating effect. I mean there wasn't anyone specific to take over. She's been left with a lot of frustrated infantile needs. But she does respond to someone who's sympathetic. You know what you should do? Get hold of them as soon as possible and talk to them, today if you can, get to know them as individuals. If you earn their trust you could have a lot of influence on them.'

A few minutes later the siren went. Jone looked round. Other novices, she noticed, also looked round. No one else gave the slightest indication anything had happened and went on drinking their fruitjuices and chatting. Then, at a mystic moment, neither too early nor too late, the fruitjuices were drunk, the seedcake swallowed, conversation dead, and the comm emptied itself. Outside, the 'wild animals' seemed to be in a tame mood, induced, Jone guessed, by their apathy about being back at the Abbey. Only when Reverend Leeam and another senior minister came up to the barrier at the door did they spring to life in a rush to be at the front. Reverend Leeam whipped out his microphone and began to organise them, first into male and female, then by age from the front. His tone was steadily and smoothly sarcastic. So confident of his authority was he, that he could be almost relaxed. While he directed, the rest of the ministers moved the bodies. The novices meanwhile were given the easiest task of registering the IDs at the checkposts.

Since the youngest were to be in front, the older ones began to pretend they were young. Jone, not knowing any of them, found it difficult to tell. So many of them were so small and so underdeveloped. But the priests, who did know who was who, were roused to fury by these games and began to flourish their paralysers. Directly confronted with one, the catachumens would move to their right place, but not without broad grins of self-satisfaction at their success in providing amusement for their friends. The place was beginning to wake up. When all the sorting had been done, Reverend Leeam managed to silence them. Order reigned for a second or two; until the front crews of girls and boys moved forward. Pushing and shoving and struggling to be ahead erupted, and the priests were working hard again.

As the first group of girls approached Jone's checkpoint, one of the young male priests pounced forward and forced them to stop.

He moved towards one of them menacingly and Jone recognised at once her maternalisee, Luner NkBerber. The young minister spoke with a surprising amount of bitterness.

'How did we manage to miss you? Been hiding inside some poor little girl's coat?'

Luner returned the bitterness. 'Naw, You're just blind.'

The minister's reaction was to hold the paralyser to her throat. 'You're going to end up in deep trouble this term, that's one thing I'm certain of. Get back to your crew.'

As quick as a flash she pushed the paralyser away from her throat and was going out with her back directly to him, neatly combining defiance with avoidance of trouble.

When Luner returned through the door with her own crew, Jone gestured to her to come through her checkpoint. She was about to speak when Luner, smiling broadly, flicked the arm without the ID band past the scanner and sailed through the gate. Jone's mind had been so intent on what she was hoping to say that she was flustered, and instead of calling Luner back, she moved after her, leaving the gate open to let a dozen or so others gleefully pile through. 'Get back behind the gate!' she shouted, more aware of how unsure her voice must sound than anything else. It took her a few more moments to realise she would have to shut the gate to stop any more coming through. An older minister, quick to see something was amiss, came forward. 'What's going on here?' The ones inside the barrier turned to him with complacent smiles.

'We canny get back oot, the gate's shut.'

Jone pushed herself to maintain some control.

'Just queue up at the scanner in a line, and you'll get checked as quickly as possible.'

The older priest stood back, but made his presence felt. The cats queued up but managed to have plenty of quiet fun getting in each other's way. When it was Luner's turn, Jone said, 'Please can you wait by the console, I want to ask you something.' She was putting herself in an impossible situation. Either she made an arrangement to see Luner now and hold up the queue or have Luner hanging around waiting to be talked to, and getting up to some mischief. The third possibility of not bothering at all never crossed her mind. Reverend Milar's advice to do something right away about getting to know Luner and Geever had got stuck at the front of her mind. By the time she had finished with the queue on the inside of the barrier, the ones outside were beginning to push on it and the ministers on that side were getting furious at the bottle-neck. Jone was forced to get on with the checking and in frustration she said to Luner, 'You'd better go on.'

Luner shrugged, 'It disny matter, ma division went through the ither checkpoint ages ago. I'll help ye, Rev, make sure they dinny get through wi' oot bein' checked.'

She gave Jone a disarming smile and Jone was disarmed. At once Luner entered into the role of checker, joshing those who came through about behaving themselves. The victims took it good-humouredly and let themselves be scanned dutifully. One of those coming through was heard to comment, 'She'll be puttin' a razor to her hair an' gettin' a wee black cap next.'

'Dinny you be targy,' said Luner, and waved her arm aggressively at the speaker. This gesture was noticed by one of the other ministers who strode over to her. It was the same priest who'd had the confrontation with Luner at the door.

'What are you doing here? Why aren't you in your own division?'

Jone was too busy ID-checking to break in and Luner replied, 'The Rev here telt me tae stay here. A'm helpin'.'

'Helping? Who are you trying to kid? You've no business being here and you know it.'

Jone, incensed by the fact that he was ignoring her, slammed the gate shut and turned to him.

'I asked her to stay here. She's not doing any harm, please let me get on with the checking.'

This time she surprised herself with the firmness of her voice. The man glared at her, then turned to Luner.

'You watch your step or you'll be more than welcome on my rack.'

Jone intuited that only his loyalty to the ministry made him direct his anger at Luner and not at her. At last the line went through and Jone could tell Luner she was her maternaliser and arrange to meet her that morning. Luner was delighted and when Jone told her to go she went meekly as a lamb. Jone felt like bursting, whether with tears or laughter, she wasn't quite sure. Through sheer ineptitude, she had blundered into the role of Luner's ally against one of her evident enemies.

One hour later Jone and Luner and Geever NkBerber were sitting on the Abbey standard semi-mobile furniture in Jone's base.

Jone was sipping fruitjuice. The girls were sipping the same fruitjuice with hot water and sucrose tablets added. The instant she had offered it, the girls had brought out their capsules. Jone tapped her soul dial to restrain her shock. She had won their approval with her reaction to the priest at the checkpoint, she was not about to lose it.

'A heard aw aboot ye tellin' Skwyer where tae get off,' Geever had said as soon as she came in. 'Good on ya, Rev.'

Jone had not discouraged them and now Luner was complaining, 'He's always pickin' on me. A hate him. He's only been here a year an' he thinks he's right tough ken, goin' round thinkin' he's a spaceking, ken.'

'Which is a right laugh,' continued Geever, ''cos everybody jist takes the shard oot ae him an' he's always havin' tae use his rack. Naebody likes him, they aw think he's a gas pod. Mind you, we get a good laugh at Skwyer, but that Leeam, he's a real sado –'

Jone was worried an avalanche of hate was beginning and decided to call a halt.

'Are there any ministers you like?'

Luner looked doubtful in a way that suggested she just wasn't in a positive mood.

The more cheerful Geever responded, 'Oh aye, Rev Orlam's right nice an' Rev Direm –'

Luner interrupted, 'Maist ae them are awright, A suppose, but they're aw saints, ken whit A mean? They're aw intae the same game – trying tae make us Krischan, A mean.'

'And you don't want to be Krischan?'

'Well, A mean it's aw just playin' borin' "Apocalypse", an' the saints tellin' ye, "Dinny dae this" an' "Dinny dae that," 'cos it's agin the commandments. Ken, aw the time it's stoppin' ye daein' whit ye want, havin' tae pit these on for instance –' and she pulled at her uniform in a gesture of disgust.

'But uniforms are, well, practical. How else do you eliminate bodily secretions?'

'Oh aye, the ones that work do,' said Geever indignantly. 'But ye should see the ones we get. Saggy bits aw over the place. Look at this one –' she lifted her skirt to show a patch where there was no contact with the skin – 'See, they gie us rubbish an' then tell us off fur smellin'. It's no fair is it?'

'A dinny ken whit's wrong wi' smellin' anyway,' said Luner in a mildly sulky tone.

'Well, the way we see it is, it's distracting. I mean, say I'm looking at the Bible in here and there's a lot of noise outside. I can't concentrate. Well, distraction comes through the sense of smell, too.'

'A'm no distracted by it, an the ither senses dinny distract me either. A kin dae ma avocations at hame wi' the Vulgy full on, an' music on –'

Jone saw a way of trying to make the talk more positive again and asked Luner about her zoology and botany avocations, which had been referred to in the file. But this only got the two of them on to more complaints about not getting to do avocations at the Abbey in the daytime. Jone gave up trying to defend Jondik Abbey, 'All grace assessment units aren't like this one, you know –'

Luner interrupted angrily, 'Would ye no ken, it's always Plotin that's worse than everywhere else.'

'Aye, they're scared ae us. They think we're right savages, that's why we get the ballistics like NkDod an' Leeam,' agreed Geever.

Jone saw no reason why she could not tell them that NkDod was retiring. They had heard rumours but none of the other ministers had told them directly. It was another alliance she was forging with them and she felt good about it. The prospect of NkDod retiring conjured up wonderful pictures for the girls of being able to wear their pagan colours and listen to music.

'Well, yes, maybe, provided they're mathematical,' said Jone.

'Oh aye, there's always got tae be somethin' Krischan aboot it,' said Luner, with a weary cynicism.

Jone couldn't tell how serious it was. She looked at Luner closely. The cynicism didn't show on her face. It was smooth and would have taken a tan well in a better climate. She had long, straight, dark hair. By adjusting her soul to ignore the grease and dandruff (which wasn't that great, comparatively) Jone could see its mathematical qualities. She could see them even more in the face. There was a symmetry between the dark eyes, the straight nose and sharp chin that was computable. Geever was not uncomputable either, broader-faced with blonde, wavy hair, less appealing to Jone, but that was only a matter of taste; her appearance was just as mathematical. Maybe it was their attractiveness that made them troublemakers.

Geever was wondering why Jone wanted to see them and she told them she wanted to try to get to know them. 'Ye'll have tae come oot wi' us on Holydays then,' insisted Geever. Jone hardly gave a thought to the unorthodoxy of the suggestion, pleased they had taken to her that much. Luner suggested going to the 'wars'. Discovering Jone didn't know what wars were, the girls entered into a description with great enthusiasm. The wars were petro-mobile races which took place out in the 'wilderness', the countryside near Embra kept as a reserve free from the direct rule of the Church. The races turned out also to include fighting between the teams in the petros. Jone had to work hard with her fear-of-violence wave-lengths, an attunement she'd only just got to grips with in her pre-mission training. She was saved from committing herself by a knocking on the door. Two female friends of Luner and Geever burst in, and presented themselves to Jone as Molner and Zaner. They were less mathematical in appearance than Luner and Geever, to Jone more typical Plotinian. Zaner was thin and dark-haired. Molner was distinguished by a bad complexion that made Jone reflect angrily on their medical deprivations. Still, however they looked, the two of them were full of sharp, ebullient humour. When Jone pointed out she wasn't their maternaliser, Zaner said, 'That's awright, we'll no hold it against ye.' Her attention was drawn to Luner's files on Jone's console and Jone had to grab them from her, telling her they were confidential.

'Does it say horrible things aboot her?'

'No, it's just a record of Luner's Krischan progress.'

'It must be empty, then,' said Molner.

'Dinny be targy,' said Luner, evidently hurt.

Jone was surprised at first, given Luner's negative attitude to Krischan indoctrination. Then it clicked. She had called it 'progress' and progress implied failure and no one wants to be labelled a failure. She had a lot to learn about handling them sensitively. She locked the files in the drawer and said,

'It isn't horrible. Whoever compiled it, and I don't know who it was, obviously likes you. It's really pretty enthusiastic.'

Luner flushed. Jone guessed she was both pleased and annoyed she didn't have something to get aggressive about. Luner diverted the embarrassment by turning to Molner.

'Rev Grifan wants tae get tae know us an' A suggested she should come wi' us tae the wars on Sabbath.'

'Oh aye, it's the Krados vee the Dokes –'

'Yes, I've heard. I think I'm not ready for that yet. The smell of petrol might make me faint.' This had come into her head as an easier option than talking about violence.

'Ooh,' said Zaner, 'ye dinny huv tae worry aboot the smell o' petrol. Naebody wears uniforms in the wilderness.'

'Aye, but she disny huv tae worry aboot stinkin' folk,' added Molner. 'She'll be too busy bokin' at the stink ae dogs' trodge.'

The girls collapsed in fits of laughter at Jone's expression. She was disgusted of course, but by using her soul to control it and making no critical remarks, she hoped she was gaining their confidence by allowing them to make fun of her.

The talk continued for another twenty minutes or so. Jone tried to keep roughly to her script by asking them about the morning's medical inspection, but the girls were singularly uninterested in their own state of health, physical or mental. They were much more interested in poking fun at either the machinery or the medical officers, or in expressing their annoyance at being 'told off'. Being told carbohydrates or cholesterol weren't good for them was being stopped from doing what they wanted, and anyway that was what the medical inspections were for: to get their nutritional injections.

When they had gone through all this Jone felt she had had enough and sent them off. After they had gone, she realised the session had tired her. It was having to hold back criticism and 'telling off'. No, it wasn't that. It was also being unable to put the Krischan case more positively. Yes, that was the real cause of her fatigue. And could she really blame them for their chaotic barbarities? Born and bred in such an ugly environment? Oh, she knew the dogmas very well. If they were freely given environmental provisions, they would destroy them. Spiritual brains had to come from spiritual habitats. She also knew the heretical answer: no one had ever tried giving them all the provisions saints enjoyed and seeing what really happened. If only she could do it, if only she could have a little fusion plant of her own – what a silly dream. Not only did she not have her own fusion plant, she had no idea what she did have to give.

3

It was Turquoday morning and Crew Delta, denomination Thyatira, were in NkCroom's playroom with NkCroom and Jone. Today's competition was between Thyatira Church and the Latonian Barbarians, and NkCroom had spent a lengthy period at the beginning of playtime tediously extracting drops of blood from stones: the names of the Bits in the competition.

'Now, it's important to remember what these bits stand for. What was Thyatira, Zaner?'

'A church in the Kayos times, Reverend.'

'Yes, yes, a bit more, a bit more. You always give the answer that needs the least effort. Come on, girl, open your mouth and speak.'

'Well, eh, church meant different frae what we mean. Like wi' us the church is where you go an' register yer virtue points an' that, but in they days –'

'Which days?'

'Before the coming of the Kingdom, Rev, in the Kayos. Eh, churches were like groups, eh, krischans who, like, lived tegether when everyone else wis heathen.'

'All right, someone else. Daner, what did the Thyatirans do?'

Daner was one of the more cooperative girls. 'They guarded a nuclear missile site frae the barbarians, who'd have used it tae blow up the world again, Rev.'

NkCroom stood back and thought for a moment. 'Right. You see, ah, I know you think it's just shapes on a viewing screen but I want you to see the real people behind those symbols. Those brave, brave, people who struggled to make the world fit for the coming of the Kingdom. Don't do that!' His face went even redder than it normally was. 'Girl, you are not an animal in a zoological park. I will not tolerate any instinctual gestures in this room.'

If one of the girls at the front had not blushed and squirmed, Jone would not have known whom he was talking to, and she certainly had no idea what she had been doing.

NkCroom went on, 'Don't disturb my train of thought again. As I say, if you could see these images on the screen as people fighting and dying to preserve the light of rationality in the darkness of idistic kayos, you'd have the motivation to win. Try and think yourself into them.'

Someone raised their hand. 'Rev, ye said you were gontae tell us aboot Michael this week.' Other cats quietly but eagerly chorused. 'Yeh, go on, Rev.'

NkCroom turned to Jone and smiled at her left shoulder, 'I can see they're thinking, let the old fellow blab on and we won't have to do any competitions.'

Jone replied, 'Well, I admit I'd like to hear the story of Michael myself, I think us saints can think too abstractly about "Apocalypse" too.'

NkCroom paused, then decided to quiz some of the crew on where they were up to in the competition that week. He moved among them extracting promises from them to finish the move they were at. Then he returned to his console and leaned on it. Everyone was on tenterhooks. 'Aye, well, I'll tell you about Michael.' A ripple of relief went round the room. NkCroom leaned back and gazed out of the window.

'The Kayos had gone on for, oh, over a century when Michael was born – in one of the matriarchies called Astarty. There wasn't much left of pre-Armageddon mirakelisms, earth was sinking back to the Stone Age, and that's no exaggeration. Astarty was one of the few exceptions. They had a remarkable number of mirakelisms inside their fortified city, though they didn't have nuclear warheads. So how did they escape being captured by barbarians? It was their knowledge that protected them. They were healers and fortune-tellers and people came from far and wide, especially the barbarian soldiers, to be cured by them. So they made treaties with some of the barbarian armies, who protected them in return for their healing services. They also sent their young men to join those armies. So much for matriarchy having no truck with machophrenia.

'Well, Michael, who's name was Alber then, wasn't sent off to a barbarian army. He was so good a theologian, they kept him in their Academy of Sciences. What's science, Dabbur?'

'It's what we call theology, Reverend.'

'Aye, I'm glad to hear you're concentrating. Anyone who thinks NkCroom's stories are just an excuse for taking a nap is a fool. Yes, science means theology, but there is a difference in the words you know. Science just means "knowing" and theology means "knowledge of Gawd". And that shows the difference. Our knowledge has a purpose, the construction of Almyty Gawd. Before Armageddon, scientists just pursued knowledge for its own sake, or, I'm sad to say, even worse, just did what their idistic power-maniac Elect told them to do, usually build bigger bombs. And we all know what that led up to. Anyhow, Alber studied at their Academy of Sciences, and it was there he got to thinking about how Armageddon had happened, and about how the world could be rescued from the abyss of savagery. It was through all the talk among Alber and his friends that they realised the truth: the cause of Armageddon and the Kayos was the irrationality within each human brain and the solution was to eliminate that from each human brain. Now that was a totally unacceptable idea in Astartȳ, obviously, for the Astartians only used science in the service of their mythomania, their ludicrous worship of invisible female forces and so on. Alber and his friends soon realised there was no place for them in Astarty. But where else could they be scientists in that demoniac violent world? Nowhere. And that's why they fled from Astarty and made their way to Zibeera. Why Zibeera, Bandur?'

The response was quick, the cats were listening: 'Is that no where the first moon shuttles went frae?'

'Exactly.' NkCroom was clearly delighted at the attention he was getting. 'That's where they could get to the moon from, and the moon would be the perfect place for them to pursue the science they needed. As some of you may know, the moon population was wiped out by neutron bombing and, of course, Armageddon stopped anyone getting back there.

'Well it was a terrible journey they made, but that's another story. When they got to the base, beautifully preserved in the frozen wastes, they found it was guarded by another group of mythomaniacs called Krischans, followers of Krischianity, a mythomania that had been very popular in BA times. They were a very primitive superstitious lot. They spent all their time studying this old book. You know what books are do you?'

'Like hand bibles, only they're written on paper an' ye canny wipe them oot.'

'Well done, yes, this book they studied, they said it predicted the whole history of the world. Anyone smart enough to know what book that was?'

'The Revelation of Saint John.'

'Oh they're not as dull-witted as they let on when they're playing, are they Reverend Grifan? Yes our "Apocalypse" is based on this book of theirs. But for us it's play, not mythomania. Now the trouble with mythomaniac beliefs is that because they have no objectivity, because they're completely irrational, everyone disagrees about them and these Krischans spent all their time quarrelling about what this old book really did say about the future. The only thing they were agreed on was that one day, out of the sky, down would come these beings called Angels, who would save the world.

'The scientists realised almost at once how they could take advantage of this situation. One of them stole into the base, got a copy of the book, and the scientists proceeded to master every word of it. Combining this with their knowledge of science, which to most people was like magic then, they soon gained power over these simple, superstitious people. They said they were the Angels and that they had come down to observe the humans in secret, and now that they knew all about them they had to return to "Heaven" and plan their takeover of the world. The Krischans bowed down to them, and so they took over the shuttle station, which the Krischans had guarded so wonderfully well.'

Daner put up her hand. NkCroom nodded to her to speak. 'Was it no wrong tae, well, make fools ae these Krischans?'

'You've a right to ask that and it shows you're thinking about what I'm saying. I don't think it was, because it was all to the good. And weren't they really Angels anyway? Not creatures from some fantasy place up in the sky, but human ones. After all they did save the world didn't they? Anyhow it's from that time that we use our Krischan language.

'So they got to the moon and there they planned their takeover of the earth, and the civilisation that would follow. First they would have to clean the world of the scourge of radiation. How could they do that?'

'They invented the radabs, Rev.'

'Right, and then they had to find a source of safe and abundant energy, so what did they invent then?'

24

'The Tormags, Rev.'

'Our nuclear fusion plants, right. Well they were greatly helped by the designs left behind by the BA moon colonists. Some people speculate that if the Tormags had been invented before Armageddon, it might not have happened, but that's quite wrong. Societies ruled by irrationals destroy themselves whatever weapons they have, whether it's nuclear bombs or elbows and fists. It shows the wisdom of the Angels that they began by solving the material problems and then moved on to what really mattered: the problem of the human brain.

'Now in order to change the brain they had to understand it, and for that they needed live human brains to experiment with. It was Michael himself who came up with the answer. Why not use the lepers? the people whose genes had been mutated by radiation. Wouldn't they be willing to trade their miserable outcast lives for what really would be a heaven? The Angels got their Krischan devotees to go round the leper camps, selling the idea of wonder-cures to be obtained in the frozen wastes of Zibeera. Once they had gathered enough of them they were shuttled up, and the great experiment began.

'At this point I have to bring in Tiamat. She and some friends had fled Astarty and made their way to Zibeera. It's amazing how news can still travel in a world without bibles. The fact is that mythomania was corroding what was left of science in Astarty, and Tiamat was devoted to science. She had heard the weird tales of the Angels, and realising what it was really about, was determined to get to the moon itself. And she succeeded. Of course we all know what Tiamat is famous for now, don't we?'

'She started Bablylonianism, Rev.'

'Aye well, there's a lot I could say on that topic, but I'll get on with the story. Michael and Tiamat "fell in love" as they say – and I don't see why you should giggle. In BA days romantophilia was sometimes a very noble thing. It led to many lifelong partnerships, a remarkable thing when you consider its irrationality. That was one of the most terrible effects of the Kayos, it destroyed that great tradition of romantophiliac partnerships between males and females.

'At all events she and Michael solved the problem of how to examine the living brain. Tiamat synthesised Bhudanium, the substance that emits psi-radiation. When Bhudanium was released into the brain it showed up whatever thought and feeling patterns were working at any given time. Michael's neurograph receiver then translated this into images. So our neurones and synapses were mapped at last. From Bhudanium she got the idea of an electrode implant able to emit chemicals into the brain at any time – in other words, the soul. And from there she moved on to synthesising the first purification drugs.

'All this time they were investigating the lepers' brains and getting them to record all their thoughts, to coordinate subjective and objective experience. It was this close contact with the lepers that led to Tiamat's downfall. Tiamat fell in love with one of them, a woman called Nildan. Well, what could you expect from a woman like Tiamat brought up in a matriarchy, a place where hormonal arousal by your own gender – I mean sex, of course – was so normal they even used insemination instead of repro-rituals. You see, childhood conditioning is all-important and that's why we have nurseries. And I hope we can all have them soon. As long as we have this Kayos gender separation we'll have the danger of outbreaks of sex-mania and machophrenia. Oh, not that I'm blaming the women of those days for that gender divide. When men took to wandering about in murderous gangs how else could women avoid being slaves? But civilisation has returned and there's no need of it anymore.

'But to get back to the story. This Nildan ranted on about how the lepers should have equal control of the moon colony with the scientists. Lepers, I ask you! When you consider how well they were treated on the moon, how badly treated back on earth! It reminds me of some of the heretics of today! It's always the same. Give people something for free and they throw it back in your face. Well, the colony was ripped apart, when these two began propagandising. There were waves of unrest among the lepers and even some other scientists were swayed by Nildan's ravings. Fortunately a rebellion led by hysterical females didn't have much weight when the leading Angels set about to curb it.'

'Heh Rev, are you sayin' lassies canny fight, Rev?'

'Now, Zaner, don't interrupt with aggressive remarks like that. The fact is, that to be effective in a military sense, you need very cool-headed leadership, and though I'm not saying you girls are more irrational than the boys, you are more susceptible to outbreaks of hysteria. That's just an unfortunate genetic inheritance. One day, we'll be able to bree

finish the story.

'Michael was very deeply wounded b

was the horror of that which made him t

amor-radiation into the program. He re

instincts, whether repro-ist or sexual that

interactions. Scrapping them had to be the

from animal behaviour altogether. From there

see if they could purify idism from the brai

could never be perfect, he came to the conclusio

part of humanity would have to be removed, an   pure

consciousness. It was the use of the lepers' recor that led him

to the answer, that led him to his vision of Almyty Gawd: the

gathering together of all purified experience.

'Meanwhile Tiamat was sent back to earth, which I think was a
grave mistake, but I'll talk about that some other time. Five years
later the Angels did come down to earth, it was the most peaceful
conquest the world had ever known. It was like spring after a very
long winter, plants and animals that hadn't been seen for hundreds
of years returned, babies were born pink and healthy. Oh, you can't
imagine what a difference the Kingdom made to the world. You
may grumble all you like about the Abbey, but if there was no
Krischan Kingdom here, by this day and age, you'd be barely
scraping a living from the soil, if you were lucky enough to have
even survived beyond infancy. As to Michael, he stayed on the
moon, composing psalms for the rest of his life. I don't believe he
was a happy man. His devotion to Tiamat went very deep, and I'm
not talking about carnal passion. Don't ever imagine Krischanism
isn't about emotion. I know you think that, but it's totally untrue.
We believe very much in emotion, as long as its purified and
spiritualised. And Michael's devotion to Tiamat was noble and
spiritual. His grief wasn't just at his own loss, but in his compassion
for her too, for her corruption into evil. And I say that with emotion
of my own, because you may find this hard to believe, but I've been
to Damask where the Astartians went after Tiamat's return. Yes
I've been inside a matriarchy, but that *is* another story.'

The memory of that visit seemed to throw NkCroom into a
gloomy huff. The story-teller NkCroom had vanished and become
the unapproachable introvert NkCroom. He went round behind his
console and sat down at it. Some of the cats raised their hands, their

aroused and they had no desire to go back to
out looking up NkCroom said, 'You've pleased me by
and attentive, don't ruin everything, pestering me with
ions to get you to the siren without any playing being done at

He fiddled among some of the mass of chapters on his console, his face getting redder again. The cats stayed very still, knowing better than to risk his anger when he was frustrated with practicalities. At last he found the tape, inserted it in the wall screen and told them to get on with their games. He rose and walked over to Jone, telling her that he had to leave for a few minutes. He turned to the crew, 'My shadow stays here, when I'm not in the room. Watch out for it.' Jone guessed he might be doing this to see how she would cope on her own. She decided to try to act as purposefully as she could, and strode across to NkCroom's console. She stood beside it firmly, grasping it tightly as if it might transmit his authority through her hand. She waited for the silence to break. It took about five minutes, with one or two whispered exchanges. She decided to move among them. Should she demand total silence? What if they didn't obey? Would that make it worse than if she tolerated the whispers? And if she did, how much worse would it get? Her decision was postponed by one of the girls raising her hand.

'Heh, Rev, come on o'er here, Ah'm stuck.'

Jone went over. Besser certainly was stuck. While Jone explained what she was doing wrong. Besser furrowed her brows and gazed at her screen for the first few minutes. Then her gaze suddenly shifted to Jone. Jone finished her explanation and said, 'Can you do it now?' Besser ignored the question.

'D'ya tyze Rev NkCroom then, Rev?' Jone stiffened.

'You know you're not supposed to use ethnic language in the Abbey.'

'Sorry, A mean, would ye like tae amor-radiate wi' him?'

The whole room stopped playing, all eyes were on Jone.

'What a ridiculous idea and what has it got to do with move 48 of the Thyatira/Latonia game?'

The cats were delighted, the bait had been swallowed. Besser continued. She sounded serious.

'Aye right enough, he's too auld fer ya. Whit aboot Rev ArBrenan, would ye like tae amor-radiate wi' him?'

28

'I haven't the faintest idea. I don't know him. Amor-radiation is a rare thing. You have to find someone who can resonate on your inner frequencies and that's not at all easy, and certainly doesn't happen with strangers.'

Besser was undeterred. 'But dae ye no get a wee thrill when somebody, ken, looks ye in the eye an ye' think tae yersel' mm, A wonder if he'd resonate on ma whitever it was ye said.'

'I might get a mild hormonal arousal from someone. So yes, I admit perhaps I'd try to get to know them, to see whether I like them or not, which doesn't necessarily follow from the attraction.'

'Am A annoyin' ye, Rev?'

'A bit. You seem to think amor-radiation is just a saintly version of repro-ritual. It isn't.'

'Well it canny be much fun, if ye canny just get yer hormone arousal and hae a wee bit plug in wi' yer wires, ken, like we'd have a wee bit kiss an' cuddle.'

'I thank fusion I don't. Look at all the violence that surrounds repro-rituals. Doesn't sound like fun to me.'

Now a boy's voice came in.

'Aw come on, Rev, it's no aw violence. There's only violence when the lassies two-time ye, then they deserve whit they get.'

The girls turned to him angrily, and Jone woke up to the fact that order in the room had disintegrated. People had moved out of their seats to be nearer the conversation and one boy was even sitting on top of someone else's play unit. Jone mustered all her strength and threatened them with NkCroom. It worked and they began to move back to their seats. Unfortunately, the boy on the play unit, Skinur, clambered off clumsily and brushed against its scramble knob. The girl sitting at the unit shrieked at the sight of the random patterns shooting all over her display screen. Skinur began furiously fiddling with the keyboard, imagining he could put it right.

'What do you think you're doing, lad?' NkCroom was at the door, fixing his eyes on Skinur with fury. A few minutes before, he had seemed a cocky little fellow. Now he looked pale and feeble as he stood there frozen with fear.

'Did you hear me say my shadow stays here? Didn't you believe me?'

'Eh no, eh yeh, Reverend.'

NkCroom walked towards him and pounded on the screen which continued to erupt light beams like fireworks.

'This is what happens when control is lost for even a minute. This is why there must be no disobedience. Don't you see?' He drummed his fingers on the display screen. 'This isn't just a machine, this is a symbol, a picture of your brain. And there it is, Kayos unleashed. I will not tolerate disobedience. It is the only possible way you will learn self-control and you will learn it. Get over to the rack.'

The boy shuffled over to the pain stimulator and sat down. As NkCroom began to fix on the electrode helmet the boy burst into sobs.

'Holy deuterium, learn to take your punishment like a Krischan, control yourself.' NkCroom spoke with a mixture of contempt and anxiety at the boy's weakness.

The act of administering the pain was over in a second or two, but the effect was disastrous. The boy yelped and then began to tremble all over. It was an epileptic fit. Some of the girls squealed. Others ran forward. NkCroom shouted at them to sit down. He pulled at the helmet, in a state of high agitation. Jone came to the rescue. She loosened the boy's collar and stuffed his waist-sash between his teeth. NkCroom stood back and fidgeted anxiously.

'Sacred deuterium, I only had it on level one. I had no information about this.'

In the meantime the siren had gone. None of the cats made a move. Jone turned to one of the girls nearby.

'Call through to the medical facility. Say it's an epileptic fit.'

The girls looked at NkCroom. He nodded and she ran across to the intercom. Two minutes later the orderly arrived to give the boy an injection and he calmed down. NkCroom dismissed the rest of the cats, who filed out in silence. NkCroom was still visibly upset. He spoke to the orderly.

'I had no idea, no idea. There's nothing about it on his record. I only put it to level one. The lad said nothing, we had no warning.'

The orderly looked at him impassively and said, 'We'll have to take him to the facility, will you come?' NkCroom replied, 'No, no, Reverend Grifan will go with you. She can handle this sort of thing better than I can.' The orderly leaned over the boy, 'Can you get up?' He looked at her in pathetic gratitude as if she had rescued him from the brink of death, and nodded. She pulled him up gently and both she and Jone held him by the arms and led him out.

At the facility another orderly took the boy into an exam booth while the first orderly went off to the office to record the event, suggesting to Jone she should have a look in Shinur's file. Until then, Jone had been so absorbed in practicalities, she hadn't had time to reflect. Now she was filled with the horror of it. Ever since she'd been told about the rack she'd been in a turmoil about what she should do. She had an innate revulsion to the idea of using it, but she feared she had no choice. While she was with NkCroom she'd put it at the back of her mind, until now. It was the first time she'd seen it used. He had used it unjustly. The disorder had been her responsibility and anyway, it had been an accident what the boy had done. But that was of less importance than this. She looked down at the file, nothing about epilepsy, very little about anything else. Her horror was giving way to anger. Why? Why? She looked round the room. Only six booths, for a community this size? What was this place, a medical facility or another playroom? Medical provision had nothing to do with grace or merit. Whatever excuse they had for this deprivation it had to be an outrageous, wicked rationalisation. Preventive medicine was not a luxury in the Kingdom, it was everyone's right.

The orderly returned and told Jone she might as well go, she would take care of Skinur. Jone was stung by the orderly's coldness. She felt as if the orderly was blaming her. She protested,

'This is appalling. How can it not be in his record. How could a Diagnostician not have detected it?'

'Take a look at the state of them, and you'll see why.'

The sarcasm was bitter. Jone felt desperate to disassociate herself from this scandal.

'But it's wicked, everyone is entitled to proper sickness prevention.'

The orderly stared, in what Jone reckoned was only slightly masked disbelieving contempt. 'Tell that to Mission Control.'

'I can't believe Mission Control approves of this.'

'Oh ye think it's NkDod doin'. Everyone blames NkDod for everythin' roond here, then they dinny have tae think aboot what it's really all about. If you think Mission Control cares aboot us, then prove it, go an' tell them.'

Jone felt like sinking through the floor. She had been caught out, a novice banished to the colonies for nearly failing ordination, going off to kick up a fuss at Mission Control all by herself. It was farcical. A look, this time of undisguised contempt, flashed across the orderly's face and she marched out of the room.

31

4

Rannan NkBerber, the medical orderly who attended to Skinur that day, walked home in a mood of angry disgust. The afternoon had ended with an emergency meeting of the medical staff about Skinur's epileptic fit. The medical High Priest had brought mirakelists from the local church to examine his Diagnostician. A fault undetected by its own fail-safe mechanism had been found.

Everyone in the team had been horrified and everyone, bar one orderly, was agreed the affair should be kept 'unofficial'. If a report were filed, Mission Control would send investigators. If investigators came, word was sure to get round. If word got round, there would be sure to be one stroppy member of the boy's clan wanting to take the Abbey to the Mercy Seat, and with so many protestants around these days, would probably get support for it. Even if they could not prove that the fault in the Diagnostician had caused the boy's condition to go undetected, the publicity would be ruinous enough. Then Mission Control would look for scapegoats and nobody in the team would be safe.

The High Priest had already thought about what to do. They would report the fault in the Diagnostician, accompany it with a strongly-worded protest, and demand a replacement with a better model – 'So that this appalling mishap can be turned to good in the end,' he said piously. At this Rannan had wanted to vomit over his crisp white surplice, but instead she had wrenched at one of the keys of her hand-bible. She had said very little at the meeting. Her position in the team already was unsafe and all she could do was appease her conscience by making it clear where she stood and leave it at that.

Now, as she walked home, she had to wrestle with the problems. How long could she·go on walking this tightrope? If she stood up to fight she wouldn't just lose her post on the medical team, but with that went her Blessed status as well. To go back to making metrifacts in the playpens all day, like most of her clan sisters did, was something she could hardly bear thinking about. And there were the extra Virtue points that her clan depended on. Then the anger at the shameful cover-up came to the surface. How long could she go on accepting such dishonesty silently? She had a sense of impending doom about it. One day she might lose control and blow it all anyway.

The image of the novice pastor floated in her head, and that brought another wave of annoyance. So she had been shocked, big deal! What would she do with her shock? Hurry to her quiet holomorphic cell in the Nace residency and recover with a few stims, at her altar. Then, perhaps, go and record her wounded sensitivity in her gawdstore, and retire to her sleep module satisfied she had made her contribution to the Great Goal. Rannan cursed herself for expressing even a little of her feelings to her. She could see it hurt the novice's delicate saintly feelings. At the time she had got a kick out of it, but now, it only added to her anxiety. What if she went and talked about it? Oh grutag, so what? People's opinion of her couldn't get any lower, anyway.

She turned her thoughts forward. The clan habitats and its cacophony of bickering seniors, whining infants and never-ending vulgate space sagas blasting from every wall. Perhaps she should go straight over to Ered's domicile in Nace. No, she had said she would see Luner first, and she always hated disappointing Luner. In the last year or so they had got much closer. Rannan had been something of a substitute maternaliser for quite a while, but now that Luner was maturing into a young woman, they were much more like sisters. Luner was in Crew Delta, she could have a good moan with her about the day's events. By the time Rannan was at the hab door, she was ready to face the mobs with a humorous resignation, which broke as soon as she stepped inside.

It appeared that Shelan, Merem's womb-sister, had been beaten up by her repro-hirer and had been taken to hospital. 'It's well seein' you werny there tae keep him off her, though it wis you that was tellin' her tae leave him before the hire wis up, you wound her up tae this.'

Rannan's anger flared up at once, 'Grutag doon, Merem, are you sayin' A'm tae blame the soggert beat her up?' The two women stood there screaming at one another until one of the more senior women broke them up before they came to blows. Rannan said she would go to the hospital and stomped into the dorm to find Luner. She desperately needed some supportive company.

On the way to the hospital, she and Luner discussed what had happened. Rannan said, 'Somethin's gottae be done aboot NkMare, he canny just get away wi' it.'

'Me an' Geever an' some e' us were talkin' aboot it in the dorm. Ken whit we came up wi'? A gang e' us jumpin' on him at night, ken, at the citadel or some place like that, ken, where he'll no ken it's folk frae roond here. An we could make sure he wis by hissel', ken, get somebody we ken frae the other end. Get her tae wij wi' him, lead him up a dark alleyway then pounce frae behind, so he didny ken even how many e' us there were.'

Rannan could see it was a wonderful idea, if it worked. But would he really never find out who it was, and wouldn't he just decide who he thought it was, for obvious reasons, and wreak revenge? She'd seen the clan wars that came from this sort of thing before. It didn't change anything in the long run. 'This is where we should be usin' the Mercy Seat. Soggerts like him should be gettin' taken before it.'

Luner looked at her in astonishment. 'You ken they didny touch the repro-rituals. They dinny gie a shard aboot clan females gettin' beat up.'

'The Mercy Seat's no Mission Control. There's protestants gettin' involved in it. We kin force them tae do somethin'. It's oor only chance. Us flagratin' wi' each other's never gontae get us any where, that A'm 100 per cent sure of.'

They sank into gloomy silence and Rannan thought about Shelan. She was partly dreading seeing her. Would she be resentful and blame Rannan as Merem had done? Understandable if she did, but difficult for Rannan to face. But the dread turned out completely unnecessary. Shelan was an inspiration. She was a wonderful paradox. Physically she looked like the wilderness battlefield after a day's war, but her eyes were shining.

'A'm tellin' ye, when they brought me in, A wis jist lyin' here howlin' then aw of a sudden A thought, you grutij soggert, ye think ye've got me in the troj, don't ye? Ye think ye'll get me crawlin' back tae ye? Well ye're dead wrong. A'm free of ya, free of you forever, ya soggert.' She tried to wave her arms and raise herself in the straps, and then collapsed laughing. 'A shouldny laugh, A dinny ken whit A'm daein' tae masel' wi' these painkillers they loaded intae me.'

Then she told them just how free she intended to be. Rannan and Luner were the first to know, even Merem didn't know yet. Shelan had wanted to share the news with the sister who had helped her out of her hell. She was going to excommunicate and go to Lundin, the Yukey Island's one great city, and survive in Sewer city. 'Sewer city' was the collective nickname of anywhere that lay outside the Kingdom's jurisdiction. It was found everywhere, from the wilderness at Plotin to Strylya itself. The Church had quietly decided that to allow pagan areas that were contained, like pressure release-valves, was better than trying to suppress them altogether and inevitably stirring dissent.

Shelan was intending to go there with another female friend. They had talked about it as a dream, like a lot of others did, but now they were going to do it. Both Rannan's and Luner's jaws dropped when she made her announcement. Rannan, for all her religious radicalism, was shocked. Throwing up access to Virtue points, to Kristbanks, to Salvation, in fact to an identity in the Kingdom, was a huge risk. To go excom sounded exciting when fantasised about, but to actually do it! With sisterly concern Rannan queried Shelan, but it was clear she had thought it through and decided the risk was worth taking. Rannan ended up full of admiration for her courage. It was a complete reversal of what she'd expected, Shelan reassuring Rannan, not Rannan reassuring Shelan. 'Dinny worry aboot the rest sayin' ye put me up tae this. Ye didny, it's ma decision and naebody elses.'

There had been times before Shelan left NkMare, when Rannan had despaired of Shelan's passivity. Almost believing, to her own shame, that Shelan had unconsciously wanted to cling to her suffering. Now that was swept away. Change was possible. It was more than a delight, it threw Rannan into a turmoil. Was excommunication a choice for her too? If Shelan could throw away the security of the Kingdom's prison for the dangerous freedom of Sewer city, she surely could. Was that the way out of her dilemmas? Yes for herself, and for Shelan herself, it might well be. But what about the rest of the clan? The rest of Plotin? Everyone couldn't run away. It would do nothing for the sisters left behind, still victims of violent hirers. No, she had a responsibility here. She would go to the separatists and propose a campaign around bringing hire violence to the Mercy Seat. If change was possible, then change must be possible in Plotin. Change that would affect not just one of them but all of them.

Later that evening, Rannan was sprawled out on one of Eran NkRaze's floforms, plugged into his altar, while watching his roof visual and listening to the Booleans. It was all very pseudo-saintly fashionable, but sometimes (and tonight was one of those times), she had to admit, she revelled in it. And the meal she was digesting as well: cooked organics from the biopark. In her stroppy moods, she teased Eran mercilessly for his pretentiousness, but tonight that wasn't her mood. She was still thinking about Shelan's decision to go off to Lundin. Her conscience was wrestling with the longing to come and live here with Eran. He never badgered her. He knew that it would make her stubbornly resist, but the unspoken offer was always there. Rannan was even tempted to forget about the campaign idea. It would be so nice just to relax and escape. But the moment she had thought that, the niggling fear arose: was she avoiding mentioning the campaign because she didn't want to provoke conflict? If so, there was no point in sitting fantasising about coming to live here.

Eran who'd been watching her, noticed the gloomy frown.

'What's the matter?'

Rannan pulled the psalm stimulator helmet off, placed it slowly back in the altar and gave him an 'I want to talk, but it's difficult' look. Eran turned the music down and waited. Rannan plunged in.

'A want to bring repro-hire violence up at the meeting.' She saw he hadn't caught on immediately. She had to push the rest out. 'I mean, A want to suggest starting a campaign for letting females take violent renters to the Mercy Seat. What d'you think? Would I get anywhere?'

She saw Eran's face twitch. 'No,' he said, flatly. She waited a moment or two to see if he would elaborate. He didn't.

'Is that aw ye've got to say, "No"?'

'You asked me if you'd get anywhere with it in the sect and I said "no". It's true.'

'Would you no support me?'

'What difference would that make? I know it wouldn't get through. I've been in long enough to –'

'Eran, would you support me or no?' She could see the look of pain crossing Eran's face. He knew he was about to put his hand in the fire. Rannan was being sharply woken from her sleepy escapism. He had no choice:

'I don't think so.'

'Oh, ye think it's great to let renters go on beatin' up their hires.'

Rannan knew perfectly well he didn't think that. It was anger talking. The spark had been fanned. The heat sparked off Eran too, though his rationality knew it was folly.

'Don't insult me. You know I hate repro-violence as much as you do, but grutag's sake, it just isn't the right tactic. I happen to agree with the orthodox line. I've argued and debated it myself for years. You know it would split us apart.'

'An why? Because the separatist males areny prepared to change themselves anymore than the soggerts in the clan hooses?'

'Some of them are, but that's not the way to change them. Grutag, I've changed a megaton lot, but not because of fights in the sect. Everybody knows it's doctrine to change the whole repro-business after independence, and they're going to have to face up to it then –'

'Oh aye, the answer tae everythin', wait till after independence. Well it's trodge. If they're no prepared tae do somethin' now, a dinny trust them tae dae it then.'

'You don't have to trust them. I'll do it, we'll do it. We'll have the power to do it, when we've got our own assembly. Rannan, for fusion's sake, all these years we've been struggling just to survive and now look at us. Things are really startin' to happen. We'll get independence within ten years, I'm sure of it –'

'Ten years! Ten more years've hire batterin' an naebody givin' a quark aboot it? An' then what? Another ten years', strugglin' tae get it through the assembly, because nobody's done a thing about machophrenia in the meantime. It stinks. For fusion's sake, wi' protestants in the Mercy Seat noo, we could maybe get some legislation in two years. An even if we didny, we'd got people thinkin' aboot it, an maybe even dooin' somethin' –'

'Protestants? What are you talking about Rannan? Are you telling me the protestants'll do more for you than the separatists? Because if you are, maybe you'd better go an' join them.'

It was a laser beam to Rannan's centre and it cut her stone dead. She knew now she wasn't going to get anywhere. It wasn't that she thought he was being machophrenic, she always thought of him as gentler than she was. It was his allegiance. Separatism, and his separatist beluvids, came first, everything else, including loyalty to her, came after. Eran felt a chill too. It occurred to him that in this bitter little exchange he might have lost her. But he could do nothing, without being dishonest.

'You dinny frighten me wi' labels, Eran, A'm a female an' that counts first wi' me, an' A reckon wi' a fair few other females as well. At any rate, A'm bringin' it tae the next meetin'. Oh I know it willnae get through but I'm gontae see what support A do get, an then see what tae do. An' seein' you've said clear enough you're no gontae support me, A dinny feel like stayin' here now.'

Rannan walked into the habitat common room and wondered if she'd made a big mistake. The smell of too many un-uniformed people, of fried carb-pulp and the noisy inanities of intersteller sagas from the walls, felt like a dose of radiation. Not to mention the hostile brush-offs from Merem and her allies. Luner, she was told, was in the Music room.

Thankfully, the music room was quiet. Luner and Geever were alone, rolling about in pretend wrestling on the cushions. Luner was astonished but delighted to see Rannan. She was jealous of Eran, or rather not of him but of the temptation of his domicile.

'Why've ye come back?'

'A think Eran an' me are finished.'

It was only as she said that that she realised the probable truth of it. The relationship had never been passionate, nor central, but it had been a part of her life. She fell down on the cushion and began to cry. Luner put her arm around her.

'Whit happened?'

'Religious disagreement. He's against the campaign idea.'

Luner was puzzled, 'So am I, but ye're no splittin' up wi' me.' It was a loving threat.

'You an' me disagree on tactics, Luner, no on first principles.'

'Well A'll tell ye what my first principle is.'

'What?'

'Yalida?'

Through her tears, Rannan burst into uncontrollable laughter, quite out of proportion to the joke. Oh it was good to be home. It felt like a good time to block off from what had happened and slip into the comfort of home interaction.

'Oh aye,' she teased. 'Yalida's got the answer to everything.'

'Heh, you were gontae put on the Juno track,' said Geever. She looked at Rannan enquiringly,

'Oh yeh, put it on. A dinny want to do any more talkin'.'

The three of them huddled together to watch the wall screen. Rannan had seen visions of the great gas giant planet before, but it still took your breath away to see her. The instrumental introduction took them towards one of her near moons. It still seemed staggering, the thought of your mother planet filling up your whole sky in one direction. This would make a great visional, thought Rannan, and wished all three of them were in Eran's domicile, without Eran. Maybe she should forget about religion and do more training in medicine, get herself a Nace domicile. Oh grutag, stop thinking and just lose yourself in Juno.

There is nothing else like Juno's atmosphere, like her clouds. All the subtle swirling colouring and shape shifting, the merging and breaking, the swirling, twisting, rolling and streaming. Yalida's voice came in. Rannan focused on the words crossing the screen, as well as the images.

Oh life was pretty good, in your first time round rotation
As you simply streamed on westward in your high speed zonal jet
With nothing more to work on than ammonia condensation
High and white and bright in your S T r Z jet.

And the next nine hours point fifty-five were just as easy.
You turned right round to jet the eastern way
In adiabatic progress the convection kept on coming
and your frozen crystals kept their buoyancy.

But third time round your luck ran out
Got flung into a shear
Falling out of mean velocity, counterclockwise into fear,
In the turbulence of eddy, the spin of doom was near.

You thought that you were steering
Your deflection from the narrow strait
While all the while not knowing
The pressure of your coriolis fate
The grip of coriolis from one pressure to another.
Oh the sad illusion
Of the anti-cyclone's rising

When the straight wind grabbed back energy
you thought you were transferring.

I weep as I watch the tiny vortex so unstable
Who thinks her swirling curls are the vectors of great art
I watch her in the agony of hourly elongation
And I cry out with her pain, when I see her ripped apart.

Oh all you white aspiring ovals,
Listen to the words of one who sees.
Merge yourself with other spinning centres
And roll with counter currents as you please.

Then one day you'll raise a great red circle
Powered from your liquid core
One great single and united breaker
Surging to the heights forevermore.
And may your little sister moons
Fling ion torches out to greet you
As you circle in the ocean of their sky.
And the sisterhood be foreever folded
In Juno's sparkling wings of Aurorae.

Hearing and understanding the words for the first time, Rannan felt
her little joke about Yalida having the answer to everything had
somersaulted. It was one of those uncanny coincidences that made
you wonder if the Providence mythomaniacs weren't right after all.
Yes, join forces with other females, of course, that was the answer,
but where was she going to find them?

5

Towards the end of her third week, Jone was left on her own with Crew Delta for the first time. She had not been thrown into it blindfold, however. NkCroom had assigned Mik ArBrenan to fraternalise her, as he was in the neighbouring playroom on that morning. Jone had been feeling unhappy about sharing with NkCroom, he was so much of a solitary performer. Not only would she have learned more in a practical way if she'd been with Mik, but she might have been able to develop what still seemed like a potential for friendship. As it was, his mixture of affability in groups and shyness with a younger female one to one made the task difficult when she didn't see him that often. Today was an opportunity to improve things between them as well as having the terrors of playtime lessened for her.

Mik was as reassuring and helpful as she could have expected. He helped her locate the difference in wave-lengths between responsive nervousness, as she'd experienced in exams, and initiatory nervousness as she felt now. The sedation worked almost at once.

Jone had the idea of trying to gain the Crew's confidence by dividing them into two teams to take the Light and Darkness positions. She had diligently searched in the bibliotek for a suitable game. Each game of 'Apocalypse' has its own set of possible moves and positions. And she had come up with what looked like a brilliant choice. Antipas v. Balaam no. 12, full of simple but dramatic action. Mik was flatteringly enthusiastic,

'Yes, teams are always a good idea, provided you manage to keep a grip on them. They can get very excited. But it'll probably be such a treat for them they'll be willing to keep within bounds. They'll insist on males versus females though. You do realise that, don't you?' He gave her a shy smile and his eyes twinkled. Jone hadn't realised it till then and she felt a little conscience stricken that she would then be reinforcing their gender divide but wasn't able to say that to Mik. She suspected he didn't find it much of a problem. Relating to him was already verging on feeling complex and ambiguous.

When the playhour siren sounded he left her before the crew came in, telling her that she needn't feel embarrassed about buzzing him if there was any trouble. The crew spilled in, far noisier and more restless than they were with NkCroom, but not quite beyond control. They were keen on the idea of competition. 'Krado supporters vee Gizer supporters,' suggested one of the lads. But one of the more dominant girls scorned it. 'A'm no supportin' one ae them, they're both rubbish. The Grukes frae Ebirdin are the best.' This led to a slanging match on the merits of the various armies. In an effort to step back from the precipice of chaos, Jone found herself suggesting the male/female divide, falling back on its sheer simplicity as a way of ending arguments. The gimmick was a success in getting them involved. Never had she seen them concentrate on the wall screen so avidly. Nevertheless, it was Jone who did most of the playing. She suggested different moves and the crew chose one of them. She tried and tried to get them to come up with suggestions themselves but got nowhere. In the first few games their choices were all of a piece. Whichever move was likely to eliminate as many of the opposition bits as possible in that one move was chosen. The wholesale slaughter was, of course, accompanied by plentiful cheers and boos. Only when they had got to the last frame and saw that all the recklessness with bits had brought them to a stalemate did they realise that a bit of subtlety would be necessary for one side to actually win the game. Jone was so enormously relieved she was keeping their attention to the end, and with enough control to guarantee her survival at least, that she ignored the little voice in her brain that said all this had absolutely nothing to do with conditioning into logical, spiritual thought.

In the last game the girls showed themselves to be more intelligent than the boys, and they were just poised on the brink of victory when one of the boys, Makur, had a brainstorm. All on his own he saw a way of eliminating the girls' chief, Antipas, and thus unexpectedly enabled the boys to grasp victory. The girls were bitterly disappointed, not unjustified in feeling they had been cheated of a win they deserved. The boys were ecstatic knowing well enough one clever move had saved them from defeat.

It was Makur's finest hour. He was one of the runts of the male half of the crew, rarely, if ever, noticed. When Jone congratulated him he said, 'That's the NkMare clan for ye, top in fightin' an' top in brains too.' At the sound of the name 'NkMare', Luner's face turned scarlet. She turned to Makur.

'Fightin'? Caw that fightin'? Beatin' up hires that canny fight back?'

Makur, puffed with triumph and unaware of how serious Luner was, came back with an insolence he didn't usually dare. 'Aye, an we deal oot punishment that's deserved tae bachans an aw'.'

Before anyone could say anything, Luner leapt over and was at the boy's throat. Although smaller, the boy fought back. They held each other by the arms and kicked each other, until Luner got him on the floor. The boy screamed and struggled. Luner pinned him down, refusing to let go.

'You should be dead, callin' ma sister a bachan.'

At once everyone was crowding round and cheering the two on, as if it was a continuation of the game.

Jone couldn't believe how quickly everything had gone so completely wrong. She pressed the buzzer through to Mik and then rushed over to get the sluggard off the wall. Mik was through in a couple of seconds. He saw the gathered crowd, guessed what was happening, took the sluggard from Jone's hand, pushed his way through the crowd and fired at the pair on the floor. As the muscles relaxed they looked for a minute as if they were embracing. When Luner realised how they were entangled her eyes filled with horror, and she struggled desperately against the creeping sleepiness in her limbs to extricate herself from Makur. Jone was glad it hadn't been her own hand that had administered this humiliation. It might, with a bit of luck, make things less difficult later. Luner was supposed to be seeing her for a salvation session this afternoon. How was she going to cope with it? How was she going to deal with what had happened?

Meanwhile Mik had the rest of the crew in their seats. Jone bent over to help Luner up. She didn't look at Jone and as soon as she was on her feet she walked back to her seat with her head down. Mik addressed the two sinners:

'I don't want to hear how this came about. You know what the commandments are in these cases. Both of you must report to your ethical chaplain after playtime. Who is it? Reverend Leeam, OK,

Do you think you can do that without me having to drag you along, Luner? Makur?' The two nodded glumly. 'Luner, I'm very sad about this, you know what trouble you'be been in and this'll just be heaps more.'

'Rev, he cawed ma sister a –'

'Look Luner, I told you I don't want to know. There isn't any justification for what either of you did and you should both know that. Now I suggest you all calm down in the last few minutes by tackling the game yourselves on your own consoles.'

The crew did as he said, thankful they had managed to have a bit of fun without being punished. Mik smiled at Jone sympathetically, 'I'd better go and check my crew, I'll come back and chat after.'

When he came back he was at once reassuring.

'Don't feel bad about this. That kind of thing happens now and then. I'm sure it wasn't a direct result of the compete. What's going on in their heads usually has much more to do with what's going on in the habs than in the Abbey,' and he repeated his reassurances that she shouldn't blame herself.

Jone appreciated his comforting but was in too much of a state of shock about what she had witnessed to think about what it might have done to her confidence. What it did do was make her feel able to express her horror at violence. Mik nodded understandingly,

'I hope you don't think I'm being patronising, but that is the reaction of a born saint straight from Strylya. It's a common fact of life here. It's as much part of their everyday life as their language or music or sense pollution is. I mean, of course, we've got to be hard on them about it in the Abbey, that's the bottom line in Krischan programming. Well, you know, a fair few of us think NkDod's off-line with curbing music and language and so on, but violence is different. The least we can do is give them a haven from it here. I mean, I understand your revulsion of violence, but Luner and Makur aren't any different from the others, so it's important not to extend your revulsion to them as people. Do you see what I mean?'

Jone appreciated the advice. It made her feel a lot easier about how she would tackle seeing Luner later on. She would make sure she sedated the revulsion so that it wouldn't interfere with communication. She told Mik about the interview. He looked thoughtful.

'Oh, that's good, to tell you the truth, this may sound a bit strange, but I think you'll need to be maternal with her, I mean without being approving. Leeam's very good with the rougher lads but he's too heavy-handed with girls. Mind you, she is in need of a good sharp shock, she's been dodging around in a meteor shower for a while now. Let's hope it does the trick. I must admit I've a soft spot for her, for all her wildness. She's a bright lass. That's one of her troubles, nowhere to go with her originality. Maybe you could help there, take an interest in her avocations and all that. Anyhow, enough of big brother eh, lets go down to the comm.'

Jone was inspired to feel hopeful about Luner and turned her thoughts away from the awful playhour. She started tentatively to ask Mik about his vocation in the Abbey, to pursue her intention of getting to know him. The invisible plasma of shyness hadn't quite broken yet, but she was optimistic that now it would.

Luner and Makur dutifully went off to the office to arrange appointments with Rev Leeam. Luner was summoned to his private interaction space, just after dinnertime. As Luner walked in, he fiddled with his keyboards to look as if he was very busy.

'Sit down,' he said, without looking at her. 'Do you know what is considered to be, what everyone knows to be, the worst form of heathen wickedness in the Abbey?' He turned to look at her at last. 'Do you?' Luner bowed her head and said nothing. 'Do you?' His voice was bitter and brutal. 'Answer me.'

'Violence.'

'I take it you don't deny committing such an act.'

'But Reverend,' Luner was frightened and close to tears and only just managed to stumble out with, 'he cawed ma sister a – a really bad word, an' said she deserved it Reverend. She's in hospital, Fergin NkMare beat her up that bad –'

'You sister's in hospital, put there by an act of violence. Presumably if you hadn't been stopped, Makur would have ended up in hospital, put there by an act of violence. What makes your act of violence different from his?'

'He, he cawed my sister a –'

'I heard what he called your sister.' Reverend Leeam was warming up. He was used to overpowering people with his bulk, with his heavy-jowled features, with his quietly strong voice, 'You were provoked. Is that what you're telling me? You couldn't help it, isn't that it? Don't you think that's what this savage who injured your sister said? Isn't that what every savage the kingdom over who commits an act of violence says? "A couldny help it, A wis provoked"' He mimicked the aggrieved tone, sarcastically, 'I don't give an alpha particle what your excuse was. Violence is violence and it's wicked and heathen and there's no reason for its existence ever, anywhere, anytime.'

Luner was cowering. She had not really taken in the logic of his argument. She only feared his anger. Leeam was by no means finished. He got up, came across and leaned over her, resting his arm on the sides of the floform.

'That's not all I've got to say about your little misdemeanour, not by any means. Oh no, there's a whole lot more. I've been waiting for a chance to tell you what you are, for a long time. You're a pervert, NkBerber, a disgusting little byre sado. You swank around with your little gang as if you were getting fired all the time. You don't fool me. I know. The lads tell me that kind of thing. They wouldn't spark you off, if you paid them. You haven't got any flesh worth having. You're all one big act, you are. all that dubbing round, giving smart answers in the playroom. It's all a big sham because you haven't got anything down there. Nothing any well-oiled rod would want. But you can't get the rods at all can you? So you go after girls and when you can't get them you've got to jump on soft little dridles like Makur NkMare. You can't get any sparks from normal males so you have to go and pump it out of little boys. You know what byre sados like you are? Deep freezes. All the heat you can get is what you can manage to beat out of someone else's tank, because you're so dried out yourself. Why don't you just save all those avocation virtue points you get for the gratcher at the moonpalace and leave real girls and boys alone?'

Luner had been sobbing almost from the start of this torrent of abuse. Leeam now stood up and walked back a bit to stare at her.

'I suggest if you don't like to hear what I think of you, you make an effort to avoid ethical reports.' He sat down again and stared at his console screen, looking as if he was thinking of what to say in his report. In reality he was listening to Luner's sobs with satisfaction and thinking: that'll shut her up for quite a while.

'You can go now, or you can wait until you've regained your self-control. You can wash yourself in the hygiene-space if you want.'

Luner almost ran into the hygiene-space. There she tried desperately to stop herself sobbing and after a few long minutes succeeded and washed her face. She hesitated for a moment, unable to face the embarrassment of seeing him again. She came out with head lowered, quite unable to look at him. He turned round and said coolly, 'As I said, if you don't want to see me again, keep out of trouble. Now get going.' And she did as he said without hesitation.

In the last hour of duty Jone sat nervously, waiting for Luner to arrive with the voice of Reverend Leeam ringing in her ears. He had seemed satisfied with his ethical counselling: 'I gave her the sort of verbal exposure she's been asking for. Gave her a thorough psyche exposure in language she can understand.' She wondered what on earth that meant. What state was Luner going to be in? She worked her soul hard.

When Luner did come in, the sight astonished her. The high spirits, the friendly insolence had vanished. Instead there was this lamb-like creature, who sidled in and sat down looking as if desperation to please was her sole motive in life. Jone was so taken aback it took her a few moments to initiate talk. She was so used to responding passively to Luner's normal ebullience. Gently she gave Luner the warning she had been commissioned to give. If Luner got into trouble again she would be sent to the purgatory, and if that didn't work a pre-baptismal atonement sanctuary. Jone tried to put as much firm maternality into her voice as she could and it wasn't long before Luner was sobbing again. Jone's heart melted with compassion. Luner was obviously in a very fragile condition. Jone came as near to Luner as she could without touching her, wishing she could use her sympathy ionizer but guessing the cats didn't like such Krischan 'substitutes' for touch. She took the risk of trying to get at the truth.

'Are you upset by what Reverend Leeam said to you?'

Luner looked up, startled, 'D'ye ken what he said?'

Jone shook her head. Now she was really going to take a risk for the sake of communication 'Was he very nasty?'

Luner raised her head and gazed at Jone, only half-believing. Jone asked again silently with her gaze, hoping the barrier would break. Luner lowered her head,

'He said A wis a sado – he said A couldny get it frae the big lads cos A'm a deepfreeze an' A had tae go an' beat up wee lads tae get the heat.'

Jone, grasping the gist of this, found it quite impossible to believe. 'Are you saying he said you beat up small boys to get hormonal arousal, because you couldn't get it from normal rituals?'

'Aye, only he didny say it like that, he said it like I said it, even worse.'

'He used ethnic language?'

'You dinny believe me do ya? They aw do it, when they're on their own wi' you, wi' naebody listening in, ken. Well, no aw ae them, but some ae them. That's how the lads are feart of Leeam. He's like a real missile, like a Revenge Crusader. Ye dinny believe me do ya?'

The last sentence was pleading. Luner's desperate need to be believed made Jone feel she had no choice, if she wanted to gain Luner's trust. And how could Luner be inventing it, if this state was the result?

'I believe you,' she said.

'But am A, Rev Grifan?'

'Are you what?'

'A byre sado?'

'Byre?'

'Ken it's one've they words they use for females who only dae it wi' females, cos, ken, males dinny want them, cos they're ugly.'

'But Luner, you're not ugly. You have lovely brown eyes and black hair, and a beautiful smile.' Jone found it embarrassing to talk like this, but she forced herself for Luner's sake. Luner was not reassured.

'It's no that. It's cos A'm thin, ken. A've no got big breasts, ken.'

'I don't know what to say, Luner. I don't understand your repro-customs. I don't see how anyone could find you unattractive. Maybe females with large breasts are the most popular, but I can't believe all the males prefer them. Anyhow,' the thought struck her, 'I've seen thin females with male partners in the street. I'm sure it's not true they all think you're ugly.'

'No, maybe no, but it's true A do freeze wi' lads.'

'Well maybe that's because you haven't met anyone that arouses you. Some people are easily aroused, and other people are just naturally more fussy. Just because you haven't been aroused so far doesn't mean it'll never happen.'

'But Rev, A dinny want tae be aroused by them. A dinny like anyae them. A hate them an' A dinny want tae get hired ever.'

'Then that's why they don't like you, because they know, whether you say it or not, you hate them. They sense your phobiradons.'

'D'ye think so?' At last Luner was lifted a little.

'I'm sure so. Anyhow why are you bothered what the males think of you, if you don't like them?'

'It's fine when yer an ado, but when you get baptised you're supposed tae grow ootae it. Well ken we still sleep alongside in the habs an' that's fine as long as ye go up tae the moonpalace for the repro orgies at sabbath. An that's when folk caw ye demoniac if ye say no. A mean no everyone, but ken the real ballistics in the male clans, well, they'll come after ye, an ye kin get raped.'

Jone drew in a breath. It was a classic picture of the violence that the gospel said surrounded repro-customs. But this was no time to give a sermon on spiritualising human interaction. She had to look at it non-judgementally, like an anthropologist investigating a primitive tribe.

'OK, so the truth is you're a sexualist, a, eh, byre, right? So that puts you in a minority and minorities have always had a rough time. Look at the way the Kingdom treats even protestants. The hard fact is that if you don't want to conform you're going you have a difficult time one way or another.'

'What dae ye mean conform?'

'I mean, be the same as everyone else, or pretend to be the same as everyone else like a lot of people do. If you want to go on being different, you'll have to accept the difficulties. If you do you can be proud you have the courage to be different.'

At last Jone had made her mark. Luner's eyes were shining.

'A think you're different Rev. Ye dinny go on aboot the commandments like the restae them. It's good talkin' tae you, you make me feel better. Heh Rev, A'm gontae the Biopark tae dae some botany on the sabbath, why d'ye no come along?'

Jone gave a vague answer, but steered the conversation onto botany. It seemed right to distract Luner from her distress. Before Luner left she managed to get back to making the point about Luner avoiding trouble. She was sure Luner took it in.

When Luner had gone, Jone's mind collapsed into self-doubt again. She had been so busy trying to be reassuring, she had said nothing about Luner's act of violence. But what about Leeam's verbal racking? It was now perfectly clear what he had meant by 'using the language they understand'. Luner had been telling the truth. It was unbelievably horrifying, but now she believed it. It was horrifyingly effective. Yes, effective. There was Luner turned from an impertinent rebel into an humble listener of advice. If she stayed that way, it could be justified, justified as a means to an end. Was that the way things had to be done here? Oh, it was a harsh savage place she had come to.

6

It was two weeks before Easter and Jone was looking forward to the break just the same as any of the old hands. Mayri Theoversity now seemed like the dim and distant past. The Abbey had become the whole world. Not that she could say she was settled. Everyday brought its little crises and panics. She still dreaded being left alone with the catachumens, always nervously waiting for the Abbot to walk in, or a catachumen to jump out of a window, or her sluggard to get stolen. But though things teetered on the brink, total disaster never quite came. Until the end of term.

It was Onyxday of the last week before Easter and Jone was holding a salvation session with the girls of Thyatira Crew Delta and Gamma. That day she had decided to start a discussion about natural moral attributes. She asked them to give examples of moral qualities, like kindness and courage, perseverance and so on, in the people they knew, stressing that the examples didn't have to be in the cause of Krischanism.

The response was enthusiastic. And as usual in discussions that took off, she had difficulty trying to get them to listen to one person at a time and not fall into a general babble. This was only their fourth session with her. Crew Delta she was getting to know quite well by now, but the Crew Gamma girls she was very unsure about. A bunch of them always sat at the back of the group. They participated less, muttered among themselves and now and then cast sullen stares at her.

Most of the girls were filled with pleasure at the idea that they could see good things in ethnic culture at an abbey session. Some of their examples were inevitably muddied by the sordidness of their lives, but Jone tried to stay disinterested. The important thing was to guide them to see for themselves, to see the specks of gold in the mud. One girl talked about how her ovagenitor had produced six children and managed to love them all. Jone held back any remark about overbreeding and tried to get the girl to understand the concept in the abstract. She could not manage to stay silent, however, when someone mentioned prowess in violence as courage but this proved a positive move, since it led to a heated debate which she managed to just stay on top of.

With the focus on ethnic life, the discussion inevitably moved to other aspects of it that might be spiritual, besides natural morality. It was Mabber who brought up the subject of music. She was a big cheerful girl with sensible well-thought-out opinions. It wasn't any part of her intention to be outrageous when she suggested music could be spiritual, but the other girls giggled and watched for Jone's reaction. No sign of shock was forthcoming. She was curious to know Mabber's justifications.

'Well, see, the way you give us psalms in the Abbey, like, when we huv them in the masses. A dinny mind them, but well, see, A think A get the same enjoyment oot ae music. A mean it's no exactly the same of course but it's well, like it feels the same tae me. Well A mean psalms go tae the pleasure centres in yer brain right? Well so does music, doesn't it no?'

The group at the back began to talk noisily with their backs to Jone. She had to speak sharply to them to make herself heard. They stopped talking, but turned to look at her resentfully. The other girls expected her to be annoyed by what Mabber said but she wasn't. She was amused at this absurd idea.

'Well, yes, it's true anything that gives pleasure is linked to the pleasure centres, obviously or it wouldn't give pleasure!'

'A dinny get any pleasure frae psalms,' butted in Zaner grumpily.

'Yes, I appreciate that the trouble with psalms is that they're made to stimulate circuits that you haven't had a chance to develop yet. At your stage the pleasure circuits are linked to sensory stimulation, and because you don't have a soul, it's difficult for us to map out psalm patterns that would suit you.'

'So if we're no spiritual enough for psalms, why dae ye gie them tae us then?'

Jone had fallen into this. But Mabber was angry too.

'But you're no appreciatin' whit A wis sayin', like A think music stimulates the circuits you were talkin' aboot as well – A mean yer no sayin' we don't have any spiritual circuits at all are ya?'

'No, no, it's just that we have difficulty in tracing into them.'

'Well, A think music does. See when A listen tae music it's like meditatin' ken. A kin see these mathematical patterns in it, that take me away up tae space, like A'm seein' the universe.'

'Yer just blastin' off,' said Molner, and there were lots of giggles. Mabber was annoyed with Molner.

'No A dinny mean that. A mean somethin' spiritual. Like A canny argue wi' ye aboot the brain, but A think how A feel wi' music is spiritual. Some music A mean, no aw of it.'

Luner came in with some support, 'Whit aboot the visional? A bet you say havin' visions is spiritual, but it comes through the senses. An whit aboot that thing you use tae make sums oot ae the countryside an' that, they things ye see daft saints wandering aboot the Biopark wi'?'

'Vistameters?'

'Aye that, well that's gettin' spiritual pleasure oot ae things ye get through the senses.'

Luner sat back with a justifiable look of triumph. Jone found herself falling back on the clichés.

'Well, yes. There's nothing wrong with the senses in themselves. I've no doubt some music is spiritual, but most of it isn't. Yes, of course there's nothing wrong with senses when they're controlled by the cortex, but it's when they're still only linked to the id circuits, well that's the cause of all the problems of irrationality isn't it?'

'Oh here we go,' said Zaner, 'everytime we make a point, it gets back tae the troubles of irrationality. It gets up ma nose when the saints go on aboot music's no spiritual, this is no spiritual, that's no spiritual, everythin' we do is no spiritual. They never admit anythin' they do's no spiritual. Oh no they never do anythin' violent an' idist. Well it's rubbish. A ken fur a fact some are no as spiritual as they make oot. They just act aw spiritual in the Abbey so's they kin tell us off.'

'And in the Abbey as well,' said Luner, 'whit aboot the rack? That's violence isn't it?'

The girls had Jone cornered again. She forced herself to give the standard defence.

'To be truthful, I don't agree with the use of the rack myself. It is an instrument of violence, I agree. But all the same, there is a difference between it and idistic violence. I mean the saints here use it as a form of control, for your own good. They don't use it because they're overwhelmed by violent feeling.'

'Oh aye,' said Zaner sarcastically. 'Whit aboot Rev NkCroom. See the way his face goes aw purple when he pits you on the rack? Isn't that no violent feelings?'

Jone was rescued by Mabber. Though she had started the discussion, it was now escalating beyond her limits of nonconformity, as well as getting away from what she wanted to say.

'Aw come on Zaner, ye ken we get pretty wild if they dinny control us. If they dinny huv the rack, we'd be muckin' aboot aw the time and we'd never get spiritual.'

Now she could get back to the point.

'But honest, Rev, that's why A think some music is spiritual cos it helps you control your emotions. It makes ye feel more Krischan, ken. Could A no put on a tablet on the wall Bible an' show you what A mean?'

Jone knew she should instantly say, 'How dare you suggest such a thing. You know it's against the commandments.' That she didn't was already launching into dangerous waters. It made her so irritated, always to be faced with these contradictions of mission. It would be defending an irrational commandment against a rational objection. And wasn't their argument, that music could be mathematical, the very thing she'd argued in her student thesis? Damn the Abbot and his bigoted rules. 'Well it could be interesting. But you know how strict the Abbot is about his commandments.'

It was enough for the girls. They were like petros at the start of a race. They were determined to throw aside all objections. Two girls volunteered to stand guard at the door while someone else jumped up and switched off the intercom bible. Jone didn't have the heart to say 'No' now. Mabber jumped out and deftly inserted the tablet.

The music oozed out slowly like syrup from a maple tree. The picture was dense jungle and between the leaves, bodies slowly emerged. They were dressed, as far as Jone could see, like birds and they were playing wind instruments and guitars. It was difficult for her to stop herself from laughing. The music consisted of simple, softly-played clichés of harmony and notation. Certainly this bland inoffensive stuff wasn't going to stimulate anyone into an orgy of idism. Jone looked around to check the reactions of the Crew Gamma huddle at the back. They were perfectly straight-faced. Jone couldn't really tell if they disapproved, but she guessed they might. The rest of the girls weren't erupting into idism, at any rate. Luner and some of the others were making faces and pretending to yawn to show they thought the music was as boring as Jone thought it was. Mabber was self-consciously trying to show how much she enjoyed it. Jone fidgeted, wondering if she need leave it on. But why not? They weren't making trouble. The music came to an end at last.

'What d'you think tae it then?' asked Mabber.

'Not much, I'm afraid.'

'D'you think it could be spiritual though?'

'Well it doesn't do anything for me spiritually, but I don't think it's emotionally disturbing either. I thought it was – well, boring frankly.'

Some of the others laughed and Mabber blushed angrily and marched out to take back her tablet.

'Can we no listen tae somethin' decent?' said Luner.

Another tablet appeared. It flashed through Jone's mind that it was strange their having tablets in their pockets when there was nowhere in the Abbey they were allowed to play them.

'This is Yalida,' said Luner flushing with pride. Quite a number of the other girls cheered and chorused, 'Pit it on, Rev, Yalida's the President.'

Jone attempted to put on the brake. 'Now wait a minute. We're not just looking for opium, we're trying to see if there's any spirituality in the music, right?'

'A bet ya yer week's Virtue points that you'll think Yalida's music's mathematical,' said Luner with such conviction that Jone wondered if it could possibly be true.

'Go on, Rev,' said Zaner, 'pit it on an' we'll discuss the spirituality after, honest.'

'Please, just this once,' said Danner.

Jone knew she was succumbing. Partly due to 'doing what they want, just to be popular' and partly out of curiosity. She took the tablet and inserted it. The camera swept down to a desolate moonscape and a tiny figure in black. As the instrumental introduction gained momentum the camera zoomed in on the figure: tall and thin with a painted white face, peering out from a black robe that rose in a narrow pointed conical shape above the face. The way the figure stood so still in the landscape, combined with the stark lighting effect gave Jone a chill of fear. Then the creature opened its mouth and the song began, coming from the landscape rather than the mouth. The scene dissolved into a kaleidoscope of fade-in and fade-out bleak spacey images. The words came across the bottom of the screen.

I am the lonely hermaphrodite
How did I get to be here?
On the moon, on the moon, there was only night
I was cold cold empty dead
I could not burn with native fire
I could not flow with wet desire
My emotions were pure
My thoughts were sublime
Of cosmic truths I was perfectly sure
I did not dance to the reels of time
And yet I knew oh I knew
I was cold cold empty, dead.
The distant stars burnt with fire
But they did not sing to my desire
Silent, silent, space
Silent silent dust
And slow parabolas
In silver cells of loneliness
In lustless, rustless, vales of cleanliness
In drifting ash, in rocks of steel
I lay down lay down
Grey mountains block the way to feel.

There was a break to just the instruments again. Jone began to reflect. She had been transfixed. The patterns of the music were extraordinarily mathematical, not just well crafted, but original. This Yalida, whoever she or he was, had obviously advanced far in theology. But what was the meaning of these extraordinary words? It seemed to be saying, very clearly in fact, that spirituality was dead, and by implication that carnality was alive. Jone's conscience told her she should have been horrified. But she was drawn in, seduced by it, and she was just realising why. She had experienced the isolation it expressed. What was it? The isolation of spirituality. She had never faced up to it before this moment.

Jone's train of thought was interrupted by one of the girls from Crew Gamma standing behind her. She wanted to go to the medical facility because she had menstrual cramps. She was one of the friendlier ones, sitting in front of the hostile huddle. 'Of course,' said Jone and the girl went out. Jone's attention returned to the screen. The singing began again.

Don't die, die, die, die,
Look up, up, up, up,
And know your trap is distance
The mind that read the universe
Traced its letters in the dust in vain
Waited for the icy hurricane
That took the molecules of pearly frost
Specks of hydrogen forever lost
I knew it, knew it, knew it
One solitary lonely forever lost
I want, I want, I want
I know I want
The power of lust rose up
I fuelled the thrust. Broke through, burst free
I set a course on earth's trajectory
Oh earth embrace your newly-born
From jagged rocks of darkness torn
Burnt-out descent. My fuel's spent
I'm here, I'm here
But I can't communicate
I dance in frenzy, I gesticulate
Tell me how I am, give me something like a name
Am I land or sea? Am I cloud or rain?
Am I mind or body? Tell me, tell me
I am falling over the horizon
There is no way to return –

The door of the room burst open and in strode Reverend Leeam with the 'sick' girl behind him. He jammed the bible console off and ripped out the tablet. The silence was as death-like as Yalida's cold, dark moon. Leeam turned to Jone:

'Is your cortex completely scrambled? Have your soul threads been ripped out? What is this? A simulation of the Kayos?'

Jone gaped speechless. Leeam waved the tablet in front of the group.

'Who does this belong to? You'd better say who immediately.'

Luner timidly raised her hand. Leeam glared at her then marched across to the refuse chute and threw it in. Luner let out a pathetic squeal.

'And who else has one of these?'

Mabber raised her hand, her face white with terror. Leeam walked up to her and held his hand out. Then he took it to the chute. Mabber burst into tears. Leeam ignored her and went round asking everyone if they had any tablets, forcing them to open their bags or pockets. Nothing more was found. He returned to the front and delivered a short speech on how everyone knew music was utterly forbidden in the Abbey, and that if anyone was ever found again in possession of tablets they would be very severely punished. He neatly finished as the siren went, dismissed the rest of the group and told Mabber and Luner to report to his base.

When the room was emptied he turned to Jone with a look of disgusted contempt.

'I'm very sorry that somebody like you ever got near this place. And don't think I don't mean that. We have quite enough trouble trying to drop a minimal dose of Krischanism into these benighted heathens without having to cope with eczema like you. I don't suppose you've any idea how upset that girl was. These pathetic scraps of spiritual deprivation, clutching at the few higher goods their simple brains can consume and you go and throw them back in the mud. Isn't that charming? And you're Luner's maternaliser! That's the sickest joke I've come across in my time in this place. Her maternaliser, practically carrying her back into the hell-run. Oh, I can't be bothered going on. The Abbot'll have to deal with you. And I hope for all our sakes he does.'

When Jone arrived at the clerk's office, the Abbot was there speaking to the clerk. He didn't look at Jone but gestured her into his base. 'Just go through, Reverend Grifan,' he said in an impersonal voice. In the base she was left to sit by herself for some time. Was it a strategy to make her more fearful? She had been at work with her soul for the last hour, and had determined to maintain her point of view. It helped that she had no respect for the Abbot's. It made her a little colder. The most crippling feeling had been guilt for getting Luner into trouble. For that reason alone she should not have gone ahead with the music-playing. She had thrown away Luner's last chance through sheer naivety. It had never

58

occurred to her that one of the girls would be capable of telling tales. She had assumed all the cats were on one side of a 'them and us' barrier. But of course, that wasn't necessarily so. In an institution where rules that couldn't be questioned were imposed, there were bound to be some who equated their spiritual progress with obeying those rules, whether they understood them or not.

The majestic figure strode in, sat down on his throne and gazed down at Jone icily.

'Reverend Grifan, what am I to make of you? Either you're a pathetic demoniac as Reverend Leeam thinks, or you're a heretic intent on destroying the ethical law of this Abbey. I think perhaps, in your case, the two amount to the same thing. After all, if you were a pure satanist you would be far more devious and clever. I think the trouble with you is that you use heresy or protestantism, or whatever, to make yourself into a somebody, to compensate for your sheer spiritual inferiority. In my opinion the colleges are far too lenient. There ought to be far more desanctifications than there are, and you should have been one of them.'

He leaned back and sighed wearily. 'It will, no doubt, come as a complete surprise to you to know that you were taken on by me as a salvation case. I was persuaded to do it by an old friend of mine, Cardinal Delfin, a fine man but too soft-hearted perhaps. Had it not been for him, I certainly would never have chosen you for my ministry. The task, it appears, is even greater than I thought. My own mistake is in not telling you this before you joined. Since I didn't, my reason, though not my emotions, tells me it is only fair to give you another chance. Should this prove to be pointless, it will prove the common wisdom that mission is no place for the weak-minded. If you have, somewhere, a genuine wish to halt this reckless fall into self-destruction I suggest you go and seek some salvation treatment at Nace Cathedral. Certainly no one has time to give it to you here. Do you wish to saying anything?'

The news that she had been taken on as a 'salvation case' was shattering to Jone, but there was no time to deal with it. All she could do was pump through a suppressor at full strength. This made her go neutral and able to stick to at least her main intention.

'Since I was responsible for music being played in the session. I want to make a strong request that Mabber and Luner shouldn't be punished for it.'

'Well at least you have some decency. In the case of Mabber, certainly she's basically a good, if not very bright girl. Yes, I do hold you entirely responsible for leading her astray. It seems she had got a sister to bring a tablet in for her, because she was sure you'd let her play it. But it is quite impossible to let this go unpunished. They have to be made examples of. Mabber will have a minimum session in purgatory. It will do her good. It will strengthen her will against corruption. But Luner. It has been a fortuitous side-effect of your irresponsibility that a poisoned artery of defiance has been uncovered. She has been bringing in tablets and playing them on the recreation console bibles for some time now. I fear that purgatory will not be the solution for her. Is there anything else you wish to say?'

Jone bowed her head. What was the point in saying anything? Arguments about the irrationality of his commandments or the spiritual potential of music would be crumpled up and thrown in the refuse chute, with a few choice sarcasms. All that was left was to find out what punishment he had lined up for her. The Abbot sat up straight. Jone looked at him with the hateful awe a prisoner might have for a barbarian army general.

'Clearly you are unfit for the responsiblities you've been given. Someone in need of salvation can't be expected to save others. You will be taken off maternalising and salvation and you will not be left alone with catachumens in playtime. This particular incident is not the only one that has been reported to me, by the way, although this is undoubtedly the worst. Your general inability to handle ethnics has been noticed. Unfortunately, due to our lamentable lack of Blessed staff, I can't take you completely out of freetime. Should any sin be committed during your duty, I will have no choice but to dismiss you. Take that as your final warning.

'And so, for your last duty as a maternaliser I want you to take your charge along to the purgatory. The reason I suggest this is that I believe you owe it to the Abbey, and for that matter to the girl herself, to make her understand how you sinned: that my commandments are there to be obeyed without exception and that this breach of the moral law will never happen again. Do I have your assurance on that last point?'

Jone's 'yes' was barely necessary.

When he dismissed her, she almost staggered from the sensation of being cut adrift. She had thought she would stand up for her ideas, be able to keep in sight the wrongness of his. Nothing like that had happened. Ideas had not even been discussed. All he had done was break her self-esteem with personal insults. The worst blow was stopping her maternalising duties. She had begun to grow a little plant of hope around that, hope that there she could make her own way as a missionary. Now that plant was crushed and tossed away. She was left with nothing but the dreary round of playtime assistance. It would be like being a construction slave being directed on a monitor. Should she have stayed in Strylya as a defrocked Blessed after all? Wouldn't it have been easier than this?

Before taking Luner to the purgatory Jone went to find out exactly what was involved. One thing she could do for Luner now was try to be positive about it. For all that it made her detest the Abbot and his commandments even more, the salvation session incident had given her a fright. It was fine to be a nonconformist, but not when catachumens' lives were involved. She knew all the student protestants' criticism of purgatorial retracing: it was the subtlest way of forcing misfits to fit in. But a week in an abbey purgatory, that couldn't possibly brainwash anyone. But what could it do?

At the unit the neurological priest was very much the theological puritan, but friendly enough. He described the purgatory with a mixture of apology for its inadequacy and pride that he did his best.

'The process is pretty simple. We use drugs to sedate the idistic circuits deeply and increase cortical activity. Not to retrace any circuits, we couldn't hope to do that. Just to induce a condition of alienation while they're here. Then we give them all the usual personality tests and discuss them with them. Basically all we're trying to do is get them, for a while, into a heightened state of self-awareness by getting them to analyse their behaviour without responding idistically. The most we hope for is analytical synapses they have in their memory banks they can fall back on, when they have decisions to make. Naturally, I try to keep saintly moralisms to a minimum. I just get them to weigh up the pros and cons of what they've been doing, in a commonsense way.'

Jone felt reassured. Certainly no drastic changes were going to be made to Luner's brain. And she believed him when he said he tried to be unmoralistic. Theological puritans, she realised, were not a breed she'd met so far in the Abbey. Considering all the attention she'd get, a week of detached self-analysis might do Luner a world of good.

When Jone told Luner about the week in purgatory, Luner shrugged, in an expression of indifference. Jone was worried Luner would be hostile to her, thinking, with perfect justification, that it was Jone's fault. Jone made her inevitably inadequate apology.

'I'm really sorry I've got you into this. I tried to tell the Abbot he should only punish me and not you, but he wouldn't listen.'

'Aw it's no your fault Rev. It wis that sow, Meder, tellin' on us.'

'But it was me that was responsible for breaking the commandments.'

'Well it's stupid forbiddin' it. He's oot the system that NkDod, dinny worry aboot it. Anyway its only a week in purgy. A dinny care.'

'Except next time it won't be just purgatory, it'll be exile.'

And Jone pleaded with Luner to stay out of trouble. Then she told her about not being her maternaliser, at least for a period: 'I'm on trial too.' Luner was crestfallen which, guiltily, Jone was pleased by.

'Well I'll still see you in the playroom, and freetime. An ye kin still come tae the Biopark wi' us. Come in the holydays, please, Rev, that'd be empire.'

This time Jone promised to come, after extracting a return promise that she would keep out of trouble – 'Keep me company in good behaviour!'

Jone began to feel hopeful again. It would be good to see them away from the Abbey. She knew affiliative wave-lengths had opened between her and Luner and she wasn't going to let the Abbot's ludicrous commandments close them.

It was time to go to the purgatory. Jone started to explain what the purgatory did, but she found Luner didn't really understand or was too bored to listen.

'Well it'll be all right anyway.'

'I'm no bothered aboot it,' said Luner, in a clipped irritated voice, making Jone feel she was being over-maternal.

At the purgatory, the priest seemed more relaxed than the first time she'd gone. He took them around the place, showing Luner her living quarters, making jokes about how much better the food and facilities were than in the dormitories.

When they went back to the office he said, 'Well that's it, Reverend Grifan, you can leave her with me now.' Jone got up to go. Luner spun round on her seat and looked into Jone's eyes.

'Yer no goin' are ye Rev?'

Jone was taken aback, 'Of course, I told you you'd be all right.'

Luner reached out and grabbed her arm and gripped it tightly. 'But Rev, they'll muck aboot wi' ma brain. They'll plug me intae the cathedral. They'll make me a slave, Rev, dinny let them get intae ma brain, dinny leave me.' Luner now thrust her arms right around Jone, clutching at her tightly. A wave of nausea at the physical contact engulfed Jone, she stepped back, then turned to the priest with a look of panic. The priest signalled to an orderly who instantly jumped forward and thrust a needle in Luner's arm and she collapsed back into the seat.

'I don't understand it, she seemed perfectly all right about it.'

'Oh, they keep up the front as long as they can, but when you go that's when it collapses. They've got this deep demoniac superstition about any machinery plugged into the head, souls included, that it's the cathedral taking them over by remote control. She'll be OK when she wakes up, when she sees nothing's been attached to her. We'll be able to talk to her and put her at her ease.'

Jone hurried out. It was too much. Did Luner now believe she had let her down? Had Luner sensed her physical revulsion? Would that flinching, and leaving her that way, make Luner believe Jone had rejected her? And thus make Luner reject Jone in turn? As a way of putting her fearless mask back on? Oh, she felt so furious with herself for not understanding Luner's behaviour before they went. Was she ever going to do anything right? A whole week to go before Easter. If only she could just take off with a rucksack and a vistameter, right now.

7

The very first day of the Easter Holydays, Jone resolved to get out to the Biopark. Despite her nervousness about meeting Luner, she knew she wanted to see her and wanted things to be all right between them again. Hopefully, the short catachumen memory would be her ally. But whatever happened, she had to get out in natural surroundings, be by herself for a while and do some scenery computing. It would clean her neurones of all the jumble of data that had accumulated over the last few months, and allow her emotional batteries to recharge.

The subway from Nace ended at the eastern end of the park at the edge of a small birchwood, not far from the beach. Jone, who always felt claustrophobic in a wood, waited till she emerged out of it to take in the whole visual composition. There was no flat, but it was low-lying. To the east was one small carboniferous volcano rising from meadows that were bumpy and tough with knotted clumps of small twisted trees and stubbly patches of gorse. To the west were the crop fields of the agricults, undulating and fertile, though miniature in comparison with the miles of flat land of the mainland agricults. As she faced the sea she felt the land open itself like the palm of a hand to a high, wide, bright sky. Even the big mass of clouds to the south-west didn't close anything in. She turned her back to the sea and had the sensation that the land was sliding down to the sea. Would she compute now? No, she was too restless. She felt a tingling irritation in her legs. What was it? Running, that was it. She wanted to run. Rarely, since childhood, had she indulged in undisciplined exercise. Would she give into the urge? Why not? There was no harm in it. She was off; and didn't stop till she had run out of breath. She fell, panting. The grass was spiky and the ground was lumpy. She meditated on the touch nerve-endings all over her body. Her mind was free to do it, because the landscape had gone. In its place was an immense pit of sky and she lay warm and safe at the bottom of it. As her panting died away she raised herself on her elbows. The predominance of the visual sense and the sky's wide distance returned. She was lying on a slope that went down to boggy ground, then rose on the other side as the backside of the dunes. She looked to her left and saw a stream and it made her realise she was thirsty. She giggled. That was something else she hadn't done since childhood. Something unnecessary, for she had drink with her in her rucksack. There was no harm in it either surely, not in the Biopark. The water tasted good and she gulped it greedily, enjoying the way it untidily wet her chin and dripped on to her surplice. What would her student friends think if they could see her now! She had not been well known for indulging in minor idisms.

She clambered around the sandy pits at the side of the stream and arrived at the beach. The sight made her catch her breath. It was the light. It was quite extraordinary. She had seen nothing like it in Strylya. The low hills of Deana, across the river, the sand and rocks on the near side, the water and the sky, were all blended in many shades of dark and silvery grey, with the sunlight cascading around the forms like liquid diamonds. But she still didn't want to stop to compute. She was still restless. She charged down onto the wet sand, right down to a pile of rocks jutting out into the water. And still she was restless, she could imagine herself swimming right on to the other side. Now she was getting irritated, she had come to compute not to be taken over by inexplicable idistic impulses. Reluctantly she ended up using her soul to calm herself. It dulled the restlessness but it didn't open her meditation frequencies. Was that the soul's inadequacy or her inability to use if skilfully? How could she tell? Wasn't the answer dependent on how self-confident she felt about her spiritual abilities? And did that have objectively verifiable causes? Oh nuke it, this wasn't clearing her synapses. She was only pushing aside the jumble of input to find herself at the brink of an old familiar whirlpool of introspection.

She jumped to her feet. Perhaps the discipline of her body would do what her mind couldn't. She did a few standing yoga postures, and for a moment her brain cleared. She quickly brought out her vistagram and switched it on to one of her ready-made algebraic diagrams. For her coordinates she selected the edges of some of the rocks, the line of the eastern promontory, and the sunlit edges of one of the large clouds with the sound of the waves breaking as a base line. Then she aligned the composition with some of the postures she knew best and produced a motionmatrix. Then she climbed down onto the sand and began to perform it. The concentration didn't come but she pushed herself. It was no use. Even the soul was wearing out. She couldn't stop the adrenalin coursing through her. She couldn't even keep her eyes shut. They were restless too. They were looking for a distraction and within another two minutes they had found one: a fire in one of the bigger dunes. Her climb towards peace was over. She was rolling back down like a rock fall. The possibility of meeting the girls, she at last admitted, was the real source of her restlessness. And the people at the fire were sure to be them. Who else but a bunch of cats would be lighting a carbonising fire in the Biopark? Probably against the park commandments.

Without deciding, she found herself walking towards them. A moment later they were waving. It was them. She waved back and they gestured to her to join them. If Luner was hostile, surely they wouldn't have done that? She found herself running towards them, only slowing down when she got near enough to become self-conscious. Without looking her straight in the eye, she could see the same look of delight on Luner's face as there was on the other girls'. Her restlessness ceased.

Molner came forward; 'Here comes the demon dancer.' And she began to imitate some of Jone's movements with surprising accuracy considering the distance she had seen them from. Jone chuckled, embarrassed and flattered. Apparently, they had seen her go all the way down to the water and had yelled to her but she hadn't heard them. Molner imitated her again, this time exaggerating extravagantly, and said with a saintly sing-song voice, 'Oh isn't it wonderful to dance on the beach. Come on, Rev, dae it for us.'

'I wasn't dancing. I was just exercising different parts of my body in a –'

Everyone dissolved in fits of laughter.

'Aye they were different parts ae the body awright,' said Molner, 'No the same parts as everybody else exercises.'

'Aye you dinny exercise anythin' except openin' yer gob,' said Zaner to Molner.

'Well anyhow,' insisted Jone, 'it wasn't a dance. I don't dance.'

'A feel sorry fur they saints. They canny dae anythin'. They canny dance, they canny sing, they canny whaul –'

The rest giggled and looked at Jone to check her reaction to the word. Jone was curious to know what it meant, but also afraid to ask in case she might be disgusted. Her lack of immediate response switched their attention. They offered her some food. It turned out they had organic tubers wrapped in foil roasting in the fire, 'dochered' from the west farm. 'Ye dinny disapprove do ye, Rev?' asked Zaner, not to seek approval but as a challenge. Jone did not try to explain how different crime and carnality were to her. She had long since ceased to be moralistic about many crimes. If only coping with carnality was as simple. She smiled and asked them how they managed it. She could sense them opening to her. She was wondering how Luner was, but didn't want to embarrass her. Everything seemed normal, though she didn't actually look at Luner directly for more than a moment and neither did Luner at her.

It turned out they had all got into the park by copying Luner's botany avocation pass. Jone was surprised it was so easy to get in. But it seemed that the authorities were easy going with small numbers of ethnics coming in. It was nice to know there was some liberalism in Embra. Molner's sour comment was 'We're doin' the Inquo a favour bein' here. Gie them less folk on the street tae jump on for daein nowt.' Zaner wanted to know how Jone got in, in her usual challenging manner. When she heard missionaries had free passes she hit back at once, 'Oh aye, saints get everythin' free. They dinny huv tae cheat.' Jone cringed with guilt. Zaner quite often had that effect. Geever came in to smooth over the awkward moment and suggested Jone sit down by the fire. She flinched. She had seen them before on historical simulations, but she had never been close and not without extinguishers at hand. The girls cottoned on at once.

'She's feart o the fire,' said Molner.

'Have ye no seen one before?' asked Geever.

'Yes, but they're dangerous –'

The girls were in fits of laughter. Jone reflected on how they loved to deflate her saintly dignity.

Geever came over and pulled Jone's arm. 'Come on, diny be feart.' Molner came over and pulled too. It was surprising how much strength they had for all their unhealthy scrawnyness. Realising the entertainment value she resisted, but let them pull her nearer. As they got her right up to it, Molner suddenly jerked Jone's shoulder almost into it. She let out a yell and Molner pulled her back. With relief Jone collapsed and laughed along with them.

'It's awright. A wisny gontae push ye in.'

'I believe you,' said Jone with heavy sarcasm, and she tried to wave away the smoke and coughed. 'Woodsmoke is incredibly carcinogenic you know.'

'Aw dinny gie us yer excuses,' said Molner.

And Zaner added, 'Anyway the church is carcinogenic. It's full of carcinogens, wi' surplices, sorry, 'cept you Rev. Heh, we canny keep callin' ya Rev, reminds ye of the Abbey. Whit's yer name?'

'Jone.'

This was yet another source of total hilarity.

'Aw we canny call ye that. It'll huv tae be – A ken, Grif, frae Grifan.'

There was a chorus of agreement. For Jone it felt like some kind of baptism.

The girls turned to the fire, the tubers were ready. They rolled them out one by one with sticks. Molner handed her stick to Jone and they all watched her giggling. Bravely suppressing alarm at the sparks, she managed to get one out. The girls clapped and enjoyed Jone's grimace. Luner took some paste tubes out of her rucksack and they spread the paste over the tubers. They then lifted them in their hands and ate them greedily, the melted paste running over their fingers. Jone ignored her distaste and imitated them. By the second mouthful she'd forgotten the crudity of it. It tasted delicious. Probably it was the fresh air and the novelty of the situation.

First the fire, now the tubers. What was going to be the next test in this initiation into sin? The answer came swiftly. Geever was bringing out the straps, tubes and syringes. Canethol! She might have guessed. This was a difficult one. Not because she was afraid, just worried about her cynicism. Canethol had been taken by saints in Maeri who were into 'going heathen'. She had never been impressed by them. They were a boorish group. All canethol seemed to do was make them stupid and empty. How could anyone prefer something that had such a large-scale random depressant effect, to the neuronal precision of the psalmnodes? Certainly it was a vast improvement on the old forms of alcohol and cannabis that destroyed so many lives in the Kayos days, but that negative quality seemed to be all it had going for it. Geever was looking at Jone.

'A suppose ye've never had this before?'

'I have tried it once or twice, but I didn't get much effect from it. I don't see how it could be as euphoric as the altar psalmnodes –'

She was shouted down at once as she expected.

'Well I'll give it another try,' she said good-humouredly. Gaining acceptance was still at the forefront in her relating to them.

They set about blasting off with serious concentration. Jone, as with the tubers, went last. After the injection, she lay down on her elbows and gazed at the fire. Wondering if she could use her soul if the canethol had no effect. A few minutes later her anxieties were over. It wasn't the sublimity of the psalms. Nor was it being transported off to a distant galaxy. It was diving down into a deep warm pool. She was drowning in her own bloodstream. On the outside, the air cuddled her like a down blanket. The fire, the shore, the water, the clouds, all glowed with a fuzzy halo effect. An intense feeling of warm benevolence flowed through her, out towards the girls and everything around her. An iron cage around her head broke and liberated a ghost from her brain that was now dancing round the fire. How had this not happened before? The answer was obvious. Circumstances had changed her resistance to it. What was it doing to her? This question answered itself too. It was opening up her id-circuits. She was being opened up to a pool of formless feelingness long buried under layers of spiritual discipline. She stretched out and submitted herself. Her third initiation test was passed triumphantly.

'Are ye zerogee, Grif?' asked Luner.

'Well it feels good, I admit it.'

Luner grinned. It was the first time they had looked at each other for more than a second or two. Whatever injustice Luner might have felt, it had been forgiven and forgotten. The affiliation wave-lengths were open. Jone's mind drifted back to that conversation about whether Luner was pretty or not. She is pretty, Jone thought, those dark eyes, her smile. What am I doing? The canethol! Am I actually indulging in carnal evaluations? She was embarrassed and quickly thought of something to say:

'Actually it doesn't feel like being out of earth's gravitation to me, it's more like swimming in the ocean, like a fish!'

They all laughed again. She was glad she succeeded in entertaining them without really trying.

Zaner wanted to see her soul. None of them had seen one. Jone lifted her cap, overcoming the instinct that made her feel they were asking her to show herself naked. They crowded round her. She became actutely aware of their smell and physical closeness and frightened they might touch her. The canethol hadn't removed that. Fortunately, they didn't linger long over their look. They were disappointed, having expected something more exotic.

'A still dinny see the point've it,' said Luner.

'Well it does give you some control of yourself. You can stop yourself being violent –'

'Aw come on, it disny stop soggerts like Leeam bein' violent.'

Jone wanted to bite her tongue. 'Well it is under each individual's control. You have a lot of choice about how you use it.'

'Aye, an folk that want tae be violent dinny, so what's the use ae it?'

'A ken whit A'd like tae dae wi' Leeam's soul,' said Molner. 'Rip it off his heed an' make him bleed tae death.'

'Naw,' said Zaner. 'A'd jist rip his droolies off an' stuff them doon his mooth.'

Molner jumped to the theme, 'Aye, we could get him in one ae the shuttles an' tak his troosers doon an' rip them off.'

'Ken, we could leave messages in his console an' that,' said Zaner. 'Sayin' beware the drooly snatchers are comin' tae get ya! and get him aw feart aboot when it was gontae happen.'

Luner's eyes lit up with revenge, 'Aye, we could bring him oot here, an roast them on him over the fire an then make him eat them.'

Now Jone was shocked. The desire for revenge was understandable, but the violence of the fantasy was frightening. Were they capable of translating them into reality? She tried not to show her feelings on her face by concentrating on the fire. Now that she was getting used to it, she was beginning to see there were mathematical possibilities in the movement of the flames. Geever noticed her lack of attention.

'D'ye no like us mentioning the droolies, Grif?'

Jone laughed, 'I don't give a quark about droolies, it's a part of male anatomy I've always been supremely indifferent to.'

The girls hooted with laughter as she'd hoped.

'Actually I was trying to see if I could work out the algebra of the flames.'

This brought more laughter, and Molner's vivid imagination

began working on how the movement of the flames could be made into an 'Apocalypse' game and she began imitating a minister describing them as if they were bits on the screen. Jone's distaste moved to admiration for Molner's satirical wit. What a pity it was left unharnessed by Krischanism.

For the last half-hour, a large dark cloud had been moving up the sky and coming nearer. Now the difference in temperature could be felt and the grass was shivering. Luner pronounced it was going to rain. Zaner looked unhappy.

'Aw grutag, A huvny got a waterproof. A dinny want tae go back tae habs lookin' like an astronaut wi' a burst urine bag.'

'A love the rain,' said Molner in a melodramatic voice. 'It's the only time A get a wash.'

It was quickly decided they would go to the cabin in Birla wood. They left the fire to smoulder to ash within its circle of stones and picked up the unburnt pieces of wood, to leave at the cabin. This conscientiousness surprised Jone, being used to their resentment of obligations at the Abbey. It showed how different their attitude was to the park.

They walked through the woods to the clearing where the hut was. Suddenly, Luner stopped and the rest coming behind bumped into her. There was smoke in the hut. The girls seemed worried they might be Plotinian males, Molner especially. Jone was saddened by the gender defensiveness. There seened to be so little space for innocence in their world. The rain was beginning. They ran to the hut. Luner peered in the window. 'Aw grutag –' Zaner looked in and turned to Molner, her face whiter than ever. 'It's Stone and Grip.'

'Grutij drids, he telt me he wis gontae jettison, but A thought he wis just turbopumpin'.' She swung round. 'A'm gontae the gates, A dinny care if A get soaked.'

'Aw come on Molner, it'a gontae lash it doon. It's miles tae the Fairmead gates. They signed up last week. He must huv his brakes on.' Luner sounded impatient. She turned back. 'He's seen us, he's comin' tae the door.'

'Well hullo there, girls. Are ye no gontae come in?' He grinned and seemed genuinely friendly. Luner was unresponsive to his grin, but was prepared to make her way in. Molner hung back and pulled Zaner back with her. Jone decided she would take the initiative, hoping her presence would inhibit them. She walked towards the door saying, 'Come on, let's go in.' Her guess seemed to be right. Stone stepped back with a look of alarm. This swayed the balance for Zaner and she pulled Molner in with the others.

The girls made for the seats furthest away from the fire. Stone stood in the doorway behind them. 'Whit do we do aboot the spooklegs?'

Grip gave Jone a contemptuous once over. 'Ach, they're nothin' wioot their sluggards.' This interchange froze everyone and made Molner get up and make for the door. Stone at once turned and bolted it. Then he pushed Molner back.

'That's an insult tae hospitality, leavin' as soon as ye've arrived.'

'There's nae hospitality in it,' said Luner belligerently. 'This is no your hut.'

'Targy little byre, isn't she?' said Stone to Grip.

Grip made no comment. Instead he turned his head and stared at Molner, an intense expressionless stare. It seemed to hypnotise Molner. Stone was enjoying the show.

'Isn't Grip a lucky boy then? Aw charged up an' steamin fur it. An' guess what? His little bit've motor wheels right intae his garage.'

Grip now turned his expressionless stare to Stone and still said nothing. Stone carried on,

'Look at him, he's revvin' up. Got his mind on that nice light an' greasy cylinder. He's a flyby grutij racer this laddy. Wins everytime, don't ye pal? Ye want tae feel his pistons thrustin'. He's grutij power-packed. Go on, get yer gas firin', pal. Get yer juice pumped through –'

Grip squirmed on his seat, growled 'Shut up' and turned again to Molner.

'Come over here, A want tae talk tae you. A've been askin' roond fur ya.' His voice fitted in with his bull-like appearance.

'A dinny want tae,' said Molner, her eyes on the door.

Grip's face clouded with anger. 'Dinny you play the tease wi' me, you whauly little byre. You're ma hire.'

'She's naebody's hire,' cried Zaner, frantically. 'She's unbaptised.'

Grip was contemptuous, 'Shut it, ya whauly little freeze, dinny try tae get smart. She shouldny go tae moonfeasts an' get folk fire up, if she's no a hire then.' He got up and moved towards Molner. 'Are ye comin' over here when A ask, or dae A huv tae come an' get ya?'

Molner began to breathe heavily then screamed out, 'Gizzen off, an' leave me alane!' She was on her feet again and making for the door. This time panic had given her a rush of strength and Stone couldn't throw her back. He held her arms and she kicked and writhed and tried to bite his arm. She pulled one of her arms free and reached out to the lock but he caught the arm again in a tighter hold. Now Grip was beside them.

Up to this point the other girls had been in a shocked trance. Luner was the frist to snap out of it. She rushed wildly at Grip. The other two followed and the three were all around him trying to pull his legs and arms. But they were like flies on a bull. All this time Jone had been watching the horror show in a kind of trance too, while at the same time frantically trying to get her soul to eliminate the canethol. Now it was clear and she found that fear had made her alert, allowing her soul to move her brain into the meditation frequencies. She closed her eyes, homed into emptiness for half a minute, then spoke in a loud firm voice.

'Leave him to me.' The voice so startled everyone that they paused. 'Leave him, I can handle him,' she repeated.

The girls drew back and Grip let them go, he was so surprised. She got into a ready position, counted to three and lunged. Two karate chops and he was on the floor. She turned to Stone. He and Molner had parted in their astonishment. She grabbed Stone's arm and flung him down in a judo twist. Still fully alert, she quickly unlocked the door, turned to the girls and said, 'Come on, let's get going.' The girls needed no further invitation. Outside Jone shouted, 'This way, to the left. I came in just over there. Come on –' Grip appeared at the door and screamed out,

'A'm gonna kick start you so hard when A get you ya grutij byre, you'll be damaged fur life.' But he didn't follow.

Jone and the girls ran for all they were worth and soon reached the Nace entrance. They passed through the hatch and then collapsed against the wall. Once they had recovered their breath they turned to look at Jone with what approached wonder and devotion.

'You didny tell us ye could dae marshalarts,' said Luner.

'We're not supposed to use them for violence, only for body control, but I reckon this was justified self-defence,' Jone smiled.

An uncontrollable idist sense of pleasure was creeping inside her brain: euphoria at the thought of becoming their heroine.

73

'Where dae we go noo?' asked Zaner.

'To my mansion. Come on, here's the train.'

When they were seated on the train, the girls began to feel uncomfortable, saying they were too scruffy for the mansions. Jone had to try and reassure them over and over, they probably wouldn't be seen by anybody. She was surprised at their timidity, so different from their apparent contempt for everything saintly in the Abbey. But the Abbey was part of their life. Here they were moving into a world probably as foreign to them as Strylya.

Inside Jone's mansion, the girls put themselves down stiffly on the floforms. They gazed about at all the circles and triangles of the communion chapel and matrifacts and altar with a kind of awe. Jone offered the girls some sedatives and they took them eagerly. The immediate effect on Molner was to make her burst into tears. Zaner put her arms around her and Geever held her arm. Molner looked up at Jone.

'It's aw lies, Grif. He didny hire me. A wis dancin' an' jokin' wae him. He didny rev me up, it's a pack of lies.'

Jone was startled that she felt she had to justify herself.

'I didn't know exactly what was going on, but I'm a hundred percent sure he was in the wrong.'

But they still wanted to explain.

Zaner came in, 'We dinny go tae the moonpalace tae get hired. We just go fur the music an' that. Ye dinny huv tae go just tae get hired. We were goin' hame an' Molner was wantin' tae come wi' us, but he grabbed her an' he cawed the guards, an' he starts tellin' them she'd got hired. They believed him first, but then we tellt them we were pre-baptismal so they flung the lot ae us oot. But he's been hangin' aboot ever since. He's a grutij ape. A dinny ken how he could get free. A mean they crusaders are real ballistics.'

It was Luner who came up with the idea that they should report them to Crusader HQ. But how could they do it anonymously, if they weren't to be found out for forging their way into the Biopark? Jone at once realised she was the obvious person to do it. She could say she had taken them with her, to help them in their avocations. If she took a strong line on what an outrage it was the males were in the park, the Crusaders would overlook the small lies. She went through to the vubay, and acted the part of outraged minister very well, saying she would not let the matter rest until she heard they had been arrested. Crusade HQ was very respectful. She came back

74

and told them about it. To the girls it was another heroism, Jone was having a heady day.

The girls were unwinding. Jone brought out some fruitcake which naturally they were rude about.

'Aw its no they organic nourishers is it? They make me seek,' said Zaner.

Jone was grateful to the cake for relighting their normal sparkle.

'Just try a bit, I bet you'll like it.'

With continuing expressions of disgust they gobbled it up greedily and asked for more.

It was Luner who was first to begin exploring the pliability of the floforms. The others watched her for a couple of minutes then joined in. Soon they were all squirming and rolling around and screaming and giggling with excitement. Jone turned to look out of the window and quickly dowsed her revulsion with her soul. If she was going to be friends with the girls outside the Abbey she was going to have to deal with their habits of physical contact. When she had reacted with disgust to Luner clinging to her in the purgatory, she had rationalised it away by telling herself it had been the shock of its unexpectedness. But now she was faced with the truth. Healthy saints were supposed to view physical contact with detachment not disgust. It was a murky pool of idism in her that had been uncovered once before in a crisis of her student days. But the crisis had passed and she had let it be, and not bothered to put herself through the hard work of exorcism. A voice interrupted her thoughts.

'Are you disgusted at us bein' carnal, Grif?'

Trust Zaner to be there with the challenge. Her voice was aggressive, but thankfully not hostile. Jone coloured, she couldn't be honest and risk hurting Luner.

'No, I'm just embarrassed. Well, you know how we're conditioned away from touching –'

'Oh, aye, A ken aboot that conditionin': conditionin' tae treat us like filth an' nip off tae the moonpalace on the sly.'

'Aw come on now Zane, Grif's no like that,' said Geever.

Zaner accepted the criticism, 'Naw, A diny mean you, Grif, but there's plenty Abbey saints do that – the males anyway.'

'I believe you. I'm sorry if my embarrassment offends you. You certainly don't need to control your behaviour on account of my feelings.'

'We won't then,' said Zaner with friendly rudeness. Nevertheless the girls now sat apart from each other. Jone was compelled to fill the self-conscious gap.

'What do you think about trying out the visional?' She was worried about how they would react to putting helmets on. Fortunately, Luner knew all about visionals and could reassure the others about the helmets. Luner at once wanted to know if it could use a Yalida tablet. 'Well, it could if I had one.'

'Aw naw, A kent A should've had one wi' me the day, but see, A've got oot the habit ae carryin' them aroond.'

Luner gave Jone a significant look. At last a reference to recent events.

'Well that's a wise habit,' agreed Jone.

'Aw dinny worry Grif, A'm gontae keep ootae trouble. Remember A promised?'

How good she was to only remember the positive side of it all.

Jone had an idea, 'How about a trip to one of the planets?'

'Aw yeh, like Yalida's astral travellin' Empire, Grif.'

'I've got a good one about Heisenberg.'

'Aw aye, that's Venus on Astral Travelin',' said Luner to the others showing off.

'How d'you ken Venus is Hysen what's it?' asked Molner grumpily.

'Dae ye no read the read-oots on the tablet?'

'A dinny read at aw, it hurts ma eyes.'

'Yes, Venus is the old BA word for Heisenberg. Let's try it out, it's a good program. If you bring the Yalida with you next time, we could try it out with it, see what it's like.'

They went inside the visional and the girls began to panic again about putting helmets on, except Luner. Jone guessed that she was trying to prove something to her. Jone exerted herself to maximum to reassure them, and Luner exerted herself to back her up. At last they were settled in, and their minds merged into the program.

There was Heisenberg, the evening star. They moved towards it, as if on an invisible spaceship. It was on the other side of the sun and they felt pulled by the solar wind. As they approached, the planet became a large bright but opaque pearl-like object. Suddenly they were moved into the atmosphere. They saw the fierce sulphur and oxygen winds in ultra-violet imaging.

They descended. They smelt the burning infernal heat and the acrid smells of sulphuric acid. They became the different chemicals, as molecules forming and breaking. They reached the ground. They felt the terrible weight of atmosphere on top of them. They were surrounded by continuous lightning storms and volcanoes pouring burning ash around their feet.

Then one fissure opened below and they changed to rock itself and experienced its breaking, cracking, heaving and shuddering. Until they were right down in the melting black iron core. There was a death-like pause followed by a sudden return to the atmosphere. This time experienced differently, through infra-red sight that turned it into a dazzling sea of unearthlike colours. A purple whirlpool of coolness in the north pole, hurricanes spiralling downward from it; a huge break where one wind would meet an opposite one in a blue wall; a wild green westerly speeding round the globe; yellow cloud belts extending right round the planet; orange curving bow-waves; huge red tropical cyclones.

It's like a dream. They wake up. They are back on earth. Heisenberg is the morning star, but the mind that has been there now sees the glittering spectral colours, it's as if they are born again with a new vision.

When Jone took off the helmets she thought at first the girls were in a state of shock and was seized with alarm. Had it been too much for them? They didn't say a word until they were back on the floforms. Luner was the first to break the silence.

'Grif, it's exactly like Yalida's trip tae Venus, A swear it. They must've got it off her.'

'It's a standard Heisenberg discovery program. Yalida must have used it.'

'Maybe she made the program. She is a saint, ken.'

Luner's faith in Yalida was absolute. Jone smiled. Then again she remembered that infamous tablet. This Yalida needed investigation no doubt about that.

The girls were all sure they would be the envy of everyone down at the habs with their visional experience. Jone was a heroine yet again. After more drink and cake Geever sensitively suggested it was time to leave Grif in peace. When they had gone, Jone sat back, finding it difficult not to be pleased with herself, fantasising about having launched a new one-woman salvation program. She struck the ego wave-bands of her soul in irritation, then settled down to a rightful pride in finding a way of putting across the best of Krischanism without denigrating the girls' own culture. She could now face life in Plotin with a spring leafing of hope.

8

When Luner returned to the habs that evening, she found Rannan
curled up on a mattress in the corner of the dormitory clutching her
knees and staring at the floor deep in thought. Tonight was the
night she was going to put forward her campaign proposal, to bring
violent repro-renters before the Mercy Seat, at the separatist
meeting. She wasn't at all looking forward to it. In the habitats she
was confident and even dominant at times. At the Abbey she was
confident in her vocation, but kept a low profile for fear of
dismissal. In the separatist meetings, her confidence was almost nil.
She could see all those males, and for the first time she realised just
how male-dominated those meetings were, with their perfectly
worked-out logical arguments and their encyclopaedic knowledge
of religion and history. And now she was going to face them without
even Eran to hold her hand. She had spent the last hour wanting
some superb excuse to come along to let herself out of it, and at the
same time telling herself however difficult it was, she had to go
through with it – if she didn't do something now, she never would.

Luner's appearance was a welcome distraction though she
seemed irritatingly high. How could Luner be so excited after that
horrible encounter with Stone and Grip? All right, so their novice
pastor had been able to rescue them, so what? It was time saints put
some of their privileged training to the use of ethnics. She was
surprised and suspicious. Luner was usually so cynical about the
Abbey, why was she so enthusiastic about this ignorant nursery
hatchling? Was Luner's worship of Yalida spilling over to the
nearest available half-decent-looking saint? At any rate the episode
with Stone and Grip was enough to remind her of why she had to go
to the meeting. Not everyone in Plotin could have a handy patron
saint for every emergency. But now Luner wasn't any more
convinced about the meeting. 'Grif' it seemed, like Yalida, had an

answer for everything. 'We could get her tae indoctrinate us in marshalarts, then the fellies'd be feart ae us.' Rannan was scornful. To train in marshalarts took years of physical and mental training and anyway it wasn't just about being able to defend yourself, it was the whole repro-ritual system that needed changing. The argument got Rannan's adrenalin going, she was definitely going to the meeting now.

At the meeting Rannan made her speech. Beforehand her stomach had been like a shredder. During it, it was as if someone else was speaking. But she had done it. In the minute or two of silence following it she became aware of the tension as if the air was drawn together in a tight ball by invisible wires. If she'd been able to dematerialise in that moment she would have done it.

About four, or half a dozen, Rannan couldn't remember, stood up to comment on the speech. It was all the arguments Eran had said they would use. Beluvid NkBerber was not only being diversionary, divisive and prejudiced against all males because of the behaviour of a few, she was also ignorant of basic separatist dogma: independence came first, everything else after. This last patronising judgement cut her most, because it preyed on her lack of self-confidence though she knew it was lies. When the last male had spoken she felt the wires of tension burst. The potential threat to their unity had been removed by a reassertion of their superiority. The chairman looked at Rannan with fatherly pity.

'Do you have any reply to make to the criticisms, Beluvid?'

The tension burst in Rannan too. What was in her head avalanched out.

'No, A canny think've any arguments, an even if A could a wouldny bother to give them. It's perfectly obvious that the males in this room dinny gie a quark aboot females gettin' beaten up. Rowts like NkMare beat us up wi' fists, because they canny string two words together but rowts like you beats us up wi' your dogmas, an yer debates an discussions.'

The colour drained from the Dean's face while the rest of the meeting nearly fell off their seats with astonishment. Then they drew themselves into a stiff frozenness and looked to the Dean to remove the pile of excrement that had appeared in the midst of them. He did so. In no uncertain terms he demanded an apology and a retraction. Rannan stood up, picked up her coat, the tears could not be kept back any longer; nevertheless she managed a parting shot.

'A'll no retract anythin'. It's obvious there's no place for me here.'

As she turned, one of the other females near by jumped forward to take her arm and announced to the Dean, 'There's no place for me either.' Another female further back joined them as they passed her and the three marched out without a further backward look.

The three females beat a hasty retreat to the nearest music studio, the Admiral Spit. Music studios were the social centres of Embra's Sewer City, where ethnics, deviants and saints on going pagan met to watch tablets and inject canethol. From the meeting to the studio and for the first few minutes they simply exploded with feelings about how awful the meeting had been. To Rannan it was like the sudden appearance of rescuing Angels from the sky, her normal alienation from saints was drowned in the flow of gratitude. For the other two, Rannan was a heroine who had broken the chains of machophrenic oppression. The two women were both deviant saints, living in Blessed status domiciles. Pallad was tall and thin, and good-looking in the Yalida style, with a timid growth of hair. Nessa was smaller and dumpier with a little bit more hair, but neatly cropped around the scalp in the Blessed fashion.

After a short pause for a blast-off or two, Pallad needed to open up. The event had been a momentous break for her, more than for the other two. In walking out of the meeting she had probably walked out on a cohabitation amoradon. Thalmas, an Inlish ethnic, had been living with her for five years.

'Five years,' said Nessa, 'and it's all going to end because you've split with the separatists?'

'Oh, it's the last wire in a broken network. I've known that for a while.'

'Heh, they'll be coming here after the meeting. Do you want to move?' asked Nessa.

Pallad shook her head, 'No, I'd better see him, see what he wants to do.'

Like Rannan she knew the religious split was more than that, in her case much deeper. She and Thalmas had come together in a shared enthusiasm for metrifacts. He had been making them and getting ignored by the observatory because he was an ethnic. She had hated doing metrifacts that were used for models for building in the playpens and with his support she had deviated and they had precariously lived together on examination virtue points since. She had been able to persuade friends to get him exhibition space at the observatory, but that was where the problem arose. Her metrifacts got more praise than his and he bitterly resented it, putting it down to their prejudice, and he had turned the bitterness onto Pallad. She had eventually given up making metrifacts and put all her energy into supporting him.

'To tell you the truth, I think my walking out had as much to do with feelings about him as supporting your campaign.'

'Well it isnae just aboot the campaign is it? A mean it's aboot the males, an seein' what's relly goin on, wi' the gender divide. Under aw that fancy doctrinal troj, it's them no really wantin' females tae be independent. They want us as their servitors, one way or anither, just like they always did.'

'Yes, that's it exactly,' said Nessa, the gleam of discovery in her eyes. 'I was watching the way the males looked at you, the hatred. I tell you scales fell from my eyes. They don't want things to change. The ethnics want the moonpalace rituals and the saints,' she nodded her head at the other side of the room, 'want to creep up here with their wigs for a bit of gratching, and all of them want to leave the infant servicing to us.'

'Yes, all the equality they say there is in the Church,' said Pallad. 'It's only equality of opportunity for female saints to be like males. And as long as only a few females want to be males that's fine. The rest of us go on being servitors – like me with Thalmas, all that time I spent as an unrewarded therapist.'

All three of them began to analyse the reality of the gender divide. Why hadn't they thought of it before? They realised that to some extent they had, but hadn't articulated it, mainly because they had closed their eyes to it out of convenience. The talk was interrupted by the sight of the separatists coming in. Pallad drew her hands together over her nose and drew herself in tight. Rannan swept her eyes over the crowd without focusing on anyone and tried to look as coldly indifferent as she could.

The separatists appeared to affect the same show of indifference and sat at the opposite side of the room, with their backs to their ex-beluvids. Except for one. As Pallad expected, Thalmas came up to them, with a pained look on his face. Rannan taking a closer look when he sat down decided pain was a natural part of his face. It was lined and gaunt and shadowed, older than his athletic body. She had an immediate antipathy for him, she hated ethnic intellectuals. She also hated metrifacts, but she had swallowed that one because she understood and sympathised with Pallad's oppression on the gender divide. Thalmas ignored the other two and said to Pallad, 'They're going to expel you next time unless you agree to a reindoctrination program.' Pallad felt like spitting. It was painful to see him, but she could still muster up contempt for his organisation.

'Expelled? We've already resigned. How typically arrogant. You can tell them they can stuff their expulsions up their dubs.'

Thalmas was shocked. 'This is unbelievable, after all this time. All of a sudden separatism is bilge. What's got into you? You heard the arguments, they were totally fair.'

He understood nothing and Pallad knew she could not make him understand now. She tried, one last time, to explain her feelings. He was enraged.

'What's all this? This is grutij Bablylonianism.' His voice had risen and people nearby turned round. The wilderness studios may have been Sewer City, but heresies, which were illegal, weren't openly flaunted. Thalmas ignored the rest of the room. He looked now at Rannan and Nessa.

'I might have guessed it, you're not interested in religion, you're just Babylonian sex-maniacs.' He turned to Pallad again, 'If you want to be a filthy Babylonian byre, I'm getting out tonight.'

His loud repetition of the word Babylonian and the hush of the people around listening had attracted the attention of one of the servitors. He walked over to their bay.

'Eh, whit's goin' on here, whit's aw this aboot Babylonianism? This is a decent studio, we dinny have heretics in here.'

'Quite right, brother,' said Thalmas. 'You shouldn't have heretic byres polluting your studio.'

Rannan's fury burst out now. 'He's talking trodge, he's just mad cos his amorade's walked out on him, an' his ego's taken a beatin'.'

Thalmas lunged for Rannan's collar. 'You shut up you little byre freezer.'

The servitor pulled him. 'We dinny have fights in here either, lad, A think the lottae yous had better get oot.'

'But we've no done anythin'.' Rannan was outraged but her rage only made the servitor firmer.

'Look, whether ye're heretics or no, this situation here looks like trouble, so A'm tellin' the lot ae yous, you an all laddie, get out.'

Rannan slumped back, she could see it was pointless, 'We'd better go,' she said to the others.

'Why don't ye go to Sheeol doon the road, it's aw byres doon there,' suggested the servitor contemptuously.

They all left, with their heads bent, ignoring the stares. Thalmas spoke to one of his beluvids as he passed, asking to stay with him.

Outside, Pallad and he stood still and faced each other, each aware they were losing something. Part of Thalmas could almost have repented, but he caught Rannan's hostility in the corner of his eye and his pride took over. 'Maybe you should go along to the Sheeol, then I could go and pick up some stuff from the domicile.' Then he turned and walked off.

Pallad burst into tears and Nessa put her arms round her. Rannan felt compassion for her but also felt unable to touch her. As deviants Pallad and Nessa now practised physical contact, but it was still awkward for them. Rannan was afraid her touch would be too 'carnal'.

'What's this Sheeol, then?' asked Nessa.

Rannan pursed her lips, 'Well it's a bit of a hole–'

'I don't care,' blubbered Pallad defiantly. 'I need some more injects.'

So they went along the road. Sheeol was no paradise. It was noisy and crowded and normally Pallad wouldn't have gone near such a place but what had happened had filled her with the longing to throw herself into carnality, to throw herself into what she was conditioned to despise, because she had been labelled something that was despised. She rapidly dowsed her olfactory nerves and as many of her mathematically sensitive synapses as she could from memory.

It didn't look as if it was going to be easy to get in at first, they were stopped at the entrance and asked for their memberships. Rannan, temper still at the ready, exploded, 'Where the grutag are we supposed to go? We've just been flung oot the Admiral Spit because this rowt cawed us Babylonians.'

Fortunately it had the right effect, the attendant found it hilarious. 'Oh well, A tell ye what, A'll go an get Lazel tae code ye in, she's desperate tae meet mair Babylonians.'

Rannan shrugged at the others, 'Well A used tae think

Babylonians were just a bunch of Astartian Mythomaniacs, but it looks like A'm gontae huv tae change my opinion.'

The others laughed, feeling an emotional release. Well, yes, why not take on the despised label, it gave it all meaning somehow.

Lazel appeared, a small, strong-looking, heavily built ethnic, with a soft baby face. Rannan was attracted at once. She beamed at Rannan conspiratorially and smiled at the others more shyly. She wanted to know if they really were Babylonians.

'Well, whatever they are, that's probably us,' said Rannan and laughing they went into the dark den.

9

On the first day back at the Abbey after Easter, the first hour was taken up with Mass. The cats filed silently into the planetarium and donned their earphones. For the first fifteen minutes there was chanting of statistics of the universe. Each mass had a different set. The cats would listen to each fact, for instance, where a particular galaxy cluster was locted, or how many light years it was from earth or how many spiral galaxies the cluster contained and so on. Then they would repeat it out loud, while looking at the images of the cluster in the realisation taking place in the large domed alcove. This was followed by night sky observations for the season and events taking place from the Jeezus Space Centre on the moon. The cats had to record this on their journal bibles to be used for their personal astronomical observations. This was followed by a chapter sent from Mission Control on a particular topic. This month it was a simulation of the lifecycle of the Binaries JUC X15 in the constellation Sagan. The final part of the mass was not astronimical at all, it was Abbot NkDod's sermon.

The chanting was intended to be a form of meditation, to raise the cats' minds from petty earthly emotionalism to the vast impersonality of the cosmos. In reality, to them it was just a numbing repetition of dry facts. They were equally bored by the observations. Few of them did any observing and individuals who did were thought of as amoebas anyway. The realisation was mildly interesting, but only because it was three-dimensional. Along with the show went all the theological explanations. Despite their two dimensionalness, space exploration was more fun at home in the habs. Partly because it was usually fictionalised and partly because you could always turn the sound down at home, and play music.

The pastors were not much less bored by the content of the mass. Although they pretended to be shocked by the cats laziness about

85

observational journals, very few of them went out at night regularly with their telescopes. They spent most of the mass absorbed in watching the cats, ready to pounce on anyone who might be looking at the floor too long or moving an arm or a foot a bit too much. This proved fairly tiring and they were usually relieved to get back to the comm for their fruitjuices and chat about where they'd been at Easter.

The only person who truly enjoyed mass was Abbot NkDod. The sight of all those passive silent bodies, perfectly under control, uplifted his mind to the sublimity of an old mythological sky-father, looking down on his puny creatures. As always his sermon would begin with a theological truth. Today it was to be the fact that though hydrogen is the lightest and most common element in the universe, all the more complex elements come from it. In the same way the majority should accept how important their humble place in the great work is.

For a moment, as he rose, he felt a twinge of regret that this was his last beginning-of-the-season sermon. But he quickly pushed it away. He must play his role of embodiment-of-the-law to the last, that was his duty. He pulled himself up to his full height and went up to the pulpit and inserted the verse with the text in the lectern bible. All this he did in a slow and dignified fashion. Just as slowly he placed his hands on the edge of the lectern, leaned forward slightly and opened his mouth.

'My children – if you want to know what it's like to be free, join hands together and come along with me.'

It came out of the loudspeaker, a rhythmical sing-song voice to a musical backing, with such perfect timing, that it took everyone a while to realise what was happening. It was loud and perfectly clear and the Abbot could not talk or shout above it. It was Yalida.

'Forget about your points, forget about your play. Forget about your charity, your prayers for today. Leave it filed away in gawd. Tune into the verse of blood.'

The Abbot's face went white, then red. He gripped the lectern to control himself. He wheeled round to look for a janitor. When he saw one he gestured to him wildly to go to the door of the control room. The janitor ran up to it, pushed in his lockcode and found the door would not open. On chanted Yalida,

'Fly up to the wilderness, the wild and wicked wilderness. See the earth exploding in a rainbow cloud of gas. Drink your foam, touch your fire. Smell your sweat and see. What it could be like to be free.'

For those with the presence of mind to work it out, it was obvious. Someone had set up a circuit triggered off by Abbot NkDod's voice in the microphone and probably locking the doors at the same time.

NkDod had stared at the locked door in utter disbelief for a moment or two, then swung around to face the cats. His hands were shaking but his eyes were burning like the fire that rages after a nuclear bomb explodes. But he was far away above them and the music was getting louder. The cats began to shuffle, to whisper to each other, to make faces and gestures and giggle. The ministers were awakened from their shock and went to see if the doors to the planetarium were open. To their intense relief they were. They stepped over to start the rows at the back moving and the rest to stay to order. Abbot NkDod remained on the pulpit without moving, like an emperor in his palace balcony looking out over his ruined city.

It was two or three of the oldest cats who began joining arms to backs in the snake dance that went with the song. The movement went swiftly rippling down the lines. A couple of the younger priests moved to break it up, but the older priests gestured to them to stop. The cats were moving out in order. Trying to break up the lines would only cause the chaos they wanted to avoid. Sluggards were useless too, for the same reason.

It took them five minutes to leave, the five minutes it took to find something to open the control room doors. Yalida's call to freedom sang on unhindered.

'Sisters and brothers, comets all. Freak and fight and dance and yell. Burn your thrusters with ethanol. When we reach escape velocity, then we'll be free. Yes we'll be free. Gulp down the moon, spew out the sun. We'll make a planet of our own. We're the wolf fleet of the wilderness. Bitches and dogs roam the universe. And sing, sing everybody. This is what it's like to be free. Wooahayoo, yap, yap, yip yipee.'

Once outside and heading to the separate playrooms, the ministry reasserted control. But the hearts of the cats were light. For five-odd minutes they had tested, 'What it's like to be free'. Meanwhile the Abbot stood absolutely still, gazing down from his pulpit on the emptied planetarium.

Abbot NkDod returned to his base speaking to no one, and tuned into his altar for five minutes. Then he took the stim helmet off and thought for another five minutes. Then he buzzed his clerk: 'Bring me the file on Crew Alpha, Pergamum Division.' The crack in the ice, caused by his moment of panic and impotence in the planetarium, had closed over. The culprit had to be in that crew, they were the only ones whose knowledge of phototronics was sophisticated enough. Now, he could even afford to be contemptuous at their folly in doing something that so obviously pointed to them. His certainty was invincible, he would find out who it was.

His process of selection from the file was simple. He would interview all the 'rack-fearers'. Since the racks in the Abbey only registered up to Point Three pain stimulation, it was possible to become 'rack resistant'. He would interview those who weren't.

All morning his selections went in and out of his base. But he got nowhere. Frightened they were, and guilty, almost wanting to confess themselves, but it was perfectly obvious, they knew nothing. But the Abbot did not change his mind, he was bitterly determined to prove himself right. At last at the seventh interview, he got somewhere. Neddur NkRossan had seen two of the crew leave the dorm the night before. Neddur was pretty certain they had been sneaking off to a studio, they quite often did, but he didn't say this to the Abbot. He could see by the look on the Abbot's face that it was just what he wanted, and he was immensely relieved to be delivered from the rack.

When he had left, the Abbot sat back and smiled the smile of the self-righteous who is oblivious of any darker motives in his own behaviour. He knew the two lads quite well, hard nuts, clever and defiant. He would see them, but he was realistic enough to know that for all his abilities, they would be difficult to terrorise into making confessions. If he failed he would send them to the medical facility and order them to use ecrephanerium. Normally he saw the resort to drugs as a sign of weakness, but he healed any wounded pride by reminding himself that this was a case of mortal sin. When he had seen them, then he would have to decide how to punish the whole body of catachumens.

In the comm, there was much speculation about punishment too. Much speculation but no information, besides rumours of torture from Crew Alpha, Pergamum. As the day wore on the senior ministers became more and more annoyed that the Abbot was neither consulting them nor informing them of what he was up to. Normally they tolerated his old-fashioned dictatorial ways by getting on with things themselves quietly, but in a serious crisis like this it was unacceptable. They were afraid he would over-react and precipitate some even worse reaction back.

Blane Milar finally called some of the senior pastors into her base to discuss what to do. It was decided that Blane and Reverend Leeam should go and see the Abbot and present the senior priests demands that they should be consulted on what action was to be taken. As the two walked over to the Abbot's base a deep sense of foreboding settled on Blane. She had a feeling this was going to lead them into some kind of showdown. She had to face it, but she didn't relish it.

The Abbot was sitting in his usual stiff, upright posture when the two ministers walked through the door. He greeted them with an unsmiling nod, and a cool distant 'good afternoon'. Reverend Leeam began. To establish themselves in a position of strength they needed a direct thrust to start.

'We've come on behalf of all the senior ministry, Reverend Father, we want to know what you intend to do about this morning. We don't feel this is a decision you can make without consulting us.'

The Abbot bristled and raised his eyebrows. 'If I need to consult the ministry on decisions it is in my power to make, I consult the ministry. If I don't need to I don't. I don't think I need to in this case. The matter is quite straightforward. A matter of sin and due punishment. There are one or two options, all equally simple. I haven't decided which one, but I am perfectly capable of making the decision myself. Do you think I'm not?'

Reverend Leeam flushed slightly, 'But I think what's happened is serious enough to need consultation on what course of action would be for the best.'

'You haven't answered the question I put to you. Am I capable of making a decision or not?'

'Of course you're capable.' Reverend Leeam could see where this might lead, but couldn't see how to get away from it.

'But?' said NkDod, icily challenging.

Reverend Leeam breathed in, 'I think you should make a decision we all agree to –'

'I have never in all my years as Abbot here considered that I had to have the agreement of all my pastors with any decision I have made.'

'I think,' came in Blane with a mounting sense of frustration, 'in this case it's necessary.'

'Why?' The ice was thickening.

Blane paused to pull herself together. 'I and many others are worried that in this case you might make the wrong decision.'

A gleam appeared in the Abbot's eye, 'Ah, I take it by that you mean you think my punishment will be too harsh?'

'Yes, I'm concerned that it will.'

'Certainly it will be harsh, but it will be a punishment that fits the crime. I have always followed that principle in all my retributive dealings, and I will do so in this case. My options are perfectly clear, the only criterion of choice is which is the most practical.'

Reverend Leeam could see this was hopeless. Wearily he said, 'So basically you're refusing to consult us about this?'

'Reverend Leeam, I do not make any decision on the basis of weakly giving into demands. I have been at work all day nailing the criminals who committed this barbarism. Even if there was a need for it, which I do not believe there is, there is no time to go through the tedious business of consultation. You will hear my decision when I have made it, and it will be the right one.'

Blane felt it was time to come to the point, 'Reverend Abbot, I have to say I do not share your certainty on this. I am very concerned that you will over-react in this case and precipitate an even worse crisis. I will state here clearly that if you take a course of action which I believe to be wrong, I will oppose it in any way I can.'

'Are you trying to threaten me, Reverend Milar? If you are, you are being very foolish. I have never been intimidated by threats in my life. If you do not agree with my decision and refuse to carry out a command of mine you will be breaking your contract as a missionary here, and you must be aware of the consequence of that.'

'Are you threatening me, Reverend Abbot?'

'I am stating facts you should be aware of, Reverend Milar.' Then he thought for a moment. 'Or perhaps you have something other than breaking contracts in mind, perhaps you are intended to sneak off to those floforms in mission control. Well, you do not intimidate me with them either. It is I who have kept the lamp of civilisation alight in this dark place for thirty years and I will hold it in my hands until the end.'

Blane had had enough. 'One thing I'm sure we are agreed on is that we are wasting our time here. Obviously there's no point in wasting any more of it.' And she stood up.

The Abbot turned to Leeam and the look pushed any thought of diplomacy out of Leeam's brain. There seemed no point in steering into the iceberg. He walked out behind Reverend Milar.

The Abbot's actions were not being passively accepted in the medical facility either. The medical high priest had to call a meeting of his small staff. The Abbot, as he had expected, had got nowhere with the two lads and had sent them down to the medical facility demanding that a confession had to be got out of them by the end of the day. The high priest was not at all happy about it. Like many laymen the Abbot appeared to think ecrephanerium was able to make anyone tell the absolute truth. It was often portrayed that way in Vulgate sagas. But, of course, it wasn't. There had to be a primary decision by the recipient about what would be talked about. To do any more than that required falling back on the human art of interrogation. The high priest reluctantly set to examining the boys. It didn't take him very long to decide that the boys were telling the truth when they confessed they had been at a studio that night. What was he to do next? The Abbot was logically right in assuming Crew Alpha Pergamum were the only ones capable of it. It looked like he would have to go through the rest of the rack resistors in the crew. He called his staff and told them what they would have to do.

For Rannan it was a violent push into the confrontation she dreaded, but she could not avoid it. It was utterly immoral to use the medical staff as a substitute inquisition. The separatist meeting floated back into her mind, how easy that was compared to this. But she had no choice, she could not administer the drug. She told the high priest that she would lodge a complaint with Mission Control. Interrogation was not part of her vocation. The high priest gave his expected reply. It was her vocation to administer the drugs she was asked to. If she refused he would have to consider terminating her vocation, which was under review anyway. One of the older medics, Tam NkRomer, burst in at this point,

'Excuse me Reverend, but A think yer out of order there. I've had my religious disagreement with Blessed NkBerber, but she's as good an orderly as the rest of us, and A think she has every right to refuse. As a matter of a fact, A'm no happy about it myself, an' seein' the Blessed had the guts to speak out against it I feel ashamed I didnae myself. A don't think it is our vocation tae spend hours on end interrogating folk, we've got plenty more important things tae do.'

Rannan was astonished. Tam was ultra-orthodox in most things and the two of them had had their disagreements, sometimes unpleasant. She would never have thought of him as an ally. Tam was certainly orthodox, but he cared about the cats too and he had never liked the high priest, who, he felt, went along with any prevailing current that he thought would advance his ambitions. With Tam backing Rannan, the rest of the staff, moderates who were suspicious of Rannan's heretical opinions, felt able to ally themselves with her too. None of them felt comfortable with the idea of doing the job. Now it was the turn of the high priest to feel trapped. How could he tell the Abbot his staff refused to cooperate. Who knows what the Abbot might do?

'Look here,' he said with a kind of bullying pleading, 'we're going to have to come up with something for the Abbot. If you think it'll only be me who gets the cut you're underestimating him.'

No one did, and the pressure produced creative thought.

It was Tam who came up with the inspiration.

'It's just occurred to me. A think it's really kinna peculiar nobody knows anythin'. Maybe it's an outside job, an ex-cat. A ken there's a few of them would be up tae it.'

A memory clicked in Rannan. She had heard Badger say in the studio that he wanted to get NkDod before he went on Crusade duty. The timing was right, and he or his friends had the ingenuity to do it. Here was a chance to smooth things out for herself. Telling tales was against her instincts but on the other hand, what could NkDod do anyway? The Inquo wouldn't care about some little trick played on an Abbot.

'Eh, A've just remembered someone sayin' somethin' about gettin' back at NkDod. Aye it was a lad that's going off on Crusade, but A don't remember who, but A bet A could find out. It makes sense doesn't it?'

'All right, I suggest some prompt enquiries. It would be a welcome sign of cooperativeness, Blessed NkBerber.'

'In other words,' thought Rannan, 'I've a bit of a reprieve if I nuj.

Well why not? Anything to stop making big changes before I can cope with them.'

After the meeting the high priest recorded his report that 'as a result of interrogation, the sin had been found to be the work of an ex-catachumen. An excellent lead was going to be followed and the truth was certain to be found.' It seemed a satisfying way of dealing with it for all concerned.

Evensong came and the whole Abbey was summoned back to the planetarium. The cats filed in, quiet and timid as could be. It was clear to everyone something terrible was in store. The light of their moment of glory had quite faded out.

The Abbot mounted the pulpit, just as he had done that morning. For a second or two, as he put his hands on the lectern, the memory of his humiliation rippled through him, energising him all the more for his performance.

'I am perfectly aware that rumours have been rife among you concerning my imminent retirement. Well you need speculate no longer. I will indeed be leaving you. No doubt this thought at the moment gives you great pleasure. Filling you with wonderful fantasies of a future paradise of days spent pursuing avocations and polluting your ears with aural filth. Well you may get your paradise and much good it will do you. When you are sunk in the mire of savagery, you will one day wake to find you have nothing, that you are past hope of salvation, that you are plunged into the ever-downward spiral of sin and violence and poverty and hell. I prophesy, that many, many of you will look back and repent and wish with all your heart that you could leap into a time machine and return to here, to the peace and sanity of this ship powered by the light beams of my commandments. For many years I have had former catachumens return to give thanks to me. Often they have said how they had hated me, when they were here. Chaffed under the heavy yoke of my law. And yet years on, out in the world, how grateful they have been for the discipline which enabled them to make something of themselves in the Krischan world. And I mean people who started with nothing, who came from the bleakest and most savage of habitats, who joined up in the interplanetary Navy or the Crusaders, winning honour and rewards.

'But of course in every generation there is a tiny minority for whom the law is nothing. These are the real satanists, those who have been so infected by the cancer of barbarism that they are beyond cure. It is, as I now know, that minority who have perpetrated this morning's blasphemy. Unfortunately, my jurisdiction does not extend beyond these walls, I alone cannot stop the hurricanes of barbarism wreaking havoc out there. But I do still have the power to check sin within here. But what was your sin? That obscene little outburst of idistic movement. It was not satanism, oh no, to credit you with satanism would no doubt delight your perverted little egos. No, your sin is that you have no will of your own, and that is why you need the protecting shield of my law, to protect you from the bacteria which can so quickly infect those who have no control of themselves. My control here is a conditioning which does not yield results until you are old enough to use what has been absorbed. Until then you need its protection. Tragically this morning a tiny break in that shield allowed the bacteria of barbarism to penetrate. The only cure is innoculation. And that means a treatment of physical control. From the day after tomorrow you will be given a dose of CPK daily, in amounts depending on your age, weight and height.'

A seismometer might have registered the shock-wave that swept through his audience. Everyone had heard of coactoproskinone. It was a highly sophisticated behaviour modification drug. Its purpose was to inhibit aggressive responses to commands. Its use in the soul was quite uncontroversial, but administered externally that was something else altogether. It was still used in Redempshon and atonement colonies for the severely ethically sick but in Abbeys it was in the same category as the rack. Its use wasn't banned but things were heading that way. Mission Control, everyone knew, would not approve.

Among the pastors, there were two reactions. The progressives were disgusted. It was not only a denial of spiritual liberties, it was also in this context ineffective. Only a spiritually mature person could distinguish between its rational and irrational uses. All the effect it would have on the cats would be to dowse their aggression indiscriminately and thus sap away their creativity. The reactionaries were disgusted too. Here was the Abbot hypocritically turning his back on his own most cherished beliefs that behaviour modification could only be achieved through forcing yourself to obey commands, just because he had been made a fool of.

As for the cats, with their fear of all Krischan drugs, any drug meant they were going to be magically transformed into slaves. Already strategies of absenteeism were forming in their minds. The only person who was delighted by the news was the medical high priest. He was an old-school behaviourist. Only drugs really changed emotions. He too was contemptuous of the Abbot's hypocrisy, for he had been advocating the use of drugs for years without success. But never mind, now the chance to prove his views was laid in front of him. He would be able to record a report. When the present trend at Mission Control had passed, he would be there with the hard theological truths. And there was a bonus. His staff would have no reason to refuse, CPK was as easy as any other drug to administer, he would have every reason to dismiss anyone who refused.

NkDod watched the horrified reactions and almost smiled.

'Do I see looks of horror and outrage? How dare you? How dare you?' He lowered his voice to breathe the repeated phrase into the microphone. 'I would never think for a moment of administering such a drug to people who acted with the grace of Krischan beings. But those who act like heathen savages deserve to be treated accordingly. So don't look at me as if I had wronged you. Consider yourself lucky I am giving you treatment and not a deprivation punishment. I could be perfectly justified in putting every single one of you in an isolation tank for sin.' He paused, took his hands off the lectern and stood surveying them with a sense of satisfaction.

'I think you should be grateful that you are being given the opportunity to experience what it is like to be a disciplined Krischan. I suggest you grasp this opportunity, for I'm sure it will be the last you get. As part of this chance I am giving you, every morning after you receive the dose of CPK you will come into the planetarium and you will chant my commandments. With the fixing effects of CPK I think I can safely say, whatever you may do with your life, a knowledge of ideals of Krischan behaviour will remain in your memory banks till the end of your life.'

10

Rannan didn't go back to the habs that evening but went to Lazel's and from there the two of them went straight to Sheeol and had a few blast-offs in quick succession. There was no choice about resigning from the Abbey now. It was not even worth talking about. It was the future without it that had to be thought about now. Resigning meant Rannan would lose her Blessed status, so there was no hope of her transferring to another vocation. The choices were limited and difficult and complicated even further now because of her relationship with Lazel.

Going back to the playpens was no choice, she would do anything rather than that. Trying to get a post as a servitor of some sort in the wilderness was impossible unless you were somebody's hire or had been to Lundin first. Sewer City here was almost a club for survivors from Lundin or the continent. Should she go to Lundin then? But would Lazel come with her? Could she leave without her? The only other option was to live with Lazel, precariously existing on Lazel's Virtue and the odd point she could pick up herself.

It was soon clear enough, Lazel didn't want to leave Embra, having only recently come back. Lazel had been one of those people who had left to go to Lundin as soon as she had been baptised. She had started as a servitor in restaurants and almost inevitably wound up in the Gratcher trade. It was mindnumbing but paid decent money and that gave you access to the world of opiumation. That led to an involvement with a musician and with him she travelled Yurope on the caravan routes. At first it had been exhilarating but eventually her total dependence on him without a trade of her own and his increasingly violent possessiveness brought her to break-down. At that point she had the great good fortune to meet some Babylonians from Taleea who took her with them. It was the self-confidence and the theological indoctrinations she had got from them that had enabled her to come back to Embra and gain Venerable status.

Now she had a vocation saving girls like she had been, and though she had great contempt for the Salvation program, she loved helping them, and felt they needed someone like her around. The only place she would contemplate moving to now was Babylon, the women's settlement in Syny. But at this stage that was only a fantasy of escaping when you felt down, and probably a fantasy of what Babylon itself was like. At the same time she didn't want to lose Rannan. Having Rannan come to live with her seemed the best option to Lazel.

But it wasn't the best option for Rannan. Not confident about picking up enough Virtue points if she had no vocation, she was worried she might become too dependent on Lazel. And how long would they last under that strain? Why on earth couldn't she just stay and do the vocation unthinkingly? After all, things would change when the Abbot left. But the CPK, no! Never in a million years would she touch it. It looked like she had no choice.

She took another blast-off. She was already way over the limit. Her eyes wandered to the wall screen. She hadn't noticed till now it was Yalida. It was the fire maidens of Io and the landscape of Io filled the screen, like a great red-hot sphere of coal, oozing out poisons of white, yellow and orange sulphur from deep black holes. She was drawn to the words passing across:

Between Empire and frozen dominions
We are pushed and pulled by the tide
Boiling and melting under pressure
Our feelings have nowhere to hide

From dark pools of molten sulphur
We erupt with anger's speed
We have no crust to shield us
From the fires of naked need.

It was demonic, it was Yalida mirroring her mind again. This time it frightened her. It made her realise that before the night was out the fire of anger and naked need would erupt. 'Just what we need –' she heard Lazel mutter sarcastically. Rannan looked up to see Pallad and Nessa and one of the other deviant saints, Anal, coming towards them. Rannan swallowed hard. She still felt a loyalty to Pallad and Nessa because of the separatist walk out. Nessa she really liked, but with Pallad, and even more Anal, the differences hadn't come out in the open but the cracks were beginning to appear. It wasn't that they didn't mean well, but it was the assumptions: like Pallad when she talked about metrifacts assuming everyone had the same respect for them. And the sheer ignorance: of what life was really like with no access to Virtue points. All the time you had to control yourself, so as not to offend the pampered spores' delicate sensitivities. The pressure under the thin Ionic crust was building up.

The three of them sat down just as Yalida was moving on to Gannymede. Rannan, in no mood for chat, left the socialising to Lazel. After the blast offs, she turned to the screen.

> We are the giant ice-maidens
> Cool and grey and light
> We are the ice crystal courtiers
> Of the queen of satellites.
>
> We are the shadowy islands
> Of ancient upper crust
> Our wounds are cratered secrets
> Smoored by the plastic dust.
>
> Our thoughts are icy extrusions
> Our feelings a viscous flow
> In narrow grooves we must lead you
> If our language you long to know.

Like a high Ionic plume of sulphur dioxide, laughter burst out of Rannan.

Anal, next to her, said, 'What are you laughing at?'

'Since, yer askin': you, the ice-maidens of Gannymede, fire maidens of Io, ice-maidens of Gannymede, oh yeh, that's us an' you.

Anal went rigid, ironically confirming the caricature. She knew the song as well as the others. What kind of picture did Rannan have of her? It was grossly unfair,

'I find that insulting, I'm not ice cold.'

Rannan felt the sulphur bubbling, she was going to have a bit of combustion, good.

'It doesny say you're cold and dead, it says your slush, wi' wonderful intricate brain patterns.'

Nessa, one of life's reconcilers, jumped in. 'I think it is true of the way we've been conditioned by the church, though that's not the whole of us.' She said it to Anal in a placatory way. Put like that, yes, Anal had often said as much herself. She could now see the danger in Rannan's angry tone and nodded and said no more.

Pallad was frightened, She could see Rannan was very zerogeed, guessed something had happened but wasn't able to ask for fear of sounding patronising. Lazel was worried too. She knew Rannan wanted and needed to erupt, but she knew it might be destructive. But destructive of what? A phoney alliance? She had seen women tear each other apart before, when she was with the Taleeans. For it to happen here would be devastating. They were a tiny island of Babylonianism in a sea of hostility. Didn't they need each other? The ethnics particularly needed the support of the saints. They needed their access to the church. But grutag, why was it them who had to make the compromises, to always have to wipe their saliva off the chalice before passing it on? Was it really worth it? What were they going to be able to do anyway? Apart from talking round in circles. She decided to bring it up, hopefully to distract Rannan.

'Heh, we said we were gontae talk aboot actually takin' on some action. Anybody come up wi' anything?'

Rannan slumped back resentfully, knowing Lazel was chickening out, blasted off yet again and looked up at the screen. It was the old familiar, 'If you want to know/What freedom could be like/Get up to the wilderness –' Suddenly she had a marvellous inspiration.

'Heh, why not put a team in for the Witsun rampage? Ken, for publicity A mean, grutag doon, if we had saints in the team.'

The image of Luner's escape in the park came into her head,

'We could get you lot dain' marshalarts, heh, an' we could practise wi' a visional, if we even gottae the end, what a show!'

Lazel was bowled over by the idea. She looked at the other three, Nessa looked embarrassed and scared but not hostile. Anal looked uncomprehendingly aghast. Pallad seeing conflict erupt, froze. Rannan grinned and grabbed Pallad by the arm and felt Pallad control her instinctive repulsion.

'Heh, come on, lass, have ye no been desperate tae use yer marshalarts for somethin' really useful? Did A tell ye aboot this minister Luner met in the Biopark?' And Rannan gave a résumé with heavy ironic emphasis on the idea of a saint being of use at last. 'Aw they years of trainin' an aw ye dae with it is dance aroond motionmatricin'.

Now the reality of it all had gone through Anal and horror was eclipsing her face.

'I can't believe this, I thought we were supposed to be Babylonians and now I'm hearing the suggestion we throw ourselves into the machophrenic barbarism of war.'

Of course, rationally it was a totally fair objection. Lazel responded, 'But we'd no be gettin' involved, no really. A mean it'll just be a once off. It's true the rowts just go in fer it mostly tae get a chance ae legally beatin' each other up. But we could take advantage of that. Leave them fightin' each other at the beginnin', just fight for defence, an' we'd shoot on tae the end, and get on the vulgy. What a gospel stunt.'

Nessa and Pallad were beginning to see it intellectually, but their emotions were way behind. Anal saw nothing at all.

'This is demonic. What difference does it make fighting for self-defence? Its still fighting and fighting is machophrenic barbarism.' Her voice was going quite shrill, making her saintly accent stand out in caricature. 'I can't understand how you can think of getting involved in such horrible filthy savagery.' Rannan's point of final eruption had come at last.

'Filthy? Oh, that just sums it up, doesn't it? We dinny need aw yer moral flatulence aboot breakin' free of male machophrenia. It's oor smells ye dinny like, isn't it? An whit's this barbarism ye're talkin' about? Violence? Grutag at least the violence the rowts go in for in the wars is between themselves. Ye canny say that aboot the violence of the saints wi' their redempshon, an' their play, an aw their lies aboot self-development that keeps aw the goodies fur themselves an' deals us the troj.'

Anal looked frightened, 'I didn't mean it like that.'

'Then what dae ye mean, filthy? What's filthy? The smell ae petrol? OK, so ye dinny like the smell ae petrol. Ye kin use yer soul tae dowse it, then. Or is it the smell ae the ethnic bodies up against ye inside the petro? But yer soul could stop that an aw, or are ye scared of bein' touched? Is that what ye mean by filthy barbarism, bein' touched by one ae us?'

Anal's face had gone completely white and she was trembling. Without thinking she found herself standing up. Her voice was low and shaky but grim too. 'That's it, I'm going. I joined this sect because I thought I'd find lots of mutual sisterly sympathy. I didn't join to be attacked like this. Obviously I've joined the wrong sect.' And she walked out.

Rannan buried her head in her hands. Nessa jumped up, 'I'll go and see if I can talk to her.' Rannan began to cry. Lazel put her arms round her shoulder and Rannan spoke between sobs.

'A shouldny have lost the heed. A'm so grutij zerogee. A've nuked the sect now. Grutag ma temper. Its always makin' trouble.'

Lazel was adamantly reassuring. 'But what ye said wis true. Dinny start blamin' yourself. She chose tae walk out. Nobody telt her too. An' walkin' out's worse than gettin' angry. It's a total rejection.'

Nessa came back in to join them. 'She's not coming back but she gave me her vu' code. I've got a feeling if it hadn't been that it would have been something else. I don't think she felt she fitted in from the start.'

'Fitted in,' raged Rannan through her tears. 'Ye mean cause there's ethnics in the sect?'

'Well,' Nessa could see the point but, 'in a way, I mean I guess she's never been faced directly with ethnic anger before. So she got scared and ran away.'

'She's scared? Dae ye no think A'm scared of folks walkin' out on me, the moment A lose ma temper? OK, so A'm lettin' off steam maybe, but grutag, can A no dae it wi oot aw of a sudden bein' the big bad wolf that's eaten up the sheep?'

Now Nessa, though she could see what Rannan was saying, felt attacked too. 'All I meant by what I said was I don't think you're responsible for her walking out.'

'Oh aye, but A'm responsible for no keepin' ma mouth shut, an' keepin' the peace, right?' Nessa couldn't carry on. She put her hand over her face. Pallad's eyes fixed on her feet. Lazel hugged Rannan tighter and hung her head. They had come to an impasse as far as words were concerned, everyone knew that.

Eventually Lazel said, 'Looks like we've gottae be honest aboot this. A think the only thing we can do is promise tae keep talking an' no walk out on each other. A mean no right now, A'm sure

Rannan feels wrecked.'

The idea that the problem was going to be tackled, but not yet, appealed to all of them and the atmosphere lifted a little. Nessa the peacemaker came in as usual.

'Are we going to follow up this rampage idea? I mean, to be honest, I'm scared as well. For a start, not all saints are good at marshalarts. I hated them. I gave them up years ago. I used them as motionmatric forms, but I couldn't use them to defend myself.'

The great idea fell somewhat flat. The sect had to have a minimum of two petros, needing two marshalarts practitioners.

'Well if you think we're up against rowts that don't know any, I reckon I could show you some if we use a visional.'

Pallad was pushing herself to cope with the idea. Still she was saying 'OK.' And for the moment it put heart into them. Rannan in the calm after the storm was finding her humour again. 'Maybe Luner could get this minister she's so devout on tae join us,' and for the first time that evening her face broke in a friendly grin.

11

Rannan NkBerber didn't resign from the Abbey, Abbot NkDod did. Or to be more precise he took up a long-standing, long-refused invitation to visit the moon to receive a presentation of a valuable BA antique, a gift given to those who 'had given long and outstanding service to mission'. Blane Miler had done as she had promised, told him she would report to Mission Control and then did it. The CPK was never administered and within a week, without any ceremony, he had gone. 'Thank fusion we're spared the farewell sermon.' None mourned his passing. Some of the older generation of pastors felt fearful that now the tide of history was going to move the Abbey far away from what they were equipped to deal with, and thought more seriously about moving on themselves. Some of them were resentful that NkDod had let himself be bought by a free trip to the moon (a reward that wouldn't be coming their way) but none of them was prepared to fight in his stead. The progressive ministers, and the younger ones, were hugely relieved but also apprehensive. The era of the commandments had been like a long sleep. Now they had to wake up to freedom and that meant the work of having to act and think for themselves. It was exciting but unnerving too.

Abbot NkRaze looked and talked and acted like a classic reformer. He was well-built, sporty, more youthful-looking than his age, and brimming over with enthusiasm and ideas. Although his own canon wouldn't come into operation till the next term, some aspects of the new could be slipped in without much disruption. Outside visits was one, an idea he mentioned first while sitting one morning with the Miler Orlam group. Sitting in the comm was just one of his small innovations that had a seismic effect. After chatting about possibilities he asked Jone to come to his office.

Jone had been as delighted as anyone at the sudden change in regime. Now the opportunity to put all her ideals into practice was in front of her. Was she going to cope? Her nervousness wasn't lessened by the matey Abbot himself. His ebullient self-confidence inhibited her on a personal level just as much as NkDod's coldness and when she went to his base she said almost as little to him as she had to NkDod. It was strange, for he was saying just the kind of things she would have wanted to hear. He was suggesting she should take one of the first parties out on the history expedition and he was quite happy to accept the idea that it should be Crew Delta, Thyatira. He also said she could get Luner and Geever back as maternalisers and that Mik ArBrenan would be going with her on the outing.

Still she was relieved to leave his base and her elation at being with Luner and the crew and the real chance of getting to know Mik was dampened by worry. It was one thing to go along with events out of hours in the Biopark. It was quite another to be responsible for making protestant Krischanism work, at the Abbey.

Since the day of the fight, when Mik had helped her out in the playroom, Jone had not been alone with him but her respect for his views and liking for him had not diminished. It was good getting together to talk on a practical level, it broke down the inhibitions. There was still the kind of distance that came from his zoological upbringing but she was getting used to it and (though this was difficult to admit) finding it quite exciting.

The expedition was to be into the hills of the wilderness to the old nuclear shelter. Only forty years before, it had been the hideout of Neronian heretics, the strongest and most bitter opponents of the coming of the Kingdom. The crew were going to film the drama of the final capture of the shelter by the Crusaders. The Neronians had been betrayed by one of their own number and the Crusaders had captured the base on the night of a festival. Who was to play who in the drama was inevitably dominated by the gender divide. At first girls and boys insisted they had to be the Crusaders. No one wanted to be the losers. Then Jone came up with the idea that since the Neronians were celebrating a festival the girls could, as a substitute, find some mathematical music to do motionmatrices to. The girls were instantly converted, and soon enough the boys wanted to be Neronians as well. Until they were pacified by promises of tychee motionmatrices. 'The first stage towards marshalarts,' as Mik put it.

By the time they were ready to go, everyone including, almost, Mik and Jone, were walking on air.

The subway to the wilderness came out at Enster, so there was no way to avoid its chaotic assault on the visual senses. The buildings, the garbage, the petros and other indefinable machinery seemed like a fast-run illustration of the second law of thermodynamics. Jone had dowsed her olfactory nerves and inserted an osmotic gauze in her nose to minimise the effect of whatever poisonous molecules might be hovering around in the air but no one, she reflected, had thought of a way to eliminate visual pollution, short of totally altering the human-made environment, and Enster was vivid proof that only tyranny could do that.

Enster's citizens appeared to enjoy their freedom to choose Kayos. They strutted about in their lurid unmathematical clothes purposefully and energetically absorbed in their business. The main street was lined with little rooms with windows. Inside people were bartering for clothes, food and all sorts of unidentifiable junk. If they weren't in bartering places, they were in garages tinkering with petros, or the oddest and most amusing sight, repairing buildings with their own hands. Although Sewer City depended on slaves for its raw materials just as much as the Kingdom did, it was part of the fantasy of Kayos freedom to pretend they had nothing to do with it. Outside the factories there was not a slave in sight.

There was little time to look around. Jone and Mik needed all their strength to keep the cats from breaking ranks to go off to see this big brother and that big sister. They were aiming to get out to the country as quickly as possible. They succeeded. It gave them some much-needed optimism for the rest of the outing.

As they cleared the town their view was obscured by the town behind them and the hill in front of them, but they saw it was wilderness already. The road had become a mud track, the ground was uneven, with coarse stubbly grass, clumps of heather and protruding boulders. The concentration needed to follow the path made the discipline easier. Mik joined Jone and said, 'What do you think of Plotin's little corner of Sewer City then?'

'Fascinating, if you can cope with the visual pollution.'

She grinned ruefully and he smiled back sympathetically.

'Did you see they were buying goods in the shops with money?' he asked.

'Shops? I'd forgotten that's what they were called. No I didn't. So Sewer City has money? But how?'

'It's manufactured in Trojopolis in Roozha. That's where all the economists live. There must be, oh, just a handful of them that king the factories and the oilfields and the banks.'

'I know it would be tyrannical to wipe it out, I realise that, but is it right, or even sensible for that matter, to tolerate such a huge organisation? It's a whole kingdom not a city.'

'Well, I mean, originally they couldn't, it existed and proliferated. Yes, I think it is wise, it's a necessary outlet for idism. As long as it's contained, that's the main thing and it is. The economists see to that. Destroy Sewer City and their power is destroyed, so they keep a tight reign on heresy. It's a weird irony isn't it? It's about freedom to be idistic, yet the economists have more power in Sewer City than the cardinals in the Vatican. All the laws that keep us civilised restrict the power of those at the top. If you're a king in Sewer City you can kill someone you don't like – or pack them off to an off-world atonement opportunity.'

'Well I can see what the economists get out of it. But what about the ordinary people? I mean yes, OK, for a temporary break, to go off and play with petros, yes, I suppose I can see it, but to live in it, the terrible insecurity of it, the discomfort, what do they get out of it?'

'I've thought about that, and you know what I think it is? It's power too. I mean in global terms it's nothing, but for themselves: like supposing someone's got a piece of petro engine and someone else comes along and wants to buy it. The person who's got it thinks, if I could convince this person I'm the person who's got this particular bit of machinery in condition, I could get a lot of money out of them. And so he does, and he feels he's a king economist in his own little world, and that gives him a sense of power. See when people are judged fairly, as they are in the Kingdom Virtue point system, there's no opportunity of kidding yourself, of living in an irrational world of illusion. You've got the objective fact, perfectly quantified, of your virtue and you just have to accept it.'

Before Jone had time to digest this, they were interrupted by the expedition's first casualty. One girl had stopped in her tracks, sat herself down on a rock, taken off her shoes and was refusing point blank to go any further. Mik whipped out his first-aid kit and applied his massage beam. But it didn't make her move. Mik ran through his repertoire of persuasion. Still she refused. Finally he lost his temper. And she dragged herself to her feet with surly resentment. In the meantime two lads had wandered off the track and landed in a large clump of gorse bushes. Mik yelled at them to come back. They ignored him and carried on pushing through them. Eventually they made it, torn, scratched and shamefaced. The sight of them put the others off venturing away from the track.

They moved on up the hill. The view down to the river and over to Plotin was opening up, but they didn't take time to look. As they climbed, the moans and complaints about 'sair' feet and boots 'killing' them rose like the slope before them. Two of the girls even tried to get Mik to carry them on his back. He treated it all with good humour but refused to let them do anything else but go on, dangling the bait of the summit and extra treats for those who got there first. This spurred on the boys. The girls didn't care.

'Whit's he talkin' aboot, treats?' said Molner grumpily. 'Some fancy bit ae fruitcake muck? Isny carbopulp that's fur sure, ye canny fry things on grass.'

Mik strode out in front and Jone kept up the rear, to make sure no one fell behind. She had watched his handling of them with admiration and hoped he didn't mind her letting him have more responsibility. She felt she had a lot to learn from him. Her thoughts were interrupted by Luner coming up alongside her. Jone had been delighted at the way Luner had behaved during the preparations, as keen as any of them. She could sense it was due to Luner's liking for her as much as anything else. But there was nothing wrong in that. Affiliation wasn't a bad motive for Krischan behaviour. And anyway didn't she get as much pleasure out of Luner's affiliative behaviour as Luner did? She had been very glad to be back with the crew again.

'It's empire here, isn't it, Grif?'.

'Mmm. I was just wondering if I should get my vistameter out and do a quick calculation on the line of the hills over there.'

'Oh grut – sorry d'ye always have tae dae calculations? Can ye no sometimes just enjoy starin' at things?'

'Oh yes, I meditate too.'

'Meditate! Ye've always got tae caw it wi' a big word.'

'But meditation isn't just looking.'

'A ken whit meditation is: A dae it too. Ken sometimes A kin look at a rock or somethin' an well, imagine bein' the rock. Ken whit A mean? A'd sometimes like tae be rock on the seashore, just standin' there gettin' pummelled by the tides for thousands and thousands of years. Better than dyin' like a human bein'.'

'Are you frightened of death?'

'A suppose so. Sometimes A've got scared at night in the dorm. When A canny get tae sleep, but then somebody snores an' A get mad at them an' forget aboot it. A used tae say A'd kill masel' tae take revenge on folk, ken? Do you think aboot death?'

'Well, no not much. I mean, we're brought up to believe if we make testimonies for the gawdstores, that's the part of us that lives forever.'

'A dinny believe in this Almyty Gawd stuff. It's no ethnics' thoughts they keep forever is it?'

Jone was familiar with that criticism and knew there was no answer that wasn't insulting. 'I know, as a matter of fact I haven't recorded anything for gawd since I've been here.'

'Oh aye, muckin' aboot wi' 'niks in the Biopark isny good enough data for gawd, A ken.'

'No, no, it's not that. When I was in Mayri I recorded in our protestant gawdstore, but I haven't got in touch with them yet.'

'Oh aye, A wis forgettin' yer a bit of a heretic, Grif.'

'Now wait a minute. Protestantism and heresy are quite different.'

'A ken, A ken. Dinny start sermonisin', A wis only tryin' tae make ye mad. A like seein' ye when ye get aw bothered aboot things.'

Luner smiled and her eyes twinkled. Jone smiled back. It was perplexing the way the girls were. At one moment full of admiration for her, at the next ready to cut her down to size.

Eventually they reached the top of the hill, only to find it hadn't been much of one. Before them was the glen with Tenhorn Hill where the shelter was at the opposite end, with the steep scree side rising up to a stark jagged point. One of the cats shouted, 'Aw no, look at where the hostel is.' It stood halfway up one of the gentler sloping hills beside Tenhorn. The realisation of how much further they had to go had most of the cats ready to declare shutdown. Mik rescued the situation by promising they'd get lunch at the rocks near the burn at the bottom. Most of them rediscovered their energy and hurtled down. Mik, going red in the face, yelled at them to be careful. Luckily the worst that happened was legs that got covered with black slime from the boggy ground near the burn. Reactions were either total horror or total delight.

Everyone squatted down on the rocks or dry clumps of heather. As they bit into their sandwiches, like the girls at Jone's mansion, they moaned about 'organic rubbish' and then devoured every bit of it. After lunch the girls made a big fuss about there being no privacy to urinate and screamed protests about the boys who were going to do it standing in the open. The problem was solved by getting them to go behind the rocks in single gender groups. What unnecessary complications zoological reproduction brings to people's lives, Jone reflected.

When they moved off again, the cats were resigned to the long walk ahead. Understanding now that to go back would be worse than going on, seeing the steep slope they had just run down. So they trudged forward, mostly in resigned silence. Jone had a little time for reflection. Strong waves of positive affect welled up. Towards the cats: it was good thinking that real Krischan conditioning could be as simple as giving people the experience of walking in the hills. Towards Luner: Luner's affiliation gave their interaction a precious equality, mission through mutual learning, not just one way. Towards Mik: a little hope was bubbling up in her that maybe at last a resonance circuit or two was opening up and if not, at least the kind of companionship she had with the protestant group in theoversity.

At last they came near the hostel and the cats' energy magically revived once more, desire overcoming exhaustion. Jone and Mik had to run to catch up with them, to keep them from going further in before they'd taken their boots off. Inside, there was more hustling to get them to the showers, settled in places in the dormitories and changed into their proper surplices for supper.

Suppertime turned out to be another bit of magic. In contrast to the hell of noise and rush that dinners in the Abbey often were, the cats sat silently, concentrating on the digestion-aid verse Mik had showing on the walls. It was a geometric configuration of people on a beach. The diagrams were superimposed on the filmshots, and along with it, was a clear, but not at all serious, commentary. The cats laughed at the idea of making patterns out of people, but took it in.

After supper came the final filming discussions and, most exciting, a bit of motionmatricing. After that everyone was wiped out and most of them went to bed voluntarily. Jone and Mik sat up congratulating each other on the success of the day.

'Well, I'm really made up, they like the Booleans.' He grinned and turned away. He still didn't look Jone in the eye very often. As he turned Jone found herself drinking in his profile, noticing for the first time that his facial hair had not been very efficiently eliminated, a few strands poked through a pore or two. Did he have to cut them everyday? She felt a mixture of repulsion and fascination. Suddenly the image of Mik as a burly Kayos barbarian with long red hair and a beard flashed into her mind. It was acutely embarrassing.

'Y-yes they are good, I really believe there is mathematical music. What do you think of Yalida?'

'That grutij byre – sorry, but ethnic language expresses it best. She's a demoniac. Oh yes, very clever, very mathematical, absolutely, but I know what it's for. I've experienced it first hand. Sorry to lay the experience bit on you, I know it sounds patronising, but well she's a Babylonian.'

Jone was taken aback by Mik's reaction, the surge of intense negativity. Certainly Mik was emotional but she had always felt his emotion was just what a protestant would think was right, flowing in the service of reason. Suddenly the picture had been jarred.

'You're against Babylonianism then?' Jone was stumbling, not sure what to say. Mik was now aware of his overreaction.

'Yes, I am very much against it. Oh, I don't feel that about all heresy, I mean, I know overreaction to it is because you haven't coped with your own idism and all that. But Babylonianism, I think they twist the female–male gender divide so much it makes the gulf far more difficult to overcome. I mean OK. I'm seeing it from the point of view of a zoological, I know I've got hang-ups about it –' He grinned and looked straight at her. She blushed, with pleasure and embarrassment, because he was making himself vulnerable to her. 'But they really are trying to take us back to the Kayos, and it makes me really angry.'

'I don't quite understand, why you're so hostile. I mean they are a very small minority and as soon as we get universal nurseries that won't be a problem.'

'Oh, now you're being a naive nursery spore. If nurseries are the answer to everything, how come most of the Angels and most of Mission Control are still men? And how come most saint women end up in roles that go back to zoological nurturance? Fusion, Jone, you surprise me if you haven't thought of that.'

Jone felt humbled. She hadn't ever thought of it. Here was a zoologically-raised male, who she'd mentally stereotyped because of it, telling her the truth about gender division she'd never faced up to.

Mik could see the effect he'd had and he shot her one of his rare direct looks, filled with a kind of vulnerable longing that filled Jone with the same kind of emotion, an emotion she had rarely felt in her life. He lowered his eyes,

'I mean, come on, Jone.' This was only the second time he'd called her by name, and it sent an inexplicable shudder through her. 'Don't tell me amor-radiation hasn't still got the old customs buried in it? I mean most amorades are male-female and the ones that aren't are about statistically the same as it used to be for sex before the Kayos distorted that. Now be honest, has any of your experience of amor-radiation not started with hormonal arousal?'

'Well, to be honest, I can't say I've had much experience of amor-radiation.'

Mik grinned, 'Maybe your expectations are too high. The resonance circuits don't have to open to the whole cosmos, just to a bit of pleasure, like psalm-stims!' He smiled and looked straight at her again. The look was warm and humorous. An amor-receptor synapse opened in Jone's brain. She had not quite been telling the truth. She had had quite a few attempts at transceiving but they had been failures. But it was perfectly true they had all been with men, because they had been hormonally aroused and suggested it. But she had neither been aroused or able to open her amor-receptor synapses to them. That was why she felt she could say she had no experience genuinely enough. Perhaps she was right about her expectations being too high. Maybe an opportunity to let herself experience it was presenting itself. She surprised herself with the audacity of the thought. But why not? At last she was admitting to herself she was hormonally aroused by him. And she liked what came across of his brain too.

The next morning, the girls and Jone set off to climb up Tenhorn to find the shelter. Besides the prospect of filming the festival 'Orgy', the warden of the hostel had got them excited about the place and they approached the climb eagerly. Even when the track became steep and they had to slow down, they were still determined. When one of them complained one of the others would encourage them. Solidarity was going to get them to the top. Jone suspected their keenness also had something to do with the fact that the boys weren't with them. The girls were more natural without them. She felt able to leave them to go at their own pace and push on ahead, but she found she had company. Luner was determined to keep up with her and she did.

When they had reached the top of the ridge below the summit they stood and took in the new view. The sun was shining through thin clouds making a large band of intense brightness in the sky and on the river, with the dark shadow of the hills on the other side crossing the middle of it. The hills were rounded but massive as if they were a wall round some secret other kingdom. Luner told Jone that was Dearna, a nature reserve.

'Soon as A get biology .043, A'm goin' there. Ye can camp and do observations.'

'That would be wonderful,' said Jone, longing to be there.

'Aye well, come wi' me then,' said Luner.

Jone said nothing. She was never sure how to respond to this habit of Luner's, of including her in her dreams. No point in saying anything. After all what if Luner never got biology .043? She had to push that grim thought away to get back to enjoying the beauty of the scene. After a minute or two she turned round to look at the rest trudging up the path. 'Well come on, let's try and find this shelter before the others.'

'Aw yeh,' agreed Luner eagerly. They were to look for a metal door in a sandy pit near the summit. They set off keeping their eyes peeled. Then Luner stopped and pointed to one of the sandy pits,

'A seen something flashing in that one.'

They broke into a run. Yes it was there all right.

When they arrived at the door, they looked at each other with wordless excitement. Jone pushed in the lockcode and the door, instead of sliding, swung back inside, startling them. The steep stairs went quickly into complete dark. Luner momentarily grabbed Jone's arm. 'A'm feart.'

'Well,' said Jone, 'there'll be no one there, except ghosts.'

'Ghosts,' Luner almost shrieked.

Jone smiled, 'Come on. This is a powerful torch. The others'll be here soon.'

It was a sufficient spur. Jone turned on her torch and led the way down. At the bottom there was a wide heavy door. Jone inserted lockcode two. This time it slid. Jone's torch beamed straight across at a patch of strangely luminous yellow: a figure of some sort. She moved the torch up. Luner let out a frightened squeal, grabbed Jone's arm again and this time hung on. Fear of breaking rules of Krischan behaviour were blotted out by fear of the dark and the unknown. Jone could understand the motive and didn't flinch. There before them was the face of a lion with two horns and a glittering crown. It seemed to be staring directly at them, baring ferocious teeth. Jone moved the torch. Another head. Then another. All seemingly staring just at them. There were seven in all, attached to one body. Now it came to Jone,

'It's the beast of the Apocalypse, the epitome of evil.'

'Apocalypse?' said Luner incredulously, 'A thought they wereny spiritual.'

'Oh, they didn't use it for games. They obviously used it as a mythomaniac symbol. There must be light somewhere.' She swung the torch near the door and saw the switches.

They were still functioning perfectly. The huge room was flooded with light. They looked at the wall again. The colours were astonishing.

'It's no photoprints,' said Luner.

'No, it's paint.' said Jone. 'A poisonous chemical they spread on the surfaces with brushes held in their hands. This was obviously painted by a brilliant artist.'

'Artist?'

'Like a metrifact designer, but making patterns without using mathematics. Good ones had incredible motor-muscle control –'

'Aw it's like drawin' wi' her hands, A used tae dae that.' Luner gazed in awe. 'Wow, yeh it's empire, what's that?' She pointed at the figure sitting astride the lion: a woman in a red and gold robe, multicoloured jewellery and a cup in her hand.

'It's the Great Whore of Babylon.'

'Babylon, A ken that. It's a female settlement in Syny.'

'Yes, well it makes sense. Babylonianism is a form of Neronianism. How do you know about Babylon?'

Luner blushed and turned her head away. Jone guessed someone in her clan must be a Babylonian. It sent a little shiver up her spine. The shelter and what it stood for was brought a little closer to reality. Jone saw Luner's face go sullen. She was remembering Mik's reaction to Babylonianism. She didn't want this to be a barrier between Luner and her now.

'I don't think all heretics are evil. I think some of them are just – normal, but misguided.'

'Ma sister's no evil.'

'No I'm sure she's not.' It was Jone's turn to blush. She hoped not.

'A dinny think aw they Neronians were psychopaths either.'

Luner seemed to need to get some resentments off her chest. This sister was probably close. Jone had compassion for her predicament: a Babylonian sister saying one thing and ministers who she liked saying the opposite.

'Now we didn't say all the Neronians were psychopaths, just the terrorists, the Ironteeth.'

'But they were just fightin' for what they thought was right –'

'By murdering people?'

'Well, the Crusaders kill people an' so dae the Inquo. A ken aboot things –'

Jone sensed Luner was beginning to speak in slogans copied from the beloved sister. If she persisted arguing it would be a quarrel not a discussion. The last thing Jone wanted to jeopardise was the maternal relationship so recently restored. It was time to concede in order to make peace.

'Yes, all right. There probably are psychopaths in the Crusaders and the Inquo too.' A reckless concession but worth it. 'As I said, I believe their religion was wrong, but I'm sure some of them, probably most of them, were well-meaning people who believed in what they were doing as you say. I still think they were wrong though. Whatever its faults. I'd prefer to live in the Kingdom than in the Kayos, any day.'

Luner had run out of argument. Loyalty to her sister kept her from agreeing completely, but she was satisfied with Jone's effort to placate her. She looked at Jone and smiled and Jone smiled back. It was an affiliation resonance circuit.

Voices came from the top of the stair, Luner gestured conspiratorially. 'Heh, come on Grif, get through to the next room. So they dinny find us.' Jone nodded. The other girls would destroy the atmosphere. They went through and closed the door. It was a smaller room. Jone was about to go for the lights when Luner said,

'Naw wait a minute, shine the torch roon'. It's more spooky that way.'

Jone shone the torch round. More figures, dressed in animal costume: lions, bears, snakes. They had seen these in the stills and copied the costumes for the Verse. Seeing how ferocious they looked, Jone began to worry about her liberalism in their conversation. She swung the torch round to another wall. Both she and Luner let out a startled, 'Ah'. It was a naked woman. Quite a fat naked woman. She stood on a large, shell-like boat and was stepping off it onto land. But it was what was behind her that had startled both Jone and Luner. Multicoloured coiling waves and snakes. And the colours were rich and subtle and breathtakingly mathematical.

The truth had struck Jone and Luner simultaneously. 'It's Venus,' whispered Luner. Jone nodded. It was just the same as the vision of the heatwaves of Heisenberg's atmosphere through the infra-red. Those very same unearthly colours.

'Yes,' said Jone. 'The three BA people named the planet after an ancient mythomaniac goddess. That's obviously her.' Another shock wave went through Jone. If she needed confirmation this was it. Yalida was a Babylonian. Now two of Luner's heroines were proved to be Babylonian. How could Jone ever hope to compete with them? And how could anyone explain the extraordinary connection between a Babylonian symbol and that orthodox Krischan program in the visional? Were these Babylonians every-where? The snakewaves were beginning to make her sea-sick.

The speculations could go no further, the other girls were banging on the door. Jone smiled, 'I think we'd better open the door.'

Luner didn't hide her disappointment, 'Aye, A suppose so. A like it just the two've us. It's like we're explorin' a cave for hidden treasure.'

'Well I think we'll have to share it,' and Jone went to unlock the door.

The girls burst in. 'Whit are you two hidin' fur? Found some loot ye're no lettin' us in on?' cried Zaner. Jone and Luner laughed at the synchronisation of the idea.

'Naw,' said Luner, 'but look at this. Bet ye've seen it before.'

The girls looked and soon recognised its association with Yalida. They gaped.

'So Yalida's a satanist,' said Lambiner.

'No a satanist, a heretic, no aw heretics are satanists. Rev Grifan thinks that as well,' came in Luner defiantly.

Lambiner stared at Jone, who was obliged to give an explanation.

'I think heresy's wrong, and I certainly think it should be controlled the way it is. But it's true that heretical individuals aren't necessarily evil.'

Lambiner didn't reply. She had to take the Rev's word for it. But it was confusing. What was the point of all these savage speeches about murder they'd made up if the Rev was now saying some of them were nice people really?

The rest of the girls were unbothered about the rights and wrongs of heresy. They were just fascinated by the look of the painting. Jone felt a relief in the thought that most of their idism was just spiritual ignorance. She let them just look and made no more comment. Their attention soon moved to the other rooms. They turned out to be uncontroversial: offices, dormitories, kitchens, lounges. All perfectly preserved. Jone had no time to soak in the atmosphere. Her energy was taken up with keeping the girls from damaging anything. They were entranced by the quaintness of it all, and plied her with questions about what things were for.

Eventually she brought them back to the first room. There she hustled them into setting up the film and getting them into their costumes and lighting their torches, all the while trying to ignore the hypnotic power of the woman on the lion. The filming had to be done four or five times, to get everybody doing things correctly. In front of the cameras, the girls were much more wooden and self-conscious than in rehearsal and it took a lot of cajoling to get them to liven up. They were finally roused to enthusiasm by being reminded that they couldn't be shown up being worse than the boys. During the final take, Jone had a moment to stand back. If she concentrated on the torches rather than the girls, she could appreciate there really was some kind of pattern and imagine something useful was happening. But inevitably, her eyes strayed to the woman in the red robe. Torchlight flared across the face. Jone started. She was smiling down at Jone with an alien yet intimate smile. It was frightening. Jone blinked, turned her head and found herself looking at Luner who was smiling at her with exactly the same smile. Jone winced and turned away. What was going on? She dared to look back at the painting. The smile had gone. Of course it was a trick of the torchlight. It was in her own head, but why? Why?

116

It had frightened her, so it was obviously her own fear. Fear of what? Being sucked down into the primeval soup of carnality? But why had the hallucination been projected on Luner too? The truth dropped like a released weight. Luner's admiration was more than filial. 'Tyze', wasn't that the word? Luner tyzed her. She had to shut down the lid tightly on the seeping disgust and horror. By being friendly, by going across the barrier of Abbey minister and catachumen, she had been responsible for it. Yet she couldn't go back, but she would have to deal with it. Somehow, but how? She pushed it all out of her consciousness with her soul and returned to the dance as it finished.

When everything had been packed up, the girls were ready to leave. Being underground was losing its charm and turning creepy. Once out in the daylight, it became an exciting exploration again and they raced down the hill eager to show off to the boys about it. The girls who had made the verse were eager to talk to Jone and she entered into the talk enthusiastically. She couldn't have coped with being left on her own with Luner again. Fortunately, Luner was taken up with her little gang, who had ribbed her about leaving them behind. Perhaps she was embarrassed at being with Jone for so long. Perhaps their deep-conditioned 'us and them' mentality would stop the situation getting dangerous. It was a hope for Jone to cling to.

The last evening was given over to enthusiastic motion-matricing which veered into dancing here and there but never into uncontrolled idism. It was all very good-natured and Jone and Mik joined in, both of them showing off their mathematical abilities and both conspiratorially laughing at each other's showing off. Jone gave Luner no special attention and Luner seemed quite unbothered.

Jone and Mik weren't left alone at the end, rather to Jone's regret, but she was not going to force the situation. If developments were going to come, they would come. Instead, Jone had her work cut out quietening the girls down in the dorm. Not that it wasn't enjoyable: she felt a great warmth coming from them. When she had managed to control their now hysterical reruns of the day's events, they turned to her.

'D'ye tyze Rev ArBrenan then?' asked Lambiner.

Jone flushed and the girls jumped on it at once. She managed to wriggle out of it without saying anything that made her feel vulnerable, but the girls were perfectly satisfied. Mik and Jone were amorades as far as they were concerned. For Jone, the greatest relief was in finding no jealousy in Luner's reaction. If Luner did 'tyze' her it wasn't serious enough to bother about. When she finally got to bed, what was going through her head was one of the girl's suggestions, that she and Mik and Crew Delta should make a clan and live by themselves in the wilderness. Being a missionary in grim old Embra was beginning to feel like the most interesting time of her life.

12

When they were back in the Abbey, Jone could sense that it was a loss for all of them. They had been together in a little space-time bubble, but the bubble had burst, as they do. Not just the Krischan clan but she and Mik as amorades seemed a ridiculous fantasy. During breaks he sat at the other side of the comm in one of the other cliques and seemed a million miles away. Only during Apo hour did the clan feeling return for a little while. NkCroom got the crew to tell the story of the expedition in his usual highly disciplined manner, and their pride and pleasure in the telling filled Jone with a glow of maternal affection.

NkCroom was particularly insistent on a detailed description of the 'Great Whore'. Then he said, 'I've been to a festival of the Great Whore, you know.' A gasp went round the room.

'Oh, I had nothing to do with paying money for servicing hormonal arousal. No, no. But then that wasn't really what the Great Whore symbolises. No, she was a matriarchal symbol. Well, I suppose you want me to tell the story –'

The response was predictable.

'Well seeing you seem to have behaved so Krischan on your trip, I think you deserve it. Mm – I was a very young man at the time. I was a student of Josef Theoversity. My father was one of the few Plotinian Krischans. It was a great joy to him that he had a son studying Theology in Strylya. It's forty years ago now. You don't have to sit there puzzling it out, I'm not vain about such things. I'm 61 years old.

'As you should know now, the Yukeys had only just been conquered. The Church was victorious but not triumphant. There were pockets of resistance all over, not just here. And of course none of us, my generation of Krischans, came from nurseries. Well, celibacy was becoming more common. We were very dedicated to rationality. But with all our zoological conditioning it was difficult, and some still succumbed to the old customs.

'I had a friend, an amorade. He was a fine man, a good friend to me and a marvellous games player but he did have one major weakness. He was always lusting after females. And of course, we didn't have hormonal control in those days. Eventually he was caught by a case of romantophilia and he was stricken badly. He fell behind in his studies, got into a dreadully irrational state. First he was in a state of bliss, when she came to stay with him. Then she deserted him and he was plunged into deep despair. He was totally taken over by the obsession, and his life was falling to pieces. Eventually he found out she'd gone to Ur.

'Now the Kingdom had failed to take over Ur and Eridu, its brother city. They were a kind of catch-all for all the hostile elements. They would have had to massacre them to take them over, and the Kingdom had come to put an end to that. The Urites were beginning to call themselves Babylonians by that time, because like us they were using symbols from the Revelation. What they were doing was taking the symbols of evil in the Apocalypse, like Babylon and the Great Whore, and turning them upside down, from their point of view. So to them these were symbols of good. As you probably know they still exist in Syny today, and I'm told they have a few followers in the occult world. I don't know if I think they should be allowed to exist at all, though I know the arguments about that say if you try to completely ban something, it makes people want it more.'

Jone glanced at Luner. Her head was bowed as if she was brooding deeply. Was she afraid of what she would hear? It would be difficult to resist the word of someone with first-hand experience of a Babylonian city.

'Anyhow, my friend decided to go to Ur to find her. He was determined to rescue her from corruption. A praiseworthy idea, if that had been his only motive. But of course it wasn't. He just desperately wanted her back again. And as long as he could hope, the obsession would be possessing him. At first I tried to stop him going, but then I realised that going there would be the only cure. Either he would rescue her or he would face the truth he'd lost her forever. I frankly thought the latter would be the case. I never did understand how he valued her so much.

'During the early summer, the beginning of their year, when the city was open to any unarmed visitors of either gender he decided to go and he asked me to come along with him. I said yes at once. I was very anxious about his state of mind and I was afraid he might be susceptible to corruption. Besides that, I was curious. Of course I was. What was the power of such a place to make people stand against the Church at the risk of their own destruction?

'Well it was quite an experience. In the Revelation there's a famous phrase. Reverend Grifan will be familiar with the Anagram we make of it in the Heavenly Games. It says: "I marvelled at her", talking about the Great Whore. It doesn't make her or heresy any less evil to say it was marvellous. Evil always has its seductive surface beauty, and that was Ur. Like a brightly coloured flower, gorgeous to look at with a fruit that's poisoned.

'It was particularly beautiful then, during the festival. The buildings were all decked out with flowers and bunting. There were stalls, and exhibitions and performing booths and cafés and dancing places set up in the streets. Everyone wore their brightest clothes and there was music and singing and performing athletic contests going on everywhere. There wasn't any pollution, no petro-freaking for instance. Outside the town they had races, like people in little carts pulled by horses. The whole population and their visitors, mostly from Eridu where the Neronian men lived, spent their whole time eating, drinking and dancing, totally given over to carnal hedonism. Of course, there was orgying too. After all it was their mating time. But we didn't really see that. It went on in the temples and we stayed away from them.

'Oh, but it was exciting. I was much more susceptible to the excitation of the senses then than I am now. As you get older, you see through it more, through the superficial attractions to the ultimate emptiness underneath. But I can understand the temptations of sensual stimulation for the young. We met this group of very sweet young lassies. That is, my friend got to know them. I was a very shy young man. They were really very innocent. They had been born there. They didn't know any better and they seemed to know nothing of corruption. Well, I say corruption and you must be wondering what I'm talking about: no doubt it all seems very nice to you so far. Well, as we keep trying to tell you carnality promotes idism and idism leads to violence. There, it wasn't violence as we get here, the fighting masculine bravado. No, it was much more insidious. The female version, all bound up with involvement in sex.

What that leads to is getting hormonal and genital stimulation from inflicting suffering on each other in all sorts of horrible unimaginable ways. Well, these lassies knew nothing of that. The young are obviously kept out of it. They are initiated into it later on, in the temples. I tell you, we felt truly sorry to think of the fate that awaited them. We would love to have taken them away with us, but how could we? That was their home.

'The last day of the festival was the most spectacular. The day of the Great Whore's peace, they called it. The nightly dancing and merrymaking came to a halt at midnight and the streets were cleaned of all the temporary buildings, except for the one high platform in the central square. Everyone slept till late morning, until they were woken up by a group of women playing trumpets and drums. That was a signal for everyone to get dressed in beautiful robes and headdresses. When they were ready everyone went out into the streets and got organised in clan groups and each of the clans had an allotted space. This was so everyone would get a turn to be in the square. I must admit it was very well ordered and when the announcement was made the Great Whore was about to appear, everyone fell silent. It was astonishing to see such a close-packed mob of people, all standing still and silent.

'Now the Great Whore was acted by one of the older women: a different one was chosen each year. The musicians on the steps of the Great Temple sounded the gongs and sounded their trumpets and the Great Whore appeared riding on a huge statue made of wood and paper, the beast with seven heads and ten horns. It was covered with pictures of men fighting and murdering and raping. Our friends told us the beast represented violence and the woman sitting on her throne on top of it represented the triumph over violence. It seemed obvious to me that she and the beast were really one and the same, but of course, it wasn't to them.

'Her purple and scarlet robe was very beautiful. Well, you've seen the very same in the picture. She mounted the platform and the men chosen to represent the Kings of the Earth, as they're called in the book, stood below her. They carried her up there and bowed to symbolise their defeat. Then they took her and placed her on another throne and put the beast on a bonfire, but they didn't light it as yet. Then the Great Whore raised her cup and a man was led up and he masturbated some sperm into it and she drank it. Next, two priestesses took a doll out from under her cloak. This was the symbolic birth of the New Year. Then the Great Whore took some coins, big imitation coins to represent greed for money, and put them in the cup. Then she took a large wooden dagger to represent violence and put that into the cup. Then she was carried over near the fire and she threw the coins and the dagger into it. That's when it was lit and everyone cheered and banged drums and blew trumpets as they watched the flames shooting up and burning the beast. When the beast was fully alight, people threw fireworks into the fire and there was a magnificent display with the biggest one being a picture of the seven archangels and ten angels, the beast transformed so they said. After that the Great Whore walked among the crowd giving out sweets. Strange, they were very tasty. I suspect they must have been drugged for I felt very elated from then on.

'After that there were special dramatic performances on the platform about the religious life of the city. All about their struggles in the Assembly and so on. Apparently inside the Temple there were ceremonies to begin the new session of their Assembly. That's what we were told anyway. In the evening there were feasts in the clan longhouses, with speeches. Then after that it was back to dancing and music. I don't remember much about that night, I was obviously in high velocity orbit, but I know I thought I was very happy. Well, yes, carnal indulgence does bring bliss but it only lasts a very short time, then it's gone, leaving a legacy of pain. I know you think we're all against enjoyment, but it's not true. The fact is spiritual joy is the only true joy. True because it's deep and lasting and I speak as someone who has known both.'

He stopped and looked wistfully out of the window. Jone wondered, not without a twinge of annoyance, which kind of joy he was thinking of. Any hopes she'd had that his tale would be a dire warning to Luner had been dashed. Vague rumours of nasty sado-masochistic rituals was not much to go on, and could presumably be denied by the devotee. Why didn't NkCroom realise this? He was something of an innocent himself. Obviously he didn't realise the Babylonian heresy was still very much around.

Someone wanted to know if they found the woman they were looking for.

'Ah yes, of course, well, we had the greatest difficulty finding her. You see, what you were before you go there counts for nothing once you've become a citizen, they say it makes everyone equal. To me it makes everyone a nonentity, but any how, we couldn't find her through any records. They had none on their pre-Ur existence. We asked around but they tend to resist outsiders asking questions. They suspect you're trying to abduct people. They had built up a wall of secrecy to keep out spies. Frankly, I think it was a paranoid fantasy. I don't know what possible good the Kingdom would have got out of having spies there.

'Well, it was on the morning we were about to leave, she came to see him. She said she'd just heard he was there, though I think she was lying. I think she deliberately left it to the last moment. Well I'll never forget that meeting. My friend was quite overcome. He had had a speech all ready in his head, to plead with her to come back with him. But face-to-face he could say nothing. She wasn't cold or hostile, she actually seemed pleased to see him. But oh, she was very different. It was as if a whole lobe of circuits had been cut out of her brain and been transported off to another galaxy. It makes my flesh creep to think of what immorality that mind was sunk in. They talked for an hour or two and she made it quite clear she had no intention of leaving Ur. Then she said she had to go. Oh, it pains me to recall it. My friend broke down and cried like a baby. It horrified me to see such loss of dignity in a male who had been so strong, up until he had got involved with this female. She hugged him. Oh, it was gruesome to think of him being embraced by arms that had been round other bodies in truth knows what other abominations.

'Eventually to my relief he pulled himself away and retrieved some of his dignity. He grasped her hand tightly, said goodbye and turned his back on her. She went out and I saw her out the window. She was crying. For a moment I was filled with compassion for the pure spiritual self within her. That I think was its last flicker before it went out.

'So we came back to Josef. My friend was in a wretched state. I was very concerned but I was sure he would get over it in time. I suggested a cure would be to throw himself into his theological studies and he did. He shut himself away, hardly saw any one, including me. I was glad in a way. I was sure he would come out of it a stronger person. After about a month he suddenly appeared again. Quite back to his old self, except for one thing, there was no more chasing lassies. We got back to our games-playing. His abilities had improved enormously. I was delighted as I could be.

'It was another month or so when he came out with his bombshell. He announced he was going to live in Eridu, the Neronian city. I was devastated. I spent almost the next twenty-four hours arguing with him. But he was lost, irretrievably lost. He had swallowed it all. That's what he'd been studying all the time he'd been locked away. It was horrifying. We parted with great bitterness. It took me a long time to get over it. I don't know if I ever really have, there's still a part of my mind that mourns him.

'Five years later, the Kingdom had the mirakelism to capture the place overnight. They were given the ultimatum, either they would cease to exist as an independent Church or they would agree to be resettled in Syny provided they didn't wage aggressive conflict either physically or through propaganda. Well, they chose to be resettled and it proves what civilisation means, that the whole thing was settled without a drop of blood shed. Maybe you can understand why I'm not happy they exist at all. I think if even one person is corrupted it's a terrible thing. I always think of my friend, so talented and clever. Someone who could have been an Angel now if he had not been lost. Such a tragic waste. Oh, I know you can't stamp out heresy, but I tend to think allowing them any safe haven isn't doing enough to discourage it. But that I know is a bit of an old-fashioned opinion –' and he sank back into another reverie, a gloomier one.

Jone's twinge of annoyance had increased to irritation. If he was telling them he had been unable to save his friend, an adult saint, from Babylon's seductions, how then could Jone hope to save an impressionable unbaptised ethnic?

NkCroom frowned down at his console and said, 'There's only a minute or two left till the siren goes. Just sit perfectly still, there's plenty of Krischan conditioning in just being able to do that.' He had shut himself off after giving out too much of himself.

Outside NkCroom's door, some older girls had arrived early to queue up. One of them leaned on the wall, to continue relaying the important events of the night before to the group surrounding her.

'An' he says, "Ye canny give somebody up in the middle of the month" an' A says, "A can if A want tae," an' he says, "It's no allowed, ye huv tae keep wi' me till next month's moonfeast." An' A says, "Dinny talk troj. A'm pre-baptismal A'm no yer hire, there's no law aboot it." An' he says "A dinny gie a ride for laws, if

A say it's no allowed, it's no allowed." An' A says "A dinny gie a ride whit you dinny allow, A'm no stayin' wi' ya!"'

One of the listeners said, 'Good fer you. He's always walkin' oot on folk himsel'.'

'Aye, A ken. He's a two-faced git an' A telt him that an' aw, an he wis gettin' lurpier an' lurpier an' his face wis like this.' She puffed out her face and imitated his look of frustrated rage. The audience laughed appreciatively. 'An he say, "They deserved it, the grutij whauls," an' A says, "Well who wouldny be a whauler if your diridle was aw that wis on offer?"' There were squeals of astonished delight at this one. At the same time the siren went. No one reacted. The tale was far too gripping.

'Well, he grabs me an' starts shakin' me. Oh he wis ufo aw right, "You pidger byre," he shouts. "You filthy souk, don't you grutij call me names, or I'll turn your cylinders inside out." Well A wis feart, ken, but a wisny lettin' on, an' A managed to knee him one in the droolies an' he lets me go an' –'

The door opened and out strode NkCroom, 'How dare you make that barbaric noise outside this room.' He had come out so suddenly that the girl, unable to collect herself in time, was grinning as she turned to face him. NkCroom's face inflamed with rage.

'You've got nothing to smile at, you moronic slut.' His arm came up and he slapped her across the face. The girl stood rigid with fear and astonishment. NkCroom, unconcerned, was still in full steam, 'In all the years I've been here once or twice I allow myself the luxury of thinking spirituality is really winning through and just at that same moment my illusion is shattered. Shattered by some barbarous little vacuum, who hasn't even a single neutrino of Krischanism penetrating her void.'

With the initial shock of the slap over, the girl now began to cry. NkCroom pursed his lips and turned his head to the side in impatience.

'For fusion's sake, girl, you're lucky to get away with that, do you think if I could have put you on my rack it would have been more pleasurable?'

He strode back into his room and dismissed Crew Delta. Then he came out again and spoke to the whole group.

'Get in there, every single one of you. Fasten on your confessionals and make a ten-minute recording on the sins of noise. I'll tell your Salvation Chaplain about it and collect the recordings when I come back and don't imagine I won't listen to every one.'

He marched off to the comm.

Later that afternoon Reverend NkCroom was summoned to the Abbot's office. 'Hellow, Robby. Come in,' said the Abbot. When NkCroom was seated, the Abbot stretched his floform back, screwed up his face and scratched it before he spoke.

'I've just had an uncomfortable interview with Lela Jessel. I really don't know what to say. I was so staggered. Oh Robby, this time you really have gone over the event horizon with this act of physical violence. The girl was very distressed and naturally complained to her maternaliser about it. I mean I'm obviously angry it could happen at all but why didn't you come to me? Why do I have to hear from one minister in a state over a perfectly reasonable complaint against another minister? Do you think it's my job to defend your outbursts of idism?' He put his hand across his face again. 'Anyhow what's your side of the story?' There was a note of despair as he said this.

NkCroom was angry, but in control of himself. 'The girl was outside my playroom, laughing and screaming and behaving with total savagery. I administered a short sharp effective form of pain stimulation. It was a perfectly reasonable action to take. The girl was out of control and had to be brought back to her senses. If I had her on my rack she would have no doubt blubbered far more. But then, of course, she couldn't have run off to her salvation tutor and complained about it, could she? Of course she was very distressed. Being brought face to face with your sins through salutary discipline is very distressing.'

'Tritium's sake, Robby, discipline? What are you talking about? I'm talking about an act of physical violence, an act of pagan idism, perpetuated by a Krischan priest against an ethnic pre-baptismal, and you talk about it as if it's a bit of everyday punishment for a bit of uncontrolled behaviour. Are you demoniac? How can you talk about ethnic lack of self-control when you yourself have committed a clear act of indiscipline?'

'I gave the girl a justifiable tap on the cheek –'

'Robby, it was not a light tap. The girl had a mark when she went to see Lela. It was an act of physical violence and you committed it. That's what we have to talk about.'

'Oh yes, I can see what we have to talk about. We're here to talk about how old-fashioned down-to-earth discipline will tarnish your reputation as a hero of protestantism in the mission world.'

'I am perfectly willing to discuss my religious views at any other time but at the moment I insist we discuss what under any Krischan tendency, ancient or modern, is a breach of Kirschan ethics, the act of physical violence.'

Now NkCroom erupted at last. 'For fusion's sake, I know these people inside out. Ask them themselves whether they'd really prefer a quick slap on the cheek to the rack or purgatorial behaviour modification or whatever it is you want. If the girl only had people like me to deal with she'd have taken the punishment and calmed down soon enough. But she's not daft, she knows now she's sure to find some soppy reformer to bill and coo over her, so obviously she goes off to revel in the attention. If she knew no one would bother about it she'd have forgotten about it by now.'

The Abbot sank back and rubbed his forehead in a gesture of weariness. 'Robby, we're getting nowhere. Let me make my position clear. I'm as willing as anyone to understand the motivation for acts of violence but the fact of the matter is I can't allow any member of my ministry to perpetuate such a sin, no matter on what grounds. All I want to know is, do you accept that ruling?'

'All I want to know is, do you give me the trust I deserve? Do you trust that I know how to deal with these people in my own way and are you prepared to support me in the work I've been doing for twenty-odd years?'

'Robby, I support every member of the ministry, but not uncritically and certainly not committing acts of violence.'

NkCroom exploded again. 'This is ludicrous, this talk of violence. Since when has the Kingdom declared itself pacifist? Conflict is a form of violence and I don't know anyone except heretics who say we never engage in conflict. If you're not prepared to support me in the work I do, then it's obvious the alternative is to tender my resignation. I can't work in a place where I don't have the trust of the Abbot.'

The Abbot froze for a moment. He was sure NkCroom didn't mean it seriously, but what was he to do? It was clear NkCroom would never agree to his conditions, and it wasn't just the violence that was the problem. He was a great preacher, every one said, but he was a rotten chaplain and a rotten salvationist. The mission could do without him, why not call his bluff and see what happened then?

'Are you seriously giving in your resignation?'

'If you're not prepared to support me —'

'I'm not prepared to support acts of physical violence.'

NkCroom was stunned. He had tossed off his declaration without thinking about it and now he knew his pride could not let him go back on it. He spoke slowly and clearly.

'Abbot Raze, I wish to tender my resignation.'

'I accept it.'

After the interview NkCroom went straight to the ashram, for he felt quite unexpectedly lightened. The Abbot, after first making it clear he could not lie about why NkCroom was resigning, pointed out that after all his years in mission he was eligible for study at Josef. When the Abbot had said it, NkCroom's instinctive reaction had been to feel insulted, but as he left the Abbot's base he realised a burden had been lifted from him. In the ashram he slipped into his postures calmly and was soon in Nirvana. He couldn't remember when it had last been so easy. On returning to normal consciousness an inspired thought had arrived. He would join the school of prophecy. All the years he had studied and loved his favourite prophets he had wondered if he could do it himself. Now all of a sudden he was presented with the opportunity to find out. He didn't feel old and tired. He had plenty of energy. He had plenty of imagination. And as a man who had thrown away his vocation for his principles, he had plenty to say to the world.

When he went back to comm he sat smiling with detached benevolence. He said nothing about what had happened. He didn't want anybody's pity or shock. He was free.

13

Before playtime the next morning Mik ArBrenan sat down beside
Jone. He didn't look at her, but Jone was convinced he had sat
down there deliberately. He announced to the clique that there was
a great new realisation to be put on that night at the Hedonarea.
'Everyone, but everyone, is coming, including Uan –'

'Who's Uan?' muttered someone.

'The Abbot,' said Mik, surprised everyone didn't know. A senior
eyebrow or two was raised at this sign of changed times.

'Well, I think I've reached the stage of maturity that enables me
to live without going where everyone, but everyone, is going,' said
Fess Orlam. She turned to Jone. 'Sounds like the sort of thing you'd
be in on.'

'Mm, I'd like to go. I haven't been to a realisation since I came to
Plotin.'

Mik looked at Jone's chin. 'Most people will be getting there by
19.30, Uan and I are going early to grab a car.'

'I'll be there,' said Jone, trying to sound impersonally enthusiastic. Mik's eyes flickered to hers for a second, then he turned to
banter with Fess. All the despondency Jone had felt since the day
before about the ending of the wilderness idyll disappeared in that
moment. She would make sure she got there on the dot of 19.30.

Realisations are three-dimensional laser simulations, which you
watch all around you from inside a capsule, 'the car'. The latest
realisation to come to Plotin had the added excitement of being
locally made. It was a geological time-trip from the Yukey Islands
Orogeny, which had formed the North Wilderness, to the carboniferous period that had created the landscape of the inhabited
areas.

Jone set off that evening to arrive at the Hedonarea by 19.30. She
was sure it was going to be a good evening. Geology was certainly

an interest, it could feed very well into landscape calculations, but she was well aware it wasn't the geology that was pumping the adrenalin. As she sat on the subway, she tried to bring her soul-dial into equilibrium but with little success. It was hideously in the red. Would there be any exchange between her and Mik? Would the possibility of transceiving be mentioned? There was no answer now and the soul cannot deal with emotions bound up in unknown futures. She abandoned it in exasperation. Nuke the limitations of the soul! She would just have to hope the uncertainty would be resolved this evening.

It was 19.25 when she stood outside the Hedonarea. She hesitated. Supposing she'd got there first? What a fool she'd make of herself. She waited till someone else arrived and managed to peep inside as they opened the door. There were Mik and Uan and one of the other younger ministers, Ned Skwyer, the one who'd had that altercation with Luner that first day when she'd been on ID duty. How long ago that seemed. Her own opinion of him had concurred with the cats, that he was a gaspod, but that didn't matter tonight. She was very relieved someone else was there.

There was no embarrassment in being the fourth person to arrive. As she came into the car, Mik smiled straight at her, unashamedly pleased to see her. She sat down beside him, why not? They were friends now after all.

'Well I'm glad you've arrived to break up this heavyweight argument,' said Ned Skwyer.

'I don't know about that,' said Mik. 'Rev Grifan –' he nodded his head towards Jone, 'will probably join forces with you.'

They had been discussing the subject of a possible assassination attempt on the Yukey's Angel, who was visiting Lundin soon.

Jone smiled at Ned. 'No, I don't think so, Mik has already convinced me that separatists aren't assassins.'

Now Mik turned. Their eyes met and Jone's resonance circuits started firing.

'Well thank you,' he said. 'I'm flattered you're impressed by my argument.'

They got no further, as more people were coming into the car. The Abbot now leaned across Mik and congratulated Jone on the success of the Tenhorn expedition.

'It's exactly what I hoped for, proof we can take them out and have them behaving like Krischans. Well, there's going to be plenty more opportunities, especially in your division, now,' and he gave Mik an obvious knowing look that Jone was meant to pick up.

'Why especially in our division?' she asked.

'By next term you'll have a new chaplain.'

'Is Reverend NkCroom leaving?'

The Abbot told her the story. When he'd finished, the man on the other side of him, who had just caught the tail end of it, wanted to hear the story too, and the Abbot turned to tell him. The door was now wide open for Jone to gain Mik's attention.

'I was in the playroom when it happened. We saw the girl crying when we went out but I had no idea. He quite often upsets them. I must admit, when I think about it, this resignation is typical. There's so much idism that just keeps erupting out of him, in spite of all the years he's probably tried to keep it down.'

'Yes,' said Mik, agreeing vigorously, 'keeping it down, that's his whole problem. The problem of his whole generation, making the mistake of thinking rational control of the emotions meant suppression of the id circuits. OK, maybe with a cold fish like NkDod it's irrelevant, but for a passionate man like Robby, it's disastrous.'

Jone was elated by his insightfulness. 'Of course, yes, if we have overwhelming emotions, we go straight to an exorcist and get it discharged. But if you don't do that the feelings build up inside and then explode destructively. That's it, yes that's exactly how it is. He'd just been telling us about this amorade of his who'd gone off to be a Neronian, and it was obvious he had years of unexpressed grief in him about it, and then he goes and does that. It makes sense, doesn't it?'

Mik seemed just as pleased as Jone that they understood each other. It buoyed Jone up with optimism. Communication wavebands synchronising was the obvious first step to the opening of other frequencies. The two of them talked more about NkCroom until the realisation had begun. Then they fell silent, but Jone didn't feel it was a shut-down.

The realisation soon had everyone engrossed. The car moved through thousands of years in minutes. At first they were thrown about by the convection currents in the molten mantle rock. Squeals of fearful delight could be heard from other cars. The abbey group were still too shy with each other, though Jone surprised herself with the urge to hold on to Mik to stop the giddyness. Next they were moved with the continental plates as if they were clinging on to them for survival like rafts in water until there was the great downfall of molten rock as one plate slid under the other. The car was hurtled down the molten rock as if it was on a waterfall. After this came the sensation of being buried under the ever greater weight of sediment in the geosyncline until the great jaws of the plates squeezed and squeezed to throw up rock and apparently the car, like a rocket taking off. The show was rounded off with a dizzy finale: rocks folding, cracking, faulting and slipping; earthquakes, rumbling instrusions and expanding extrusions. When it was over, everyone sat back, lighthearted and relaxed.

Mik offered to connect up the next stim for Jone, while she began to find words were flowing out of her. At one point, Ned Skwyer turned to talk to them, putting the two of them together, as if it was the most obvious thing in the world. Jone was being wafted up into a sense of confidence like a glider. Something was sure to happen, somehow.

The realisation began again but this time they talked on. Jone's mind was fully awake to everything. The background: vast desert vistas, crumbling mountains, bursting volcanoes and underwater scenes of the teeming life of corals, brachiopods and all the rest, growing, dying and forming limestone. The midground: the discussion about mission matters. The foreground: ArBrenan's features, shoulders, hands forming a mathematical configuration. At moments, when the two of them seemed to be likeminded on some subject or understood what each other said more than the others did, the configuration became a crystal that their minds were complementary planes of. For those moments, she was certain the transceiving waves were coming through. Then the sensation would fade, yet leave her optimistic. If they could come through spontaneously, even just for a moment, surely there would be no problem when they wired up their orgasmodes?

When the announcement came for the carboniferous era in the realisation, Ned beamed at Mik. 'This is your speciality. Are you going to give us a running commentary?'

Mik shook his head. 'No, I'm just going to sit back and revel.' Jone was intrigued and pleased. It was something else to find out about him. All the time there was more and more she wanted to know. But it was time to sit back and revel. The car nosed its way through the densely packed forests of faint ferns and cycads. It probed upwards from squelchy bogs and thick piles of moss; up forty feet to where the ferns cast their spores to wind. They saw strange trees with leaves like crowns of swords, trunks ribbed and fluted like primitive carvings. It was a dense, luridly green-and-brown world without flowers. They felt a choking claustrophobia from the carbon dioxide and the intense humidity. They breathed with relief the slow build-up of oxygen. They followed sluggish rivers, where little amphibians like crocodiles and alligators crept about. They watched the mighty dragonflies, with their immense wingspan, swooping in shafts of sunlight, emperors of this alien world. They listened to the deep, birdless silence, broken only by rain and thunder.

Once only Mik turned to smile and share his pleasure with Jone, but it was enough to make her feel they were companions in this strange world. Now the dramatic change began. The swamps came and went. Flooded by the rising sea, collapsing in black mud, filled again by lagoons. Then the torrents of sand and gravel, brought down by heavy rains, would block up the lagoons and the swamps would return. And they in turn would be lost again, to sink and be compressed into peat then finally, down into coal.

When the show finished, the whole Hedonarea burst into applause. Hardly a usual event at a realisation, yet everyone joined in. It was the islanders, whether native or not, congratulating their own on creating something that was just as good as anything that came from Strylya. And it certainly had been.

Jone could no longer hold back on questioning Mik about his 'expertise' and found him eager to tell her. One of his historical interests were the coal mines, a major part of the North Yukeys' BA history. He loved to think of its link with the even more remote geological past. As he talked, Jone was very drawn to his passionate involvement with ethnic history and with the local landscape. It gave him a rootedness in the environment that she longed to connect herself with.

It seemed hardly any time at all till the party was breaking up. Jone was back in the realisation on the edge of the geosyncline. She had to say something or she was swallowed up for ever. She turned and smiled straight at him with as much bold nonchalance as she could muster.

He said it. 'Want to come back to my mansion for a few stims?'

So that was it. It was going to happen.

Half an hour later the two of them were lounging on Mik's floforms plugged into his very sophisticated altar. His background was there, in BA and Kayos antiquities displayed round the room. But his high virtue showed in the exquisite mathematics of the setting. Nothing yet had been said and Jone was terrified still of taking the initiative, and yet at the same time was bursting with joyful certainty that it was going to happen.

The talk swung from religious discussion to tales of their lives, though in this field Mik had more to tell and Jone much more eager to listen, still wondering when something would be said. Mik began to talk about a visit he'd made to a tropical rain forest. Then he suddenly interrupted himself. 'Actually I made a vision about it. Would you like to share it?' So this was how they would transceive, through some sort of synchronicity in the visional, they would float into a state of transception without being caught in the net of miscommunication spun from fear and inadequacy. Jone smiled and nodded and the two looked at one another with perfectly comprehensible looks.

'It's not very complicated, just flora and fauna and some BA music from this fantastically mathematical ancient musicer called Bach. We'll do,' and he shrugged his shoulders and gave her an ironic grin, 'motionmatrices to it.' A wave of nostalgia for the Tenhorn trip swept through Jone. The girls would love to know this was happening now, she thought. I'll tell them. And Luner's face looking affiliative and proud of her floated into her head. Oh Luner, she thought, I hope one day you'll have this kind of experience when you've realised your spiritual potential like Mik has.

The vision worked almost at once. The harmony of sound, colour and shape slipped Jone into Nirvana effortlessly.

When she returned to normal awareness she was jolted to discover she was dressed in only a sarong. But why? Was she showing a nasty streak of Strylyanism towards Mik? Thinking his ethnic background would make half-nakedness an embarrassment? She was ashamed of the thought. She flung her mind into the movements and as the tropical heat pressed around her she realised guiltily that the sarong was the most rational garment to wear.

They were in a jungle clearing facing each other, moving slowly towards each other, their motionmatrices meshing in perfect harmony. Was this in the program? Whether it was or wasn't, it was the crystal formed between their minds: a living one, forming, reforming, dissolving and reforming continually. If this wasn't transceiving, thought Jone, transceiving is nothing. She could have continued in this trance for hours and hours into forever. Mik began to move closer more swiftly. Jone could almost hallucinate the amor-radons coming from him, surrounding her.

Her whole being was moved with the urge to merge with him into one whole. She, too, moved closer more swiftly. At last their eyes locked and she wanted to swim in the amor-radiation waves deep down into the amormagnetic field behind his eyes, closer and closer, until the poles began to spin, north became south, south became north, he became she, she became he. A flood of insight engulfed her. Of course, this was the perfect instrument of transception. However spiritual they were, they still had bodies, and they had to synchronise if the minds were to do so.

They were right beside one another and Jone felt herself poised to plunge into an abyss: a sustaining abyss, like the void that gives birth to new particles. Should she do it? Oh yes, she would do it. And she threw herself down, down – aagh – she screamed. Something hard had thrust itself inside her. She was in pain. It was like a sword. What was happening? What was going wrong? She woke up from her trance to realise what it was. Mik had thrown aside his sarong and he was holding her tightly, so tightly it was painful and his erect penis had been pushed inside her vagina. She gave a loud gasp of horror and began to struggle free. His grip tightened. It was as if she was skewered on a hard piece of rock, down a cave where the suction and lack of air had made her stick. She couldn't get out, she couldn't breathe, she couldn't move. She was helpless. A scream tried to rise but couldn't come out. She was trapped forever. Then at last the scream forced its way through. She ripped off her helmet to wake up to the darkness of the visional chamber. She was fully clothed. No one was touching her. She gulped for air, as if she'd been holding her breath and stumbled out of the module into the light of the room.

Still reeling from the shock, she fumbled about for her coat and made for the door. But she wasn't quick enough. Mik had emerged from the visional, his face red with anger, staring through her and into her.

'Just a minute.' Jone turned to face him, feeling his gaze fix her like a laser beam. 'Don't you come the outraged floating spirit virgin to me. Oh, I know you holy prudes and your hypocritical faking troj about pure intellectual movement. You were wet, you were as wet as a burst waterbed. You wanted it. You think I programmed a motionmatrix in that, it was a dance, and you were right in there, dancing. It was sheer grutij instinct all down the line. You were revving me up and I was revving you up and that was all of it. I didn't put that greased cylinder of yours into the program. That was your oil running and nobody else's, and if it wasn't because I got it pumping, what was it? Were you busy fantasising about little girls? Was that it? Is the gossip true then? And don't kid me you don't know what I'm talking about. Don't think everybody doesn't know about your little orgies in the Biopark. Oh yeh. And if you try crying rape on me, I'll give back just as good, and if you don't know what I'm saying is the truth, it's time you faced up to it. We're all carnal beasts, when you get down to it, whether we're clean white snowflake saints or stinking fry-fat ethnics.'

All Jone could think of was that she wanted to be back hidden in her sleep-module, oblivious of everything. Now she could only try and extract herself from the torture of his gaze. She turned towards the door. He hadn't quite finished.

'My advice to you is make yourself a vision of little girls and gratch away to that but don't try baiting any real people, or you'll just get yourself in trouble.'

She ran out of the door at last.

She managed to make her way home by instinct, for she had no awareness of her surroundings, her head was filled only with his words. Round and round, over and over, cutting bleeding wounds in her self-esteem. She could not objectify what he had said or argue with it. Everything turned round and round to the one thing. She could bear the words but they kept repeating themselves. Her 'cylinder' had been greased. She had been 'fired'. Now it was brutally obvious why she had never transceived before. She had never been ignitioned. That was the barbaric carnal truth. And she could not detach. She could not use her soul. How could she? When she didn't know what it was she should objectify. Anger surged up in her against the soul. She felt like tearing it out, running straight off to the moonpalace and burying herself in debauchery. If we really are all carnal beasts, why not go the whole way? She began to feel sick. That was stupidly demoniac. She didn't want rituals. So what did she want? Who was she? What was this physical arousal about? The pain turned her gut upside down and she ran to the excretan and the excrement poured out of her like lava from a fumarole.

Eventually she climbed into her sleep capsule and dowsed herself heavily into sleep. But there she didn't find rest, she was in a dark heavy silent forest of giant ferns and cycads. She was hot and wet with a hot wetness that made her feel like a sponge, filled with water that couldn't be squeezed out. She was choking in an unbreathable atmosphere. She tried moving but she couldn't, she was covered in moss, thick wet moss that was growing round her, weighing on her, pressing on her. She saw trees and tried to climb out through the ferns. Slowly inch by inch she reached them and tried to climb, but they were rubbery and wet. Her hands slid down. She turned and saw a sluggish thick river swarming with tiny little amphibians that crawled out of it and clung to her. She looked up and saw a gigantic dragonfly whirring towards her. It hovered over her and its long thin body flicked and twitched down before her eyes. She screamed but there was no noise from her mouth. She let the river and the moss pull her down into darkness.

14

Jone woke up the next morning feeling utterly unrested. A whole chunk of her seemed to have been broken off and swallowed up by a darkness. She didn't know what it was, except that it was part of her identity. She remembered that today she was supposed to be going to the Abbey, but when she thought of seeing Mik ArBrenan, she knew it was impossible. She would vu' in sick, but that meant contacting the High Priest in her mansions. Well, so what? She was sick, no doubt of that, and he would send her to the exorcist, no doubt of that too. Well, maybe that's what she needed. Her thoughts went back to three years before, when she had started a course with an exorcist. She had given up when her lifestyle at the time had improved. Now she saw what a mistake that had been. The well of anger and disgust and aversion and despair she'd uncovered then was still there. Of course it was. How could she have thought otherwise?

She vu'd in sick for two days and went to the High Priest. Jone said very little about the incident, just making it clear that she realised the problem she had with her feelings. The High Priest gave her some heavy sedatives and recommended a full treatment of exorcism, which Jone readily agreed to. She also suggested Jone keep away from any activity likely to excite emotion and confine herself to supervising play as far as possible.

After two days Jone returned to the Abbey. The sedation worked on her reaction to Mik. But anyhow he stayed far away from her in the comm and ignored her existence. She arranged with Blane as the Thyatira Salvation Chaplain to confine herself to playroom activities because she needed a 'rest'. When she saw her, it was difficult to cover over her state of sedated apathy, and Blane could see it. But it took her a lot of effort to get Jone to talk. Eventually when she did, Jone felt it was like removing pieces of glass from a cut. Where the exorcist had refrained from commenting, Blane did and threw her on to sharp edges of reality. None of the horror and disgust that Jone had felt, just a benevolent sad sympathy.

'I really do think young women straight from Strylya should be warned of this. Hasn't anything like this really happened before? Oh dear, oh dear. Now that I think about it, I saw the effect he had on you the other day. But I suppose I thought you could take care of yourself. In some things you do seem worldly wise. Oh my dear, I do feel guilty not saying anything. If you don't want to get involved in that kind of thing keep away from being alone with men you don't know well. I thought maybe theoversity had changed since my day, become more part of the real world. Don't misunderstand me, I dislike it all as much as you do. But you just have to learn to accept the gross imperfections of the world outside celestial games. I'm not being sarcastic, believe me. I do sympathise. I had to learn some hard lessons myself.'

As she listened to these words, Jone felt herself caving in like the cracking edge of a tectonic plate. Was this what it was all about? All this hatred and disgust. It was all irrelevant, she was just a naive Strylyan who had been sheltered from reality. That was all it was. But what about her carnal response to him? She wasn't innocent.

'But I responded carnally at first, that's what's so awful about it.'

'No, it's not so awful, the instincts are in all of us. Transception isn't something completely different from carnal rituals. That's a modern delusion, isn't it? The first Angels would never have said that. It's a refinement. I mean that's what we're here for, not to suppress like Abbot NkDod tried to do, we're here to refine. But I do think Mik was being irresponsible, do you want me to talk to him?'

Jone panicked. She would have to tell Blane the rest of it. 'Oh no, no. Please don't do that. I know what he'll say. You see, he came out with this horrible gossip about me being – sexual – because I'd met Luner and her friends in the Biopark. I mean that was an accident. They got into this dreadful harassment situation with some young males. So I took them back to my residency to recover, that's all it was.'

'Oh gossip. It can be really horrible, but that's another thing you'll have to get used to. Oh yes, it's a long way from the Kayos to Almyti Gawd, sure enough. Of course your motives were pure, I'm sure they were, Jone. But I'm afraid when somebody does something that, well, it isn't the accepted thing, the rumours do fly. Oh I know the gossip's wrong and hurtful, but to be honest, dear, I don't think it's at all wise to socialise with the cats outside the Abbey. They begin to see you as just one of them and begin to lose their respect for you. And that's no good. They do desperately need models and well, you can see we have too many faults and weaknesses ourselves. We can't afford to expose them.'

'But isn't that hypocritical?'

'I don't think so. You're not pretending to be doing good while you're doing evil. It's just realising your limitations. The truth is (this is an image I've thought of before), it's as if we've just crawled out of the slime of savagery and we're hanging on to a ledge with our hands, with our feet still in it. They're tied to us by a rope, but they only have their heads out. If we let them pull us down, we're all lost. Do you see what I mean?'

A strong unnamable fear welled up in Jone, an image of herself sinking into a swamp. It was like a memory but she couldn't grasp it. Blane could see Jone's emotion and began to change tack.

'Jone, just forget about what happened. File it away as an experience not to be repeated. Concentrate on your vocation in mission. I think you did a marvellous job on the expedition and I think you're doing really well as a maternaliser and in therapy sessions. There's plenty of opportunity for you in mission to express your charity towards the cats. Concentrate on that. I really do think, with the wisdom of experience, you'll be one of the best of missionaries.'

Jone was warmed by the flattery she could see was sincere. Yes, Blane was right no doubt. As far as the Abbey was concerned she should forget it, and concentrate on the mission she was capable of. The trouble was that right now she found she had not the slightest spark of interest in mission or anything else. All she could feel was a sense of being very small and very, very empty.

That afternoon, Jone was to supervise Crew Delta in a revival hour. Normally this meant sitting at a console in the corner of the gym keeping an eye on things while the cats played competitions of any kind. Today Jone would have relished keeping passive watch, but of course it was not to be. As soon as she walked in the door they were jumping around her demanding motionmatrices. Jone had to work her soul hard to stop herself vomiting at the sound of the word.

After trying as many rational arguments as she could without success she burst out with NkCroom-like fury. 'I just don't feel like doing – motionmatrices – today.' And the girls stopped pestering her at once. Her observer mind could think in passing: I can see the effectiveness of NkCroom's emotionalism for asserting authority.

The girls retreated to their normal activities and Jone tried to concentrate on some recording work, but her mind constantly wandered. It was only two days after it had happened, something was bound to jolt her into remembering. But how long would this go on happening? Proper exorcism took a long time, and in the meantime? The image of the swamp came into her head, a strange, flesh-creeping, horrible memory. What was it? The realisation, that was it. And then the dream came back, she had been in the mire of savagery. She felt herself moving into one of NkCroom's 'spiritual blackouts'. Now she understood that – There was somebody standing behind her. For a moment she tried to pretend to ignore them, but she couldn't. It was Luner and Geever.

'Are ya OK?' asked Geever.

'Oh yes, I'm fine, absolutely fine,' she wanted to snap but she saw the sympathy in their eyes and could only turn away and close her own. It would have been wonderful to be able to cry but her inner thoughts were too bleak and too dark for crying. And she was remembering Blane's advice.

'Has somebody been messing ya over? Is it one ae the cats?' said Geever.

Jone shook her head.

'One ae the priests?'

Jone nodded.

'Was it last night at the Hedonarea?'

It was astonishing how much they always knew. Now Luner came in.

'Was it Rev ArBrenan? Has he oot-taken ya? Does he –' she stopped and stared at Jone. At the mention of the name the nausea had come over Jone. She had to say something before there were any more mistakes.

'No he didn't out-take me, he ugh, I don't want to talk about it.'

Luner's eyes opened wide, 'Did he ram it up ya', the grutij soggert? Just let me get tae him. A'll ram his droolies doon his throat –'

'Luner.' Jone was surprised at the indignation she could muster.

'I know you mean well, but please don't talk like that, I don't want to hear that language right now.'

Luner hung her head, and Jone could see she had stung her. But at the moment she couldn't be sensitive. The memory of Mik poisoned the language with the act, she could not make a distinction. Luner had found her hostility.

'But, Grif, ye can see what we say about the rowts, they're aw the same, priests or 'niks there's nae difference. They're efter the same thing, doin' females over.'

Jone sighed, she was beginning to regret letting them speak freely to her. Now she was getting the Kayos gender simplicities: males are evil and that was it. If only it was, but the tortured sense of meaninglessness she had been plunged into stopped her grabbing hold of certainties.

'You should take him tae the Abbot,' came in Geever. 'Get him flung oot.'

'Oh Geever its not as simple as that –'

Luner was enraged. 'Look Grif, if ye didny want him tae dae it, an' he did, he's a soggert. Sorry A canny think of other words. He's a satan an' that's it.'

Jone looked at Luner and the dancing electrons of passionate partisan support of Jone, the simple belief that Jone was right and he was wrong broke through to her, not because she believed it, but because she felt Luner's belief in her. It felt more like amor-radiation than anything she'd felt before. Suddenly she was no longer afraid of the sexual element, it just didn't seem to be there any more. She was happy to accept it, if only she could feel about herself the way Luner did. She shook her head and growled. 'I don't want to talk about it, it's nice of you to be concerned, but I really don't want to talk about it.'

'Well,' said Geever practically, 'it's no gontae help sittin' there broodin'.'

'But I don't want to do motionmatricing.'

'Heh, whit aboot some marshalarts, Grif, maybe a bit ae fightin' would do you good?'

Luner obviously wanted some marshalarts instruction and was throwing the last part in as a means of persuasion. For the first time since yesterday evening Jone could almost grin. She was aware from the expedition how much strength these pale, malnourished, too thin or too fat ethnics could have.

She decided to give up brooding. The girls were ecstatic and she had to calm them by pointing out how limited the instructions could be. But it did feel better to do something, to plunge into activity as a screen that hid all the unresolved traumas.

Once launched into action she found herself being quite creative and the girls didn't disturb her emotions. At one point she stood and reflected that actually she had never seen carnality among them, physicality yes, but affiliative and not carnal, like little animals. The only carnality she had seen was Stone and Grip and what Luner had said about Art Leeam, and now him. Were Luner's Kayos simplicities right after all?

Her thoughts were interrupted by the girls clamouring for more advice. Luner was wanting to know if she could free herself from being pinned down.

'Ken, suppose yer lyin' sleepin' on the grass an' some rowt jumps on top of you –'

'Well, we could see. I'll show you what I would do –' and she lay down. 'OK, I'm on my front, now see if you can pin me down.'

Luner jumped down, pressing her knees on Jone's legs and gripped her arms, with the still surprising strength.

'OK,' said Jone, 'I'll just push you to show I'm not going to do it by force. Since of course a male is likely to be even stronger than Luner.'

'Oh yeh!' said Luner, cheerfully aggressive, and pushed down on Jone so tightly it was painful. Jone grinned back. For a moment their eyes met and Jone found herself carried on a wave of amor-radons. She could intuitively measure their spin, but she could not locate the circuits they were coming from. It stopped her reacting and made Luner relax her grip. The seconds expanded into slow time. It was as if they were floating in the air looking down on themselves. What on earth was happening?

'What on earth is going on here?' The voice was like a stone thrown through glass. The circle of girls parted. Luner jumped up and Jone sat up blinking, slightly dazed. The figure of Reverend Dinsen, the Revival Chaplain, materialised before her, horror written plainly across her face. 'Reverend Grifan, this is a Revival chapel, not a habitat dormitory.'

Abbot Raze was still livid with fury when he had Jone ushered into his base. 'I'm having a wonderful time with undisciplined priests this week. First it's physical violence and now it's carnal touching. If these poor catachumens didn't have my compassion before they certainly have it now. Why should I demand Krischan behaviour from them when I can't get it from my priests?'

Jone, who'd been sitting in the comm for the last half-hour in a stew of equal fright and indignation, tried to summon up all her strength. 'I don't know what you mean. I was giving a self-defence lesson. There was no carnal touching.'

'Self-defence? Deuterium save us, Jone. What on earth gave you the idea you could simply go ahead giving indoctrinations in something involving that amount of physical contact between people who haven't the remotest clue about the distinction? How can you possibly imagine these poor deprivates can, dragged through the morass of carnality as they are? I just can't believe the blind naivety of it. Yes, we all know I don't believe in these ridiculously repressive commandments the Abbey's been burdened with, but that doesn't mean I've opened the door for every fool to throw off all the restraints of Krischan decency and throw these fragile spirits to the wolves of total licence. How on earth you could interpret my program of creationism as permitting you to oversee an orgy of physical contact is beyond belief. What on earth did you think indoctrinating them in self-defence can possibly do for their spiritual development? Do please tell me?'

'I – I didn't think about that.'

'No, I'm sure you didn't really think at all. They asked you to show them marshalarts so you went ahead and did what they wanted without a moment's thought. Jone, do you think this is a unique situation, don't you think they're always clamouring for someone to show them marshalarts? And why do you think that is? Because they see it as the only machophrenic barbarian prowess stunt that puts us above their petro-freaking kings. Oh Jone, I just don't know whether to see you as totally innocent or totally irresponsible. Unfortunately, when it comes to being in charge of the spiritual welfare of deprivates, the effect of both is the same.'

Jone clung to the raft of ready-made argument amid the wreckage. 'But I think the fact is, they do need to learn some form of self-protection. I think that does concern their spiritual welfare. It can give them a sense of dignity.' She had pulled this idea out from somewhere, though she didn't expect it to stand up for long. And it didn't.

'Jone, what do you think we've got an Inquisition for? These people, whether they acknowledge it or not, live in a civilised Krischan society, not a barbarian stockade. They have recourse to the official instruments of justice. The sad fact is that the female clans follow the prejudices of the dominant males and will not use them to protect themselves against the excesses of machophrenic demoniacs.'

Jone now had only one plank left, if it broke she would go under. 'I still believe the contact wasn't carnal.'

The Abbot was finding himself unable to restrain his contempt. 'You believe it wasn't carnal. What is this belief based on? Did you write a thesis at theoversity about how pagans' touch neurones interpret signals from their nerve endings?' Jone gaped at him. The sarcasm sounded just like NkDod's. The Abbot read her look. 'I'm sorry Jone but you just aren't qualified to make that kind of judgement. It takes years of experience in biofeedback techniques to make that kind of discrimination. I wouldn't attempt it and I've had a lot of experience in mission, that much at least you can concede me.'

Jone finally fell from the ledge into the swamp. Wasn't what he was saying perfectly true? What had happened in the Revival chapel? That moment of what seemed like transception. Was it just an interchange of carnal longing? Wasn't it just the same as last night? If she had been naked wouldn't she have found the same grease in the cylinder? She wished the slime was real enough to suffocate her. She looked at the Abbot and could see he was puzzled. He must have thought she was like a sullen catachumen being told off. She should have been sitting there arguing in her own defence, arguing that her intentions were pure even if her acts were unthought out. But she couldn't. She could only feel her own sick misery. Was what Mik had said true then? It didn't make it any less horrible and hateful. But the nastiness didn't make it necessarily untrue either. All this went through her mind and could not be spoken of.

The Abbot for his part was beginning to think that perhaps what one or two of the senior priests had said to him was right, that this Jone was a misfit not suited for mission. He sighed.

'I'm sorry to have to do this, Jone, but this incident wasn't just a little mistake. I hate having to play the repressive disciplinarian, but you've left me no choice. I'm going to have to take you off any duties outside playroom supervision, at present anyway. I'm also going to move you, tomorrow, to Fess Orlam's playroom. Well, I think you need to make a fresh start with a different crew and I think Fess will be a much more helpful guide than Robby's been. That includes not being Luner and Geever's maternaliser any more. I've heard about you interacting with them in the Biopark. I know the temptation to break down the 'us and them' barriers. But it doesn't work like that. The real barriers come down through breaking into a space where they can be creatively Krischan. Not by us going pagan. Of course, I have no control over your extra-Abbey activities. But I do strongly suggest if you want to stay out of danger, please don't get mixed up with clan life. Hopefully by next term, we can review your position.'

Jone heard what he said but was no longer taking it in. The only emotion she could bring to consciousness was the desire to get away, out of this room, out of the Abbey, away from Plotin, away from the Yukeys. To where she didn't know. If she could it would have been NkCroom's Ur, to lose herself in an orgy of whatever orgies they indulged in, to disappear without a trace from the Krischan world. Perhaps to go into the desert and walk back in time to the Kayos, to join a barbarian army and go ravaging and killing until she could be killed herself. She was going mad. She had better get out. 'I'll go now,' she said. The Abbot was still registering incomprehension at her silence. She didn't give a quark.

'You'll join Fess in the playroom tomorrow, then?' he asked. She nodded and left.

15

By the second session with the exorcist, Jone was able to admit she had been infected by a romantophiliac attachment to Luner. And by the second week she could understand why. The exorcist had taken her straight back to the incident in her student days that had taken her to an exorcist the first time.

During a period of great loneliness, in a moment of despair, she had contacted one of her old nurses. The nurse had come at once, and being an old-fashioned ethnic maternaliser who had no truck with phototronic sympathiters had been sure what Jone needed was some physical comfort. The result had been an explosion of disgust in Jone, so overwhelming she'd even had to give up marshalarts training to avoid physical contact. One or two sessions with an exorcist had made the disgust die down and in the meantime she'd made one or two friends and she had stopped bothering about it. A grave mistake she now knew.

Hypnotic regression now unearthed the repressed relationship with the nurse. She had had an unhealthy motherly attachment to Jone, had tried to keep physical contact with Jone for longer than she should have, and even after Jone had finally managed to break the physicality, had retained a possessive emotional hold on Jone. The disgust was really Jone's hatred of herself for wanting/not wanting to break free of this control. Her attachment to Luner was a twisted form of gaining control by taking over the nurse's role. At the moment it was romantophilia, the next moment it could turn to disgust. It was a whirlpool of unpurified feelings.

All this she understood quite quickly, but understanding does not clear an infection. As soon as she walked into the Abbey each morning she knew how deep the infection was. She would see Luner at mass and at once the burst of romantrons would dissolve the gauze of sedation in the infected circuits. She now understood why romantophiliacs she had known had breakdowns. It was an agonising game of contradictions. She would try not to look and she would feel Luner's eyes on her. Feel the romantrons and phobons and amor-radons, and she could not but turn to look. Luner would stare for a moment with passionate love and resentment and then turn away and Jone would feel utterly bereft. Once they had passed each other at the shuttle, Jone had wanted to say she was sorry but the Abbot had forced her to give up as Luner's maternaliser. It wasn't what she was supposed to say, it was what she had wanted to say at that moment but Luner had scowled and not even looked at her. She had been devastated.

This kind of contact with Luner was inflaming the disease not cooling it. If it was to be halted she had to be cut off from contact all together. Both she and the exorcist hoped the Whitsun break would do it. If it didn't, the more drastic alternative had to be faced, she might have to leave Embra. To her surprise the exorcist was positive about this. It was the only good thing emerging from the sessions so far. Jone was now able to contemplate losing her sainthood to return to Strylya. She had learned enough from seeing the contrast between saintly abundance with ethnic deprivation to think that being a Blessed in Strylya was no great sacrifice. And the exorcist had helped her to believe in her talent for landscape computing, to believe developing it was a realistic option.

This hope kept her staggering through to the last day of term. But that day brought her to a crisis. When she walked out of the building she knew for certain that the Holydays would not halt the disease. Imagination could flourish just as well out of sight, and the break was not long enough. A drastic method had to be found and that evening as she watched the verse of herself talking about the nurse, she found it. She would have to see Luner and let Luner express her feelings and touch her, and the disgust would come. It was using and hurting Luner but it was the only way. She was convinced of it. Yet she didn't tell the exorcist. She was too ashamed, but she would do it. She would go to the Biopark every day. Luner was bound to appear sometime. And in the meantime she could try and work out some computations.

First thing the next morning she set off. She was glad of all the subtle sedations the exorcist had given her from her neurograph readings. The soul seemed to be of some use, for the first time since she'd been here. It was all there below the surface, but the surface

149

free of abbey tensions could function pretty well.

She made her way to the seashore as quickly as possible. It was a sunny day, with the fresh sunlight that comes after a day or two of wind and rain. The sky was blue behind lots of white, thin, fluffy clouds. The sun was behind the clouds and cast a wide area of diffuse glitter on the water. The water was calm, with almost no crests on the waves, breaking on the shore with a lopping sound. The tide was in to the edge of the soft dry sand where the winds of the previous days had left a thick border of seaweed. Jone walked along it, cracking razor-shells and bladderwrack under her feet. Her mind was opening to sensation. She decided to get to the big clump of black volcanic rock emerging out of the water on to the sand. There she would stop and take out her vistameter.

When she settled down she looked for any sign of people. None. Disappointment, then relief. She decided to make a general schema of as wide an area as possible. The bay from here was a clearly defined crescent, with Fairmead promontory to the right and Killane Point to the left, seeming to move together like pincers, although, in fact, quite far apart. She would use them as her parameters, both for the fixed composition and later when she moved on and they changed their relative size and direction. As she watched, a large dark cloud loomed up to the south-west, like a crouching animal. Then the sun came out from a cloud, flooding the sky and sea with white light, making the Killane promontory and the rain cloud darker in contrast. On the other side of the rocks from where she'd come, the waves seemed even slower and oilier, with seaweed weighing them down. She incorporated their timing as the baseline, underpinning the other proportions. Having fed it all in, she turned landward and added in the contours of the hills and the houses of Plotin, showing clearly in the sunlight.

With enough data from a fixed point, she could move on, registering the changes. She went towards the place where the sea came inland in a river. When the tide was out you could walk over the river bed. When it was in, it was very deep. She would have to walk upstream, round the corner of the high bank above the sand. This would completely alter the perspective in the vistameter. She had forgotten what an adventure landscape computing could be. Round the corner were steep-sided dunes going down to the river. Fairmead promontory was now out of sight. Killane promontory was its grassy back rearing up to the sky. The river was narrowing and cutting deeper. She would have to follow it till it narrowed to a stream in the marshy grass. The dunes were very steep with only a tiny ledge above the stream, so Jone's head was down watching her feet. Landscape had to be neglected.

She turned a corner and the land ahead opened on to the marsh. She looked up and froze, with astonishment, pleasure and fear. There was Luner, crossing the stream. It hadn't narrowed much, only got shallower, and Luner was wading across in her bare feet, shoes in hand. She hadn't seen Jone. She was too absorbed in negotiating the stream. There was time for Jone to panic and run, but she didn't. She stood there and waited. Luner reached the bank and looked up. She also stood, and froze and frowned. Jone, frightened but desperate to get it over with, moved towards her. The frown changed to a sullen stare. Luner's eyes filled with grieving resentment. Then embarrassed by the self-exposure, she swivelled her eyes to the vistameter hanging over Jone's shoulder.

'Dain' yer daft wee sums again, eh?' And she hesitated before the next sentence. 'Aye, sums is aw you care aboot.' She turned away and muttered just loud enough for Jone to pick it up, 'It's no us that's for sure.'

All Jone could think to say was, 'I was hoping you might be down here. I wanted to see you.' Without being able to control it, the tone was of longing. But the tone did not impress Luner. On the contrary her eyes flashed with fury.

'Why? Ye didny want tae see me before. What's made ye change yer mind? Oh, A ken ye've come tae tell me not tae use the Biopark when you're here in case ye get a sexual disease.' Seeing Jone's face turned white, Luner fired her arrows home. 'Well, A'll tell ye somethin' that'll gie ya a big surprise, Rev supernova, you're gaspoddin' yersell if you think A'd want tae get physical wi' you for any reason, A wouldny bring masel' that low.'

Everything had turned completely upside down. Jone felt utterly humbled. In being frightened of Luner's desire she had completely ignored her pride. Her Strylyan arrogance crumpled to dust. 'I couldn't talk to you, they'd have thrown me out. I couldn't face that, not yet.'

Now at last Luner softened, 'But why, Grif? Ye didny do anythin'.'

'I broke the abbey code of Krischan ethics, an act of non-medical physical contact.'

'But A thought Raze was abolishin' the commandments.'

'Not that one.'

'But we didny dae nought wrong, we were just fightin', we wereny bein' carnal.'

'Reverend Dinsen thought we were, you remember when she came in –'

Now already the moment of truth had been reached. Luner's anger blazed again. 'If A wis bein' carnal, then so were you.'

Jone felt herself shaking, 'Exactly. And that's why they have stopped the contact.' She could feel tears coming.

'Did it upset ye, Grif?'

'Yes it did. I don't blame you, believe me it's my problem, it's my conditioning –'

'Aw A get it, wis aw that high an' holy conditioning, you canny control yersel. Well, grutag doon on it then, because A can control it. A ken when a kin be carnal and when no, A'm no a slave.'

All Jone's defences had melted away, and all she could do was look into Luner's eyes and let the amor-radons flow. How dare she plan to be disgusted in the face of such integrity? Up to this moment she had known nothing about ethnics, nothing at all.

It was Luner who looked away first, embarrassed. 'So ye're no gontae be allowed tae see us ever again?'

'I have to tell you the truth. I'm planning to leave the Abbey in the summer.'

'Why?'

'I don't think I'm cut out for mission.'

'But, Grif, yer an empire missionary. Everybody in Crew Delta says so, ask them.'

'I'm not, I break the rules without thinking, that's not good mission, it gets you lot into trouble.'

'But the rules are troj.'

'Yes, but a good missionary works to change them, she doesn't blunder about forgetting them and causing more trouble for the cats. Besides that, as a matter of fact, I don't actually want to be a missionary.'

'Whit are ye goin' tae do then?'

'Go back to Strylya.'

'Why?'

'What else can I do if I'm not in mission?'

'Ye kin deviate! Rannan's got friends that are deviant saints. You could live in Nace.'

That possibility had never occurred to Jone. Why should it have? What would be the point in staying here, to see Luner? She felt herself back on a tectonic plate about to crash. So there was amor-radiation between then, she could never deny it now, but what else did they have? They were light years apart in everything except their liking for each other.

'I've got protestant friends in Strylya, that's where the real changes have to be.' She knew it sounded lame.

'Grutag Strylya, you've got friends here, me an Geever an Molner an Zaner. And there's protestants here too, protestant women. You should get intae that, Grif. You ken whit the rowts are about as well as any of us.'

'I know I've had a bad experience, but that hasn't made me a Kayos matriarchalist.'

'Ye dinny huv tae be, Grif, come tae the meetin' the night. See what A mean. The prows are wantin' tae fight for a fair deal for the females here. An' saints kin help cause even the deviants are better at some kindae things, like talkin' tae the Cathedral an' that. Ye dinny have tae go tae Strylya tae fight, stay here an' fight wi us.'

Jone was lost in a whirlpool of confusion, she flung up her arms in reckless despairing abandon. 'I don't know what I'm going to do, what I'm going to be, who I am.'

Luner's eyes opened wide at this totally uncharacteristic melodrama and then she burst into laughter, and Jone caught the virus. Then they looked at each other and transception wave-lengths vibrated in harmony. It was Jone who looked away first. Afraid, not of physicality, but of falling through a wormhole into a parallel universe.

Her eyes caught the top of Killane Point. 'Have you just been there? I'd like to go up there.' Luner was ready at once to retrace her steps and go back over the point. Jone promptly took off her boots and waded across the stream and began the ascent behind Luner.

It was Luner who broke the silence. 'So d'you think you'd come tae the meetin'? We're gontae be plannin' the strategy fur the Whitsun rampage.'

'The what?'

'See, Grif, the prows, the protestant women A mean, are puttin' in two teams. It's like the wars, ken, but anybody kin go in fur it.'

153

'You mean a petro-race with fighting?' Jone felt the whole thing becoming demoniac – but.

'Yeh, see you an' Pallad could use yer marshalarts, it'd be empire.'

'Luner, don't be demoniac, me in a petro!'

'But Pallad's a saint. She's usin' her soul tae dowse the smells an' aw that, it wouldny be that hard.' Luner was wanting Jone to be a heroine again. Jone felt that elation she had felt she would never recover again. A war hero! It was ludicrously demoniac. It was the most irresponsible stupid idea. It was fantastic. She was back in the swamp, but she wasn't drowning, she was swimming. Why ever not? What did she have to lose?

'What if someone saw me? Then I'd really be for excommunication.'

'You could disguise yourself, Grif. Wear a tartan bunnet over yer bald heed. We could get a wig.'

Jone laughed, 'Well maybe I'll think about it.'

'An' there's a Yalidas concert the night after, you could come wi' us.'

Jone thought about that infamous salvation session, and about the mass, and about the painting in the shelter. Yalida the Babylonian saint, who seemed to glimmer through the murky waters of confusion like luminous tropical fish. Oh yes, it would be very interesting. But she wasn't going to let on to Luner just yet. She wanted to tantalise, to play celestial anagrams of emotion. It was completely demoniac and she wanted to chart every particle of it.

At the top of Killane Point, they sat down, leaning against an outcrop of grey and yellow lichen-stained rock, near enough to the edge of the cliff to see the rocks below: soft rock misshapen into monstrous animals by the sea. So weirdly shaped they looked artificially carved, like a setting for a Bible chapter on some remote planet. To reduce it all to solvable equations was a challenge. A challenge Jone couldn't resist. But what would Luner's reaction be to her absorbing herself in landscape computing?

'Do you mind if I do a bit of this?' Luner shrugged and made a face that Jone assumed was jokey indifference.

'You dae yer sums an' A'll have a nap,' and she lay down and closed her eyes.

Jone turned to the rocks, but couldn't find the figures coming together. The distraction was her disappointment at being unable to share her most loved occupation with Luner. It was an impassable barrier. The computations she used were way beyond Luner's comprehension, and it was very unlikely that would change. Could a vistameter be adapted to simpler sums and still be mathematically satisfying? It seemed doubtful. It made her grieve and put her off continuing. If she hadn't felt self-conscious about exposing herself she would have stopped. Instead she pretended to carry on. Suddenly the vistameter was pushed out of her hands. Luner had sat up and was looking at her with an insolent 'what are you going to do about that' look.

'A'm bored, Grif, time tae get movin'.'

Jone looked down at the vistameter, looked up at Luner's face waiting for Jone's annoyance and burst out laughing.

'Yes, good idea.'

Luner was a bit put out at not getting a fight. Jone added, 'I couldn't get any of the figures to work out anyway.'

'A keep tellin' ye that thing's a waste of time.'

The truth hit Jone that not only was it a barrier but that Luner was jealous of it too. It was as insoluble as the equations she'd just been trying to work out. Oh, down a wormhole with it. She jumped up.

'Come on I'll race you to the bottom.'

Without further persuasion, Luner was off ahead of Jone and stayed ahead on the top until they reached the place where the hill dropped down in diagonal strips of brown rock. Luner had to stop to decide whether to carry on to meet the path much further round or clamber down the rocks. She leaned over, felt a twinge of height giddiness and grumpily set off for the path, meanwhile Jone looked down, felt a twinge not of giddiness but of guilt. Her experience of rock-climbing made the climb-down look easy. She scrambled down in half the time it took Luner and sat on a big tree trunk that had been washed up on the shore. There she waited, hoping Luner wasn't too mad.

When Luner did reach her, she was fairly annoyed. 'Oh, smart dub rock climber, are ya?'

'Well, yes, I have done quite a bit, I must admit.'

'Is there anything ye've no done?'

'Lots, I've never been in a petro, even in a visional, yet –'

'Does that mean ye've made up yer mind?'

'No I haven't made up my mind yet.'

Luner sat down, she was going to play the game too. She began to talk about the Whitsun rampage 'If' Jone came on it.

After a few minutes, silence fell. They looked at branches strewn around the trunk. They were white-clean and they reminded Jone of the dry bones that were raised to life in the old BA myth. It was quite different on this side of Killane Point. The promontory with its steep side was like the wall of a fortress. It was as if they had stepped into another world. The sand here was yellower, the grass greener, and the river bluer and more sparkling. The sun now over the land instead of the water was a different sun, a private sun for a hidden-away world. Jone picked up a small branch and she felt the amor-radons flow from her hand onto it, to make it come alive. Now she looked up and saw the whole scene resonate with transceiving harmonies, vibrating back and forth from oneness to manyness. She was almost breaking with pleasure. The branch snapped, the gyroscope of the scene stopped, and put her back in everyday life. She looked at Luner and grinned. Luner grinned back, understanding.

They had been in the other world together. Jone wanted to say something but couldn't, frightened of what it could all be about. Luner, with no intention of saying anything, decided it was time to carry on along the sand to Enster. On the way she recounted stories of when she came to this beach as a child. She was in a hurry to tell the tales as if she also had something to cover up. Jone was grateful for the reminder that she wasn't the only one to suffer from confusions. When they parted at the subway, Jone had a flicker of fear that Luner would reach out and touch her and then was shamed by the thought. Luner said she would 'vu Jone, 'tae see if yer comin' tae the meetin',' grinned cheekily and was off. Jone decided to go home and make use of her recently acquired supply of canethol.

16

The starting point of the Whitsun rampage was a big field at the edge of Enster, that became a fairground over the Whitsun Holydays: a grossly unmathematical muddle of noise, colour and crowds much loved by the ethnic population of Embra. Unless, like Rannan NkBerber, that morning you were in a mood to hate the whole world, especially in its noisy, colourful and crowded aspects. Rannan was wondering what on earth they were doing here. It was she who had come up with the demoniac fantasy when she had thought she had no vocation anymore. Now of course she was still in the Abbey medical team and the medical high priest, fed up with reformism already, was going off to work in an atonement colony at the end of term. What with new facilities arriving too, a Kingdom vocation wasn't looking so bad after all.

Everything had turned upside down. While she was deciding staying around wasn't such a bad idea, Lazal, fired by renewed religious fervour, had begun to think maybe they should go to Babylon. Staying in vocations was a betrayal of their beliefs, they should opt out the whole rotten system, not prop it up by taking care of its casualties. The added tension building up to this foolish rampage idea had caused them to have a blazing row about their plans the night before.

Rannan had stormed back home to the habs to be faced with Luner in a state because Jone hadn't turned up to the meeting and now she couldn't get her on the 'vu. Luner had been so sure Jone would come. Rannan was doubly annoyed both at Jone for not appearing and at Luner for her romantophiliac obsession. However this saint felt, it would only end in tears for Luner. Luner's faith in her heroine was infuriating. In Luner's eyes she appeared to be capable of throwing all the competitors over her shoulder and winning the war single-handed. As it was, this morning, with or without her, the whole enterprise looked completely ridiculous.

Rannan and Luner got to the pit early. Rannan decided to busy herself with last-minute fiddling about with the engine. Actually the engine looked fine but she proceeded to loosen and tighten a few nuts and bolts just to keep herself from hitting Luner or anybody with a spanner. For a while it looked like nobody was turning up. Maybe they'd got cold feet and the rest of them could just go home. Then she felt Luner jabbing her excitedly. The bonnet shook and Rannan almost hoped it would fall down and slice her head off. 'It's Grif, she's here!' Luner gripped Rannan's arm so tightly Rannan was forced to come out from under the bonnet.

Wandering alone, either very heavily soul-sedated or zerogee, was this ludicrous figure in ethnic colours uncomfortably hung around her with an obvious wig on top with Pallad behind looking as if she was ready to catch her if she fell. Luner collapsed laughing and Rannan found it hard not to join in. Grif came up and grinned at Luner.

'I'm sorry I didn't come to the meeting,' and she shrugged. 'Well I hope I can still be of some use.'

Rannan squirmed, hating the saintly self-effacement and cursing herself for her grumpiness. She smiled thinly. 'We kin sure use another marshalartist. You can come with me an' Luner an' Geever.' In her head she was thinking, I suppose I can forgive you, letting yourself be made to look so ridiculous.

It turned out that Jone had gone to the occult gawd store last night and got waylaid until it was too late for the meeting. She had then gone to Pallad's domicile. Luner had to suppress a surge of angry jealousy. While she had been frantically wondering where Jone was, Jone had been rapping the night away with Pallad. Anyhow she was here. It was going to be a fantastic day.

Everyone else was now arriving and they busied themselves getting ready. Nessa was delighted to be replaced by Jone and said she would meet them at the refreshment break and tell them how the rampage was progressing. No one had much else to say. They were all too nervous. Rannan and Lazel had exchanged wry forgiving smiles and got on with the business. Lazel was driving the other petro with Pallad, Molner and Geever. They drove up to the starting-line to watch the pre-rampage dance displays.

Once behind the wheel, Rannan felt more normal again, nervous, excited, and hopeful their strategy would work. The ridiculous dances made her giggle and the giggling infected the others. The adrenalin was flowing. When they heard the announcement to switch on engines in two minutes, Rannan put her hand on the seat behind her. 'Good luck, protestant women.' Everyone reached out and they all grasped hands, even Jone. It made Rannan warm to her a little.

The first part of the race was through Leper Town, as it was still called. This was the old BA town of Enster, that had been left a heap of rubble by the post-hit firestorms of Armaggedon. Here in the Kayos days, the mutants had come to live in makeshift dwellings from rubble. After the Coming of the Kingdom, when mutants went to the moon or died off, sinners and heretics took it over. Then there was the invention of tectoplasm and the present Enster was built leaving the old town just as it was, an impressive ruin that made the flesh creep from its intense atmosphere of very different times.

The prows had a strategy for Leper Town with a high probability score of success. They had mapped a route through alleyways and tracks in the partly rebuilt ruins, where there was no room for overtaking. The worst hitch would have been if they had been trapped in an alleyway by petros coming at them from opposite ends, but that was unlikely, since they would hardly be noticed. They would cross main roads when they were empty, and use buildings to keep themselves out of sight. They were pretty certain the other competitors would be too busy with battling one another. Leper Town, with its numerous criss-crossing roads, was regarded as the battleground of the race. Here was where the male machos were separated from the mouse-like mops. To trap someone in an alleyway was no glorious bumper-to-bumper chase. The prows' only real worry was damaging the petros on the rough ground, but here the practice in the visional had been invaluable in improving Rannan and Lazel's driving skills. Fortunately, the one concession to Kingdom mirakelism besides the all-round bumpers were the tyres.

The drive through Leper Town gave Rannan a surge of confidence. She drove carefully, neither too fast nor too slow. She felt alert and in control. The petro felt smooth and strong. She was glad now they were going through with it. Since so many of the other petros were locked in battle they reached the pit-stop below Lammas Heights in sixth and seventh positions. They tried to control their elation. There was a long way to go, but they were energised by their strategy working.

Over Lammas Heights they were taking more of a risk, by following the much longer route over Merlan Crags. Because it was a clifftop route, battles were forbidden. But in avoiding battles they were adding a lot of time and putting their petro's cooling and fuel system to the test. If anything went wrong up there, which they couldn't put right themselves that would be the petro out of the race. Since the rescue vans didn't patrol up there, by the time one got to them, they would be disqualified by the length of time they'd waited.

It was a long steep climb, and trouble did loom. Lazel, out in front, radioed to Rannan, 'Rannan the engine's chugging. A'm gontae stoop at the top an' have a look. It's probably just somethin' that's come loose at the points or somethin'.' Rannan's lightness immediately left her, and all the ill-feeling from the night before seemed to flow up uncontrollably. Lazel's nonchalant confidence about her ability to play around with the engine had always irritated her.

'Is it chugging badly?' Rannan asked, hearing the sharpness in her voice and not being able to stop it.

It wasn't, but that made Lazel feel sure it was worth stopping to look at before it got any worse. Since the exhaust was looking fine, she was convinced it must be oil leads needing tightening or points oiling again. Rannan was convinced they could make it to the pit-stop, and that they were wasting time stopping up here. The argument carried on for some long minutes, the bitterness mounting with every response. Until Lazel decided to stop since the argument was making her lose concentration anyway.

Rannan realised she had become so emotional that she would have to stop to calm herself. They stopped. Everyone got out. The atmosphere around Rannan and Lazel was thick. They glowered and barely looked at each other. Jone was bewildered by how quickly the hostility had escalated. She knew from Pallad they were sexual amorades, and she knew what kind of comment that would elicit from the Church point of view. She felt the need to escape and wandered over to the edge of the cliff. It was a day of perfect visibility with white, thick, well-defined, separated-out cumulus moving steadily high up in the sky. Rain might come by evening, but now in the sunshine it was fresh and warm. Jone looked down at the cliff they'd been climbing, a red-brown sill with deep horizontal striations and vertical grooves looking as if it had just oozed out of the grassy bank beneath it. She turned in the direction of the road ahead to see Merlan Seat, the volcanic plug at the end of the cliff, and it struck her that she knew this place.

She rummaged through her memory banks: of course, the realisation they'd watched that night at the Hedonarea. This was the very volcano and its vents they'd watched forming. It all came back, that whole evening, the excitement, the horror and the deep pain. And yet it wasn't as it was then. She remembered the pain vividly, but she no longer felt it. She looked at the cliff again and could see it as it was when it was formed in the carboniferous era: burning and melting its way through layers of sediment. It was a metaphor for the pain of that night, a pain that had cut through layers of buried feeling. Over millions of years the layer that had once been on top of the volcanic intrusion had worn away, exposing the intrusion as the cliff they now saw. Like the sill, the pain was now exposed, but frozen so it could be clearly defined. The sedimentary layer of saintly detachment on top had worn away, but in an infinitely quicker time than the rock. It had taken from the walk by the shore two days ago, through the long talk with Pallad last night to the race here today. Whatever the cost, she was sure something good was happening. She glanced around. Luner came up beside her. 'Are ye dain yer daft sums?' What could she say? She had no training in speaking about feelings. She shook her head and tried to speak of her affect towards Luner with her eyes. Luner turned away, embarrassed. Jone crumpled. If this unexpected shyness of Luner's persisted, it would be up to her to say something, in which case nothing would be said and the excruciating suspense would go on forever. She looked over at the volcanic plug again and imagined the hard basalt melting back down into the vent, like a reversed reel of a chapter. There was a lifetime's solidification plugging the flow inside her. Could that reel reversal happen? It had to somehow, but she didn't know how.

Lazel had sorted out the problem. The gap in the points had needed adjusting. The argument was unresolved. It might well have lasted to the pit-stop. It might well have not. The drivers went back to their seats. Each knowing they had to turn their minds to the driving and forget their differences. But the euphoria had gone. It would depend on where they came in at the markers whether it would revive again.

There were no further mishaps and they found themselves in fourteenth and fifteenth places. It wasn't bad, but to be sure of getting on the vulgy at the end, they really had to be in the first ten. At this point in the race, no one was in the least interested in them. The larkules with the cameras had already picked out their bagwans during the battle of Leper Town and would stay with them or their conquerors, or the petros well in front, to the end of the race. All this was to the prows' advantage. It wouldn't do to be found out they were females. That was to be the big surprise at the end.

Pit-stop Two was the official refreshment stop. If the prows' secret got out in the canteen, everyone would be after them as 'easy prey', so they stayed outside round the side of the building and kept their helmets on. Nessa was to bring them food and drink. She was there to greet them, full of praise and optimism. It was just what they needed. With all the big rivalries going on between the top teams she reckoned they could slip home with a maximum of three battles each. The crews fell silent at that. Having got to Pit-stop Two without any fights made the anticipation of them harder, but they couldn't give up now.

The next phase of the race was through the wood. It would be much more difficult to avoid a fight, there were too many variables on the wood roads, too many blind crossroads and T-junctions, and there would be petros, now desperate for kills. The practice in the visional had been most useful for this part. Rannan was able to swerve and dodge, with a technique far superior to most of the enemies. But inevitably they were caught at one of the crossroads, between two petros coming at them from opposite directions. One of them managed to ram them into the ditch. It was their first battle.

Jone's unexpected marshalarts won the fight, but it was hard. Tactics and skill were up against brute force and it was exhausting, physically and emotionally.

As soon as they had made their kill they raced off. The three fighters sat in a daze trying to draw themselves together again. Another T-junction loomed ahead. Rannan decided to risk taking it quickly, and found the worst possible result: a petro right in the centre of the road. She swerved but she was too fast. She was in the verge, stalled. The men in the other petro were out at once, standing in line, a fit and confident-looking bunch.

As the prows got out Geever muttered to Jone, 'Look at him on the end.' He was standing in a karate stance. No wonder they looked so fresh. Jone made straight for him and swung out her arm to see how he blocked. He was good enough. This was no time to engage in a contest. It was time to take a gamble. Jone opened herself a little. He aimed a blow at her stomach. Before it landed, she threw herself on her back. He brought a clamp out, then kneeled down to grab her arms. At once she sat up and taking advantage of his momentary surprise, reached out for his caryotid nerve, and had him down. The others were much less fortunate, they were engaged in wrestling locks, having to strain every muscle and squeeze every drop of willpower they had to stay tussling. As soon as she had her own attacker clamped, Jone rushed for Geever's attacker. This time she was going to have to hurt. She made straight for his nose with a side-hand hit. He reeled back. Geever with all her might wrenched herself free. Jone kicked him in the legs and he was down. Rannan clamped him at once. By now Luner was screaming, her attacker had twisted her arm behind her. Jone hit him in the face, stronger and swifter than she'd ever done before. She hadn't known she had such reserves of hate, for that was what had fuelled it. The man screamed and toppled over. His nose was bleeding profusely. Jone ignored him and clamped him. Luner was moaning with the pain in her arm. Rannan brought out the first-aid kit and injected a painkiller.

Rannan's concern for Luner had put clamping the enemy petro right out of her mind. The driver had climbed in, revved up and was off. They survived a horrendous battle and now they had nothing to show for it. Meanwhile the driver could find another stranded crew.

They climbed in the petro and sat in silence for a moment.

Rannan looked at Luner. 'I'll fight next time.'

'No,' said Geever. 'We kin take the moor road.'

'We wouldny huv a place now. There's no point. If we'd gone there first we'd have had a chance.'

'A'll fight,' muttered Luner.

Rannan looked concerned. 'Naw, Luner it's no worth it, ye're wounded. Anar was right, it is nasty filthy savagery.'

Geever was poring over the map. 'Look, here's another route, plenty uv corners an' less junctions, could be less petros. Heh, ye know what? If we got a petro alongside we could shove them on the verge an' get on, lose them instead of fightin'.'

'Yeh, king idea,' said Rannan. 'OK, let's go. But dinny feel up tae it, Luner.'

When they were on the road again, Rannan opened the radio to Lazel. The other team were in a completely opposite mood. They hadn't been in a fight but had taken a kill. After a mile or two's chase their opponent driver had lost control of his steering and landed in a ditch with the petro on its side. They had raised a surrender flag and the prows had to help them out the top side of the petro. When one of them suddenly realised they were female, he was furious. Lazel had quipped back, 'Dinny bother regrettin' it, we're black belt marshalarts, how d'ya think we got here?' When Rannan said how they'd fared she was full of sympathy. 'Dae whit ye want. Right enough, it's no really much ae a laugh this, is it?'

Rannan had to switch off to concentrate on the corners. In a little while she was able to get some speed again, glad she wasn't recovering from a fight. They were pursued for a mile or two but managed to lose them with extra turns. Then they had an oncoming challenge. Rannan dodged them, quickly reversed and rammed them into the verge and left them. Coming up behind were their original pursuers who naturally stopped for the first available fight. The prows cheered. It was the lucky break they needed.

It was another fifteen minutes before they met with another petro. This time the tactic didn't quite work. The driver was as deft at dodging as Rannan and the two swung back and forth for the next two miles. Geever suggested taking a longer route, on the chance that he might not want to waste time. The others agreed. It worked. As soon as they saw he was not behind, Rannan stalled and suggested they take the risk of going back. The others agreed. She didn't say it was because she thought something was going wrong with the steering. After all the swerving it was understandable. She guessed that was why they hadn't been followed, the other petro driver probably had the same worry.

Things seemed OK until the first sharp bend, and that was it. It was as if the body and the front were coming apart. The petro threw itself across the ditch. The others screamed as the petro turned, but they were lucky. The ditch stopped them going into a tree and the petro stayed on its wheels. But the axle, and with it the petro, was gone. No one was hurt but they were numb with shock. Rannan contacted Lazel. A raging sobbing voice came through. 'We're nuked, we've surrendered, this fightin's terrible. Why the pidjer did we think this wis a good idea?'

When Rannan switched off she broke into quiet sobs. None of the rest could be bothered getting out of the petro, but stayed fixed in their seats in dumb silence. The question of what they were going to do next hovered in the air, but no one felt like voicing it. A minute or two later the question was answered for them. A petro was approaching. Rannan dried her tears, but otherwise never moved. The petro stopped. Its team sat for a moment, astonished to see a petro sitting on the verge fully occupied. Then the driver got out, walked over and peered at Rannan. He started, then stared again, this time at all four of them, pushing his head a bit further in. The prows didn't return his look. He stood back and turned to his mates.

'Heh, lads, come on o'er here, come an' see if A'm seein' right.'

The other three males came across and surrounded the petro, poking their noses in the window. The prows still turned away. The men were open mouthed with astonishment.

'They're lassies, are they no?' said the driver. The others agreed and one of them said, 'How the pidger did they get this far?'

'Mustae sweet talked the lads ootae fightin'.'

The driver leaned on the door and surveyed them again. 'Heh, come on lassies, dinny look sae glum, we'll no fight ya. Ye dinny need tae be scared. We're gentlemen, are we no lads? We dinny fight lassies.'

The other men grinned. Suddenly his eyes caught the ribbon on Rannan's jacket.

'How did ye get that, ye didny fight did ya?'

Rannan flashed a quick significant look at Jone and then said, 'Naw, they surrendered.'

'So ye've managed tae dodge aw this way.' He was patronisingly admiring. One of the others with a red face wasn't admiring.

'How the pidger did they learn to drive?' He obviously didn't like the idea.

'Maybe they canny,' said the third one, a small and wiry blond. 'Maybe they just came frae the woods lookin' for a kill.'

Luner was about to protest but Rannan silenced her with a quiet hiss.

The gruff red-faced one was still wanting to express his displeasure. 'It's no right, lassies petro-freakin'.'

'Och, Arf,' said the driver, 'dinny be an auld barbarian. Why should lassies no petro-freak? We should gie them their own race. Would it no be king watchin' lassies fight?' He turned back to

Rannan and grinned. 'Seems a right shame fur a bunch ae lovely lassies tae be left stranded in the woods.'

The fourth man who had a plaster on his nose poked his head in. 'Why dae we no take them in wi' us?'

Red-faced Arf snorted. 'Dinny be ridiculous.'

'Why no?' said plaster-nose. 'It wouldny slow us up. We'd get oorsels on the vulgy for sure, rescuin' damsels in distress. The rest ae the lads would be ragin' jealous.' He turned back to the women. 'Can ye no take yer helmets off now girls, ye dinny need them now.' Rannan looked at the others, and signalled with her eyes to do as he said. Unfortunately as Jone took her helmet off her wig came off too. 'Ooh,' said Plaster-nose. 'It's a saint. Aw ma mate Arf here gets real revved up on saints, especially ones intae ethnic culture.' He chuckled and Arf blushed and stared at Jone.

As the women got out, the driver said, 'Aye, they're no a bad-lookin' bunch. Cheer up, lassies, we're a real Krischan bunch ae lads, ye dinny need tae worry aboot us. Come on over tae the mobile, ye kin sit on oor knees.' He winked at Jone. 'Sit on Arf's knee, he'd be made up. Dinny worry, he's harmless.'

Jone looked at Rannan, she felt unreal. She could see that being aggressive might provoke them, but were they really going to go through with this?

'Come on, girls. What do ye say?' He was sure his offer was desirable.

'OK,' said Rannan, almost sounding pleasant, and started towards their petro. The men were delighted. Even Arf betrayed some pleasure. Jone was dumbfounded. They seemed to be oblivious of what the women were actually feeling.

The men climbed in, and then Rannan and Luner and Geever followed. Rannan looked worried, whatever strategy she had in mind wasn't working. Geever looked frightened. Luner was glowering with suppressed rage. Jone hung back. Arf climbed in last, turned to Jone and patted his knee. 'Come on, sit here, there's enough fat there.'

Jone was beginning to feel nauseous. She walked slowly towards him. The next thing he would do, she guessed, was reach out for her. She would probably vomit. His arm came out towards her.

'Don't touch me!' her sharpness startled him and he dropped his arm. Then he frowned at the insult, and grabbed her waist. 'Don't touch me, don't touch me!' she shrieked and in an overwhelming fury twisted his arm and yanked him onto the ground as he screamed with pain. Without a thought Jone had whipped out her clamps and tightened them on his arms and legs. The other men gazed in astonishment.

Rannan turned to the driver and sounding as innocently girlish as she could manage, said, 'She goes right ufo if you touch her.'

'Maybe we'd better leave her behind.'

Arf lifted his head and screamed 'Yer no leavin' me behind.' The driver made a face and climbed out the petro and came round to Jone.

'Heh, come on now darlin'. He's harmless, honest,' he nodded towards Rannan. 'She kin sit on his knee an' you kin sit in the middle.'

Jone's furious disgust was still intense but part of her mind was also aware that this was worth exaggerating. It wasn't difficult. She gave the driver a wild look and repeated, 'Don't touch me.'

'It's awright, love, A'm no gontae touch ya,' he bent down and took out his keys. Jone threw a kick at his face. He fell, she grabbed his arm and twisted it. He screamed. She put on the clamps.

'Grutij drids,' said plaster-nose, 'she's right oot the galaxy.' He and his companion held on tight to Luner and Geever. 'Grutij rods, Mak, get the pidjer demon,' cried the driver, between groans of pain. The two got out reluctantly, staring at Jone, as if she was a demon. Jone backed away a little, acting a demoniac look for all she was worth. The two of them approached gingerly.

'You grutij soggerts,' screamed the driver. 'For pidjer's sake, the two ae ya kin take her.'

But before they had time to move, Jone had chopped at plaster-nose's neck, and brought him down, swung round and kicked the other one in the knees. The rest of the women reacted at once. Rannan brought out the clamps and clamped them while the other two held them down. Rannan then threw herself back in the petro and turned the ignition on. 'Come on, let's git.' The rest jumped in at once and they were off.

After a minute or two of incredulous silence, the whole group burst into hysterical tears and laughter. Luner leaned over to Rannan, 'Wis this the plan?' and they burst into more laughter, including Jone. Now words came pouring out of Rannan, all the possible strategies that had been racing through her mind. By the time they were getting into the men's petro, the only possibility that seemed feasible was waiting for them to have another fight and then stealing the petro. Now they were all ready to shower praise on Jone, but seeing her embarrassment, they toned it down. Jone was worried now about them being reported for cheating. The others dismissed it. Everybody cheated, nobody was disqualified unless they had been filmed. cheating.

'Anyhow,' said Rannan, 'you were defendin' yersel against carnal violation.'

'I thought I was going to throw up, but I managed to throw him instead,' said Jone. They collapsed in more helpless laughter. Jone slumped back exhausted.

'This is definitely prows' last Whitsun rampage,' said Rannan and everyone wholeheartedly agreed.

During the remainder of the journey, they were passed by two petros and passed one. None of them trying to ram. Placing was now what mattered. Rannan drove as smooth and as fast as she could, using reserves of willpower to maintain her level of concentration. Now that they could make it, they had to.

About half an hour later, they were riding past the finishing line. Up went the blazing neon sign '10'. They had just made it. They screamed with delight. As they slowed down, people were crowding round with cameras and one man with a mike shoved his head through the window.

'How does it feel to –' Then he saw Rannan's still uncovered head. 'You're female.'

'We're aw female,' said Rannan.

The reporter's jaw dropped. 'How on earth did you manage to –?'

'We'll tell ya after.'

'You bet.' The reporter turned to talk excitedly to a camera. Then he turned back. 'Go and see them over there and we'll arrange a proper interview.'

Once in the pit, Jone, who'd put her helmet back on, jumped out and disappeared inside the competitors' rooms. There she bumped into Lazel and the others and was seized with terror in case they would hug her.

'I feel sick,' she stuttered. 'The others are just behind,' and she rushed past them to the toilets. 'We made it,' she shouted and got away. Inside the toilet she was sick.

In the early evening the prows, including Jone gathered in Nessa's domicile to watch the interview. The whole group had discussed what to say in the competitors' rooms and Lazel and Pallad had volunteered to give it.

'Congratulations,' said the smooth interviewer, 'on being the first females not only to take part in the Whitsun rampage, but to gain a place in it too. Quite an extraordinary achievement. How did you manage it?'

'We mainly did it through learning driving skills in a visional,' said Pallad, 'that's the part we're really proud of as far as gaining a place is concerned. We strongly believe there should be more petro-freaking competitions without any fighting. I'm not saying do away with ramming, that's fun, but the fighting is barbarous and it's what keeps females out of the petro-freaks.'

The interview shifted to Lazel. 'But you did actually survive by fighting, didn't you?'

'Well, obviously we had tae fight, but we found it distressin'. It's because of the fighting we don't intend to compete in another rampage. We hate it. But one of the main reasons we took part, in spite of that, was to show that females kin learn to defend themselves, by learning marshalarts. In fact our sect is hopin' to –'

'Before you mention your sect, can you say something about your takeover of the last petro? We believe its team has complained you were cheating. They say they weren't fighting you but you suddenly attacked them. What do you say about that?'

'The truth is they were carnally harassing us. Our marshalarts expert defended herself against her carnal harasser and then against the rest of the team who were threatening her. It wasn't a fight, it was one female defending herself against four male harassers. You see what we mean when we say we want to show that females can defend themselves.'

'And,' Pallad jumped in before the interviewer could deflect them, 'our sect, the Plotinian Protestant Womanists, are hoping to set up self-defence training sessions for the females. So look out for our propaganda.'

The interviewer turned to the camera. 'Well, if this self-defence catches on, there'll be quite a few of us poor males fearful of walking the streets, with armies of belligerent females on the warpath. Let's see what one or two of the male competitors thought,' and he turned to one of the men sitting on his other side.

'They cheated. That's rubbish aboot carnal harassment. Typical sexist lies. The lads were just bein' matey, an' they turned on them, because they're just a bunch've – sexualists. It's a disgrace. Just proves they're no fit tae take part in the rampage.'

The interviewer turned to the other male competitor. 'A think it's rubbish aw this talk aboot the girls' cheatin'. Everybody cheats when the cameras are no on them. As a matter of a fact A agree there should be petro-freaks wi'oot fightin'. A lot of us are fed up wi' it.'

The interviewer turned to the camera. 'Well, the idea of a rampage without fightin' is already becoming a big talking point. I went around some of the spectators to find out their views.' The opinions canvassed swung from one extreme to another, but there seemed to be a groundswell of support for a no-fighting rampage, or at least, having it as well as the fighting one. 'Whatever happens,' concluded the interviewer, 'these protestant womanists have caused quite a stir. Is this the demise of the machophrenic male or the rise of the machophrenic female?'

There was a chorus of boos in Nessa's domicile and the vulgy was switched off and a tablet inserted. Despite the idiotic interviewer the group were jubilant. The publicity that had been the religious point of the whole enterprise had certainly been achieved. The emotional and physical batterings of the event were put aside, and the talk moved on to how they could build on the interest they were bound to have generated. Jone, helping herself to generous quantities of canethol, entered into the atmosphere, and left the great heap of unresolved feeling slumped inarticulately at the bottom of the swamp.

17

The concert was being held in the civic temple in the citadel. By the time the prows reached it, the place was thronged with music devotees dressed in extravagant pagan costumes. Normally the citadel was a saintly sober place. Its buildings were where the business of colonial government was carried out.

But on a concert night, it was like it had been captured by an invasion force, and almost could have been, were it not for the lines of inquo around the perimeters, menacing, silent, still and watchful, like birds of prey, waiting to swoop. Jone had never seen so many of them all in one place before. It made her shudder. But she forgot about them when she turned back to look at the crowd. It was like a fantasy bubble of freedom and happiness with everyone a big united clan. Jone, though she was aware she wasn't part of it, was now, perhaps because of the canethol, able to appreciate it and ignore the unmathematical chaos of sense impressions and breathe in the emotional particles of freedom and happiness.

Inside, the temple was bare of seating for the concert. The prows with their tokens had got in early and squatted on the floor near the front. Jone found herself beside Luner. Had they willed it or hadn't they? All day, apart from on Lammas Heights, there had been no private contact between them. Yet there had been looks and smiles that had confirmed their unspoken intimacy. Now they landed beside each other in a way that was natural, without any self-conscious strain. All the same there were still no words between them. Luner was absorbed in gossip with the others about people they knew in the audience.

It left Jone free, for the first time since she'd been sick in the toilet, to drift off into her own head. And the same thing came to the fore: the incident with Arf and his team. In all the talk they'd had about the day's events that evening, no one had concentrated on Jone's feelings of disgust. It was all talk of machophrenic harassment, talking about it on the assumption she'd been perfectly justified because they were males. But her anger and disgust had not been at his maleness. Did they realise that? Or were they rationalising to themselves that it was disgust at his maleness not his carnality? No one had asked her directly about her feelings. Were they frightened of the truth? It was puzzling though. All evening they had been freely touching each other, especially Rannan and Lazel. Weren't they just as carnal as Arf? Yet none of them had touched her. Wasn't the real difference not maleness and female-ness but that they were sensitive and he was an ignorant oaf?

She had no more time to puzzle it out. The place was filling up and her nose was being penetrated by body odours. It seemed she was learning to live with them or was she desensitised by the canethol? She felt a nudge, Luner was passing her the syringe.

There was a rumbling sound from the audience, as the place went completely dark. A moment or two of total silence. The lights switched on at either side of the stage, to reveal the music synthesizer complex. Two people, of uncertain gender, sat before it in robes, coloured in broad stripes in shades of red and green. The crowd roared. The musicians kept their backs to them. They waited till the silence returned and then began to play, low, soft, melodious sounds, keyboard and wind sounds. First it was slow, then it started to get gradually quicker, with other unidentifiable noises added. It became harsher, sharper, more staccato.

Then realisations high up around the walls were switched on. They weren't fully three-dimensional like at the Hedonarea, but more like bible screens, giving an illusion of three-dimensionality. But the height of the walls and ceiling made them just as impressive. On the side walls was a cratered moonscape. Above it was a dark sky with planets and comets moving swiftly across it and nebulus exploding and forming, but over all a sense of deep darkness. Behind the stage a cratered mountain opened to reveal a cavern, which, because of the three-dimensionality, seemed very high and very deep, many miles deep. It glittered with ice on its weirdly-shaped walls, its stalactites and stalagmites. The music was still getting louder, almost savage, with an incessant drum beat that was hypnotising heads and shoulders in the audience into movement. It gave you a feeling of aggressive power, that turned an agglomora-tion of little insignificant individuals into one supra-person, a conquering emperor.

Suddenly it stopped and a giant black-robed, hooded figure appeared at the end of the long cave. Then the truth struck. It was Yalida herself on the stage, turned into a giant by the illusion of the cave. The image went back and forth, now huge and far away, now ordinary size and close, at least close enough to be a real person standing there, not a realisation. Then a voice came from the figure, echoed from the sides and back of the hall. Like a sing-song whisper: 'Don't touch me. Don't touch me.' Jone almost fainted. She began to shake like a leaf. It was as if the voice was a scalpel opening up her own head. She could not believe it, was she dreaming? She turned her head to find Luner half-smiling with intense sympathy at this totally unexpected exposure of Jone's thoughts. Trying to say with her eyes, 'Yes, we did think of this when you said it, but we didn't want to embarrass you with it.' Jone turned back to Yalida, mesmerised by every word.

The voice was machophrenic, hard and rasping, but very clear:

Don't touch me, don't touch me, I am
The hermit celibate bone with no marrow
Hanging like a hook from my shoulder
Bitter sharp pain unreal
Teeth skull and fingernail
Pinned to the wall
Watching you crawl
Squirm ooze everywhere
You slug slime swamp
You creeping cornucopia
Don't come near me leave me alone
I am the picked-clean dry desert bone
Let the sand trickle through my hollow back
Ah let the sun burn my mouth and lips black
And the desert dry my eyes in horizon
When you smile your face drips slowly waxily
I shall wipe your fatty buttery melting mucus
From my pure white brittle vertebrae
When you speak you smell with the food you gorge
Don't put your pudgy fingers near your breast
And squirt your milk at me
Let me out Let me out

173

Don't come near Don't come near
You don't know who I am
My vagina is a flour cave
My penis and testicles I gave
to the worms
I am above the earth and far beyond
My mind is a supernova diamond
The crystals are infinite in number time and space
You try to drag me down in your morass
You try to seep your earth into my pores
You will try to bring your tidal wave to my shore
Engulfing me with algae coelenterates and diatoms
You are earth, you are the sea, I am the stratosphere
I am the purest gases above the highest mountain
You are the murky depths beneath the deepest ocean
You are flesh flesh I am spirit spirit
Noli me tangere Noli me tangere Noli me tangere.

Jone could hardly believe it, yet it was true. It was really happening. A burning knife of words, each one perfectly expressing her feelings, had cut her open and let years of poison flow out. If her body had floated to the ceiling, freed of its burden, she would not have been surprised.

The song rose to an ear-shattering climax when Yalida screamed out the ancient language and at the same time raised her arms as if she was hanging on a tree. Her hood fell. Beneath was a mask with a skull on it. The audience gasped and some even screamed. Yalida leaned back slowly until she was lying flat. A coffin rose up underneath her. The cave darkened and became a lunar mountain seen from the outside. Gradually it darkened, and the rest of the landscape, until there was total darkness and silence. Then the woodwind/string melody there had been at the beginning returned. Light appeared at the back of the stage, a speeded-up dawn. A rocky shore emerged in the growing sunlight. A shoreline similar to the wildernesses but rockier, with higher mountains behind. It had the cool, fresh feel of the north Yukey country. The coffin now lay on the rocks, merged into the realisation. The music played a low, gentle tune. Yalida appeared from the side of the stage, with an old, stringed instrument strapped to her shoulder. She was dressed in a white robe and she looked quite ordinary, with long hair.

Her voice had become female, strong and natural. She seemed very close to the audience. As she sang, the words were acted out in the realisation.

They took away my body and put it in a box
They flung it in the ocean and it came up on the rocks
There were mountains to the north
Sandy beaches to west
The sun came up and lit the water
And a tern swooped on its nest
Someone came down to the shore
Collecting driftwood for her fire
She saw the box and clambered over
And she tried to prise it open
Something stirred inside the coffin
Fingers moved toes stretched head swivelled
The lid creaked the lock bent I struggled
I burst through I opened my eyes
I heard the waves I saw the towering skies
A frightened woman gazed at me
But she didn't go away
I longed for grass sap, sea spray, gull cry,
            rainfall, windlift and life.
And I whispered 'Touch me kind tender woman,
Touch me',
And she leaned across and gently
And she gently gently gently
Touched my cheek

As she heard the words 'touch me' Jone was filled with yearning, yearning for all the years of isolation to vanish and all the poison of disgust to be healed by a touch, the kind of touch in the song, a touch like ancient BA magicians were supposed to have, a touch that could raise the dead.

She found herself turning to Luner and the yearning poured out from her eyes. Luner smiled, an infinitely gentle maternal smile, then looked down at Jone's hands, clenched on her crossed legs. Jone loosened one hand from the other, opened the palm of one of them upward and moved it, slowly, towards Luner. Luner's hand, palm downward, moved over it, and just as the song finished, after

175

a moment's hesitation, lowered it to grasp Jone's.

Jone's sense of relief was like a flood. There was no disgust, only the pouring out of affection. The two looked at each other, smiled and turned away embarrassed, but their hands stayed glued together until everyone rose to clap and cheer and they were too self-conscious not to join in. It gave Jone an intense sense of loss. Were the hands going to get back together again? Everyone sat down again and Yalida spoke.

'Hello Embra, good to see you again' (roars and cheers from the audience). She waited till they died down. 'I wrote the words of that song a long time ago, just after I was defrocked –' (more cheers and applause). 'Well, getting into carnal sin (more cheers) was like being born again. Quite a few of my songs seem to be on the death and resurrection thing. They just seem to turn out that way. One of my favourites is on "Astral Travelling" (more cheers). It's called "The Birth of Venus" (more cheering).'

Luner turned to Jone, gripped her arm and whispered 'This is it,' and her hand slipped down and took Jone's hand again. It brought a hot spark to Jones genitals. So she was hormonally aroused, was she? Well, it was to be expected. She told herself to keep calm about it. All the same it made her feel giddy, as if she was standing at the top of a cliff, about to be hurled into an abyss. Did she want to fall? She was terrified, but yes, she did want to fall.

Yalida carried on: 'This one's about the death and rebirth you go through when you're very lonely and you go through hell, then all of a sudden things change, you're surrounded by lots of friends, something like that. Just as a point of interest, the realisation that goes with the song was one I made when I was a student, about Heisenberg. You can still get it in college bibloteks.'

Jone and Luner gaped at one another. They knew very well what the realisation would be. Their hands squeezed each other's tightly. Yalida stayed at the front of the stage, but changed her instruments to a small keyboard connected to the other machines. The music combined a dreamy melodious front tune, pinned down with solid tracks and rhythms, symbolising the atmosphere and body of a plant.

One night my astral soul left my body seeking her,
Knowing I could only find wisdom in the heart of fire
She who seeks a change that is truly alchemical

Must burn and burn again in the fiery womb of hell.
To the far side of the sun I sped, powered by the solar wind
I saw her luminescent face, outshining all bejewelled Venus.
I gyred into insertion and launched my mind down,
Now its Terran-Lunar curtain was forever torn
Into the burning bath of yellow cloud I descended
In sulphuric acid rain my ego was boiled.
In fiery spits of HC1 self-seeking was dissolved.
In HSO F's corrosion, dishonesty was atomised.
In choking fumes of CO security was vapourised
Deep into her body my dying soul descended
Solidified to rock that heaved and cracked and groaned
Magma's tide rolled the carcass from the shore
To melt in the death of the black iron core.

Awake! my pain cried outgassing through my fissures
Vibrating into echoes from my four billion years
Know now the triumph of soul's initiation
Understand the truth in retrograde rotation
And I saw the thermal ocean pour forth around my head
And I read the micrometers of my spirit's infra-red
And all the waves were blazing jewelled serpents of flame
Radiating colours that a terran cannot name.

Jone's gaze had stayed transfixed on Yalida's face through all of
this. The voice was deep and rich, the emotions it expressed deep
and rich.

Now there was an instrumental break and the realisation showed
the body of the planet, it's mountain contours like a face, while the
waves of the atmosphere became swirling hair that was also snakes.
Jone and Luner looked at each other again as they both
remembered how they had seen the painting in the shelter together.

The two musicians, who could now be seen to be women, moved
across to join Yalida with their keyboards in front of them, and the
three of them sang the song to the heatwaves, joyful, upbeat
exuberant.

Guide me on the thermal tides, O pythons of Venus
Let me surf and dive in your sweltering blazing breezes
Radiant purple queens of the cool north whirlpool

Bring down the spiralling hurricanes of revelation
Lucid blue banshees of the clear high shear collar
Open my chords to your words of divination
Vividgreen harlots of the west speeding winds
Propagate within my blood the flow of inspiration
Sungold strumpets of the resonating belts
Draw through my intestines fierce illumination
Sacral orange amazons of the curving bow waves
Fire in my genitals the spark of inspiration
Rootred witches of the subsolar cauldron
Stir inside my womb an immaculate conception

Now Yalida sang the ending herself, with a slow emotionalism that
brought tears to the eyes.

For seven months or more we travelled on that night
Till I saw close by me the blue planet's light
From my dream I woke to see her
Bright crescent of the morning
While flames of wisdom like a fountain
Over me were pouring
When they faded in the day I knew within my soul
That I was born again from the fiery womb of hell.

There was thunderous clapping and shouts of 'more'. Yalida and
her musicians smiled and clapped the audience, then they walked
off. The stage lights went off. It was Embra's last sight of Yalida.

When the lights came on again a manager came on to announce
that Yalida had been taken suddenly ill and that everyone was to
make their way to the entrance where their tokens would be
refunded. For a few minutes there was the silence of unbelief, then
the buzzing began. Word went round quickly. Illegal injects must
have been found backstage, she must have been arrested. The
expression of astonishment changed to rumbles of anger. Some
people at the front took it into their heads to jump up on the stage.
One of them shouted to the audience, 'We'll get the truth outae
them.'

There were cheers from his friends below who began to chant,
'We want Yalida! We want Yalida!' It quickly spread. Now more
people were climbing on to the stage. But the truth was not to be

got. Black uniforms were in the way. Not just one or two, but a whole phalanx. They spread out across the stage and pushed the intruders back, then threw them off. There were howls of protest from those thrown off and those below.

Now everybody was sure illness had nothing to do with it. The howls and angry chants of 'We want Yalida!' came from everywhere. Things were hurled at the inquos on stage. The orderly progress out, which had started at the back, collapsed. Some people began to rush to the doors. They could be heard shouting, 'There's inquos out here too.' Some people behind the prows began to sing: 'If you want to know what it's like to be free.' At once it was picked up and spread around the hall:

Join hands together and come along with me
Forget about your points, forget about your play
Forget about your charity, your prayers for today.
Leave it filed away in Gawd. Tune into the verse of blood.
Fly up to the wilderness, the wild and wicked wilderness.
See the earth exploding in a rainbow cloud of gas
Drink your foam, touch your fire.
Smell your sweat and see
This is what it could be like to be free.

By the end everyone was jumping up and down waving arms with clenched fists and yelling the song in a chant more than singing it.

An inquo officer appeared on stage with a hand-held mike with very high amplification.

'Clear the temple in an orderly fashion now. If you don't start moving out in rows as you were told to do, we will have no choice but to turn the web-guns on you. Anyone webbed will be arrested. You have two minutes to calm down and get moving.'

The lines of inquo were spreading round the walls with their web-guns in front of them. Panic set in, pushing began from near the front. As the back was clearing, the pushing increased. Some people began running, while others stood their ground and went on singing, and caused blocks that made the pushing worse. The prows, when they found themselves being pushed, linked arms and went with the movement. They were almost at the door when they heard screaming behind. The web-guns had been turned on some of the singers. The rush became a stampede. The prows were swept out of the building.

The citadel seemed packed with milling crowds, many more than could have been inside the building. Here the chanting and singing of the 'Freedom Song' had been taken up again. Rannan saw someone she knew and spoke to him. When she turned back to the others her face was ashen.

'It wasn't injects, it's heresy. Yon Angel that's visitin' Lundin's jist been assassinated. They're sayin' she brought the assassin intae the country. They're sayin' she's a Babylonian.'

Fear shot through them all. 'We'd better get rid ae aw the stuff at home. They'll be aw over the place,' said Lazel. Pallad had chapters and tapes too, and Jone.

Rannan added her urgent plea, 'Everybody get back hame, an' make sure ye havny got any ae oor addresses. Burn aw the propaganda. We ken how tae get in touch anyway.'

Pallad, Nessa, Rannan and Lazel moved off at once. Jone was about to say to Luner 'Will you come with me?' when the ones left found themselves being pushed again. The crowds seemed to move in every direction. It looked as if the inquo were rounding people up. Geever shouted to Luner, 'You go back wi' Grif. She canny go by hersel',' and she and Molner and Zaner rushed off. Luner began to run.

'Jist keep a hold've me, Grif,' and she was dodging in and out of the crowd.

Jone had never been so terrified in her life. At one point two or three people near them got webbed and they only narrowly missed it themselves. It was the first time Jone had ever seen it close at hand. It billowed round them like froth. The fear in the faces as it glued around them was horrible to see. At last the two of them were out of the square and running for their lives in the subway. They sat down in the car close together. Luner with her arm through Jone's. Luner was worried about the inquo getting to their bases. When someone sat near them they stopped talking, spending the rest of the journey in silent agitation.

Soon they arrived at the residency and just as they walked into the lobby, the hatch of the shuttle opened and out spilled two ethnic woman in venerable ceremonial dress, followed by two male priests. Jone muttered to Luner, 'Drop your arm,' and Luner did so at once. The next moment Jone's eyes focused on one of the priests. It was Ned Skwyer. As they came past he smiled at Jone, a slimy conspiratorial smile, 'Hi Jone – and Luner.' Luner said 'Hello, Reverend Skwyer,' as if she was a model of Abbey Krischan behaviour. His party moved to the door. One of the men said something and the others laughed raucously. Had Ned seen Luner holding Jone's arm? Surely not, he was too launched to notice anything by the look of him. Luner muttered, 'Bet ya anythin' they're off tae the moonpalace, Grif. A've seen they lassies afore, up there wi' saints.' That was Jone's guess too, but there was no time to reflect on saintly hypocrisy.

A wave of calm met them, when they stepped inside the mansion. Everything was still in its place. Jone got the addresses and chapters she had acquired from Pallad and threw them down the refuse chute. When she came back into the easebay, Luner was on the vu' to Rannan. Everything was OK there too. 'Come round the morrow's morn an' we'll talk, OK?' said Rannan and rang off. For the first time, they were able to smile, then Luner came over and said, 'Is it OK if A hug ya, Grif?'

'Of course.'

Jone was surprised at the question. She assumed Luner would have no inhibitions now, underestimating her sensitivity yet again. They hugged for a minute or two then Luner went to the Bible and switched it on. Yet another deep space adventure. She consulted the clock.

'There'll be a Gospel on in five minutes.'

'Want something to eat?' said Jone.

Luner grinned and nodded and sat down on a floform. Jone brought in some food by the time the Gospel was beginning. It was interminable and depressing. All sorts of officials from here, there and everywhere were brought forth to express their shock and horror. And as for Yalida, numerous people in her train were brought protesting her innocence, but the authorities seemed unmoved. Her music was to be banned from markets and from public broadcasting in studios. There were pictures of inquos raiding markets and studios already. All sorts of dire warnings were made about anyone suspected of heresies. Protestant sects of all kinds were under suspicion. Luner cried at the banning of Yalida.

'A willnae go tae a studio now,' and Jone put a comforting arm round her shoulder.

After the message was over they switched off and they sat in depressed silence for a little while, then they injected some canethol and Luner decided she wanted to listen to her Yalida tablets.

'They willnae be comin' tae arrest us for that will they?' she said, half-mocking and half-serious.

'Nobody'll hear it in here,' said Jone. 'That I know for sure.'

And so they watched Yalida and they talked a little about the concert and what happened. But mostly they sat in silence, huddled together, their minds drifting into wondering what the future held, but of that they didn't speak to each other. When the music was played, Luner without looking directly in Jone's eyes said, in a very matter-of-fact voice, 'D'ye feel like goin' tae the sleepbay?' and Jone nodded. A little voice inside far off said: well this is it, the great moment of universe-shattering transception. The final fall over the cliff into carnality. The great goodbye to Church and sanctity and grace abounding. The most momentous act of heresy in your life. But the rest of her mind present in the room felt none of those things. All it felt was that she was going to do something as ordinary as taking a sauna or eating breakfast.

Luner got up and pulled Jone with her. Jone staggered from the effect of the canethol and Luner supported her through to the sleepbay. Once in it, Luner began to giggle, then stuttered out.

'A've never cuddled somebody suspended in air, a dinny think A'd like it.'

'Don't worry, the sleep module's only room for one. We'll use the waterbed,' said Jone.

Luner frowned, still not looking directly at Jone. 'Heh, Grif, dae ye like the idea ae cuddlin', ken? A mean we dinny need tae dae anythin' else.'

'It's all right, I feel fine. I mean whatever happens, I'll tell you if I don't want it to go on, OK?'

'Switch the lights oot, Grif, A'm gettin' embarrassed.'

Jone giggled and switched the lights off willingly. The loss of visual sensation loaded on the tactile sense and brought desire surging through Jone's body. An image came into her head that the room was a cave whose walls were dripping with honey. She longed to taste it.

By the light of the window now emerging they walked to the water bed, and moved to opposite sides of it. Luner sat down and took off her shoes and Jone sat down and looked at Luner for a moment. She was fuelled with a heat that made sparks shoot in darkness in her head like erupting volcanoes on an airless planet.

Then she followed Luner and began to take off her clothes. She glanced again over at Luner and saw her body in the dim light of the window, pale and firm, streamlined like a dolphin. She could almost burst now with desire, like a rocket firing but stuck on its launch pad. She lay down on the bed at last and then Luner joined her.

Their arms came round each other's lower backs and their hands on each other's skin were cold. They lay like that for quite a few minutes. Then Luner began to draw her hands up and down Jone's back and Jone copied her. It amazed Jone how soft the skin was. It was astonishing to discover that this softness was what she'd been missing in all these years of conditioning against touch. Her mind received the sensations from her fingertips like pictures from a probe exploring a distant planet. Her whole body was aroused with pleasure. The hands moved wider, neck, bottom, thighs. Then the kissing began and the pleasure became more intensely concentrated, as the tongues circled and the saliva flowed. It was like watching a stream run over all shapes and sizes of boulders, forming pools, fast waterfalls, deep channels or smooth films. The kissing seemed to go on forever.

Luner wrapped her legs round Jone's and after a while, Jone could not tell whose legs were whose. She was losing her sense of separate identity. Then when she came to herself again she could feel waves of affection flow out from her and the words 'I love you, I love you' floated through her mind. Luner moved over on top of her gently and began to move down to kiss Jone's neck and shoulders. A film of sweat was uniting their bodies, like twin foetuses in their amniotic fluid. Jone became aware of Luner's long black hair, lying over her skin and wanted to stroke it. She had a moment of loss of nerve. This was taking an initiative on her own, could she do it? She forced herself to begin and was very glad she had. The hair was soft and the movements her fingers could make endlessly different. Luner's head seemed so vulnerable, she wanted to protect it. Now Luner had moved down to Jone's left breast and was pulling and sucking the nipple. It was the highest point of pleasure yet. Euphoria concentrated like a spouting geyser. A groan came out of Jone. She had heard that people did this but never could have believed it would come out of her spontaneously.

Luner came back up, put her arm round Jone's neck and they were side by side again and embraced with warm affection. Jone had a moment of panic. Should she move now? No, she would feel too self-conscious. She began moving her hand again and found it moving to Luner's breast. Luner groaned a little. That was encouraging. Before she had time to think about it too much, she had moved her hand over the nipple and began to manipulate it. She felt it stiffen under her fingers and found that the same sensation of pleasure went into her head as when Luner was touching hers. Identity was lost again.

After a little while she moved her hands round to Luner's back and soon they were stroking and pressing each other more aggressively than before. Luner pushed a leg between Jone's, pressing her thigh against Jone's genitals and stroking Jone's left thigh with heavy pressure. Then she brought her hand round Jone's bottom, thrust it between her legs and touched her genitals from the back. Jone suddenly realised this area was soaking wet. She lay back and decided to leave the activity to Luner and just savour all the new sensations. Luner brought her hands round to the front. Her fingers moved round the lips of vagina and clitoris and sometimes going inside. It was as if she was moulding a clay pot.

Jone's ecstasy was focusing and changing quality from wallowing to climbing. As if she was going up the side of a mountain, a fierce beam of energy propelling her at her back. As Luner made faster strokes more concentrated round the clitoral area, Jone found her pelvis was moving up and down, trying to release something that was trapped. She wanted the release but she also wanted the climbing sensation to go on, for it felt it could mount to infinity. She felt like a nebula: climbing and thrusting like the spinning centre and at the same time hurtling free of herself like its trail of stars. The nebula spun faster, and became smaller and smaller, heavier and heavier, until suddenly pleasure turned to pain. Luner's fingers were pressing, hurting and she grabbed Luner's hand. Luner stopped at once and drew her arm up to Jone's back. Jone hugged her tightly and she felt a release as if she'd jumped from the peak of the mountain and her whole body spread out like a parachute, filled with warm air.

She floated back to earth. A detached saint inside said, 'There, you see, this crude genital stimulation can often be unsuccessful in achieving orgasm.' While her newborn Babylonian self replied: 'Two bodies wrapped together is the highest pleasure I have yet known because I have never felt so free from loneliness.' Now she began to think she must reciprocate, though she had no idea if she could do it. Her fingers moved towards Luner's genitals and the wetness rekindled the flame of desire. Luner grabbed her fingers and moved them for her, quite violently, in a hurry. She groaned wildly, then came in very little time at all.

Now Luner cuddled and kissed her lightly over her face. Jone wanted to say something but didn't know what. It was not made easier by her sense that Luner had no intention of saying anything. She put her arm around Luner's shoulders and Luner nestled into her, her head just below Jone's. Jone stroked the long hair and felt a rush of tenderness. A totally new kind of tenderness, bound up with bodies, the softness of them, the warmth of them, the vulnerability of them. Again she wanted to say something loving, but she couldn't. Why was it so difficult to speak? After long moments of trying to summon up the courage to say something, she turned to Luner, hoping for some encouragement and found she had fallen asleep. Jone smiled and lay back. She turned to look at her watch. Two hours had gone by in what seemed like minutes, and felt like light years. The light years distance from a cold dark moon in the galaxy of the Church to a warm wet blue-green planet in the galaxy of heresy.

18

Sunshine was flooding through the window when Jone woke up. She screwed her eyes against the light and reached up to her head. It felt like a metal sphere with nails driven in all over it. It took her a moment or two to realise she was somewhere different from where she usually was. She turned her head and started, at the sight of the other body in the bed. Luner was sound asleep, lying with her face towards Jone. Jone stared at the face she'd been attracted to for so long. She saw the spots, the pores. She heard the thick rattle of breathing through a gunjed up nose and the open mouth that drooped like a subnormal mutant's. Smooth skin and fine-drawn features had been replaced by misshapen blobs of flesh, awkward and ugly.

Jone drew back, frightened of touching the body. Revulsion surged through her consciousness. The day before tumbled into her mind with acute shame. The whole idiotic day, the demonic rampage, being forced to fight with those ugly stupid savages. Then the evening: how many injections of canethol had she taken? Enough to stagger through the evening in a stupefied trance and then, then, in fusion's name what had she done? Words came floating through her mind: 'You slug, slime, swamp, buttery, melting, mucus, when you speak you smell with the food you gorge'. She swung her legs to the floor and became dizzy and nauseous. She must have taken enough canethol (and she knew medically that must be a lot) to poison herself.

How stupid, how demonic, how inane. What on earth had made her think it had been the most wonderful day of her life? She cringed, her guts heaved. She stood up and ran to the excretan, vomited in the sink and then sat down to excrete a rush of liquid diarrhoea. When it was finished, she staggered, seeing stars in her head, to her medical store and injected antidotes. The digestive organs were calmed and the headache eased a little but emotionally she felt no better. She looked down at her naked body and recoiled from its stickiness.

She tiptoed back to the sleep-space, swooped up the pile of clothes, glanced at the body in the bed to check it still slept, and retreated to the shower. She wanted to wash away the night in a warm cleansing fountain, but it only increased her revulsion at the fantasy she'd been caught up in. To imagine (oh, it was painfully embarrassing to admit she'd even thought it) that she had exorcised all her disgust in the ten minutes of that song.

She crept silently back through the sleep-bay. What if Luner woke up? What if she reached up and tried to hug her? The nausea surged back. It wasn't the canethol, it was the depths of her disgust oozing into her consciousness. She went through to the kitchen, sat down and gazed up at the bright sky. She longed for her mind to fly away and leave her body and that other body, far behind.

'I am spirit spirit, you are flesh flesh. Noli me tangere, noli me tangere.'

The buzzer was going. She sprang up, startled, rushed through and switched on the viewer. It was the janitor, she looked apologetic. 'I'm sorry, Reverend Grifan, have A woken you up? A'm sorry but, d'you mind, A know its early but –'

'Just a minute –' and Jone unlocked the door. In a second it was flung wide open. The room was filled with alien creatures, three with white faces and black bodies, one with a white body. Jone almost fell back. Terror rose in her chest, like another alien creature, suddenly spurting into being inside. One of the black-bodied creatures and the white creature rushed straight through to the sleep-bay knowing exactly where they were going.

She heard Luner scream then instantly cease. She turned to see one of the black-bodied things raise something in front of her and then she really was falling. Her legs were turning to jelly, then her trunk, then arms. What was really happening? Was she dreaming or hallucinating? One of the creatures bent over her. Was it going to swallow her? Then she saw it had a face, a pale, ugly, malevolent face. It was an inquo. It had slugged her. The room was tumbling over. He was carrying her, her head upside down swinging against his back, into the sleep-bay. She could see his muscles under his tight fitting habit, rippling like slug-like creatures under the skin

The next thing she knew was that she was being lain out on the waterbed. She couldn't bear to look at Luner, the guilt at her thoughts just beforehand overwhelmed her. It was as if her own disgust had created these creatures as a kind of punishment. She could see that Luner had been slugged too. The person in white, who she now saw was female, had a scanner in her hand and was scanning Luner's finger's. Everything clicked into place at last. It was an investigation of carnal sin.

The Inquisition had received an accusation. Oh fusion, Skwyer last night! Surely not, who else? It had to be him. Why hadn't she thought of it? How stupid, how irresponsible. To be seen with an unbaptised female catachumen and imagine the rest of the world would think nothing of it. What an utter fool she was.

Her own trousers were being pulled down now, her uniform being opened. The three inquos stood behind the medical inquo, surveying Jone's nakedness like vultures, surveying her like a piece of rotten flesh, like a piece of meat. To Jone her slugged body did seem like a lump of flesh, but her mind spun in a vortex of horror and humiliation she could never have imagined before.

The white-coated female said, 'Not much point in doing her, she's had a shower. Never mind. We'll get it from the ethnic, I could still smell it on her fingers. It'll be no problem.' She dressed both of them, handling their bodies like sacks of vegetables. That done, she disappeared.

The black-clothed vultures remained. The one in the middle loomed closer. He was an officer. He leaned over them, his eyes penetrating them like burning needles.

'You filthy byres disgust me more than anybody. What's your problem then? Reverend Holesucker. What makes you have to crawl down the drains to lick the troj off little nik-rats' dubs to get your gratcher pumping? Can't get the pistons is that it? By grutag, you make me sick you saint byres that scream rape anytime a male gets a bit of natural acceleration. What you need is a few dry pistons rammed up you so hard there wouldn't be any sanctimonious piety pus left in you.'

Then he turned to Luner, 'And what about the little rat nik then?' He seized her hand, smelt her fingers and threw the arm back with a look of utter disgust and contempt. 'Do you really think you can get a bang with that bunch of worms wriggling around your hole? Or have you just been trying to crawl up out the slime, up the inside of the sanctified trousers have you? I reckon it needs a big shovel up it too, one that would get it crawling back to the moonpalace where it belongs. Getting plugged and pregnant from puberty on, that's what Plotinian souks have got a hole for.'

He stepped back, relishing the looks of total terror in the faces beneath him. Then he switched his voice to impersonal detachment, as if he had been following a routine. 'Take them down to the glider and then get back here and we'll search.'

One of the others said, 'Do you reckon it's heresy, sir?'

The officer curled his mouth, 'Heresy makes it sound special. I reckon this is just a clogged up waste-chute, needing to be flushed out.'

From the moment they were dragged out the building to the moment they entered the reception area of Inquisition HQ everything around Jone was a blur to her. She kept her eyes shut except when she was forced to walk and then they were fixed on the ground. She had never once looked directly at Luner, and Luner had never sought to gain her attention. She was obviously in as much of a state of shock as Jone was. Jone's emotions, in so far as she was aware of them, were a deep pit of fear and guilt, fear as a result of the arrest, guilt about everything that had gone before.

In the reception area they were met by Abbot Raze and Blane Milar, which only deepened the shock. Luner was taken off first and Blane went with her. Jone was taken by a female inquo into an interrogation room and was sat down in front of a table. On the other side of it was the Grand Inquisitor of Embra, Rev Mardik. In build and size he was like the Abbot, burly and athletic. In persona he was suave and cool.

He first of all informed her that she was being formally charged with the cardinal sin of carnal knowledge of an unbaptised ethnic. Then he proceeded to telling her he was here to find out whether she was a straightforward demoniac, needing to be sent off to a sanatorium immediately or whether she was a heretic, in which case she would be subjected to a public trial.

It didn't take the Inquisitor very long to decide she was too pathetic and naive to be a satanist, but the question of heresy was much more difficult to decide. As he knew (though the public would not know for some time), the Inquisition had already realised they were mistaken in thinking Yalida was mixed up with the satanist assassination of the Angel. But she had confessed to being a

Babylonian and the Inquisition leadership had already decided that it was time to wage some kind of extermination program on this heresy to prevent it taking root in Skosha. To the Inquisitor, the best way was to attack protestantism. In his experience wherever there was protestantism, heresy was hovering in the wings. And here was a perfect example: one of Plotin's fashionable new Abbot's pastors infected by an incipient case of Babylonianism. To put her on trial would be the most perfect way of discrediting Abbot Raze and his protestant new wave.

But of course, it wasn't that simple. The fashion that had brought Abbot Raze to Plotin emanated from Mission Control. The man had powerful friends. The Inquisitor would have to do it all strictly by the letter of the law, which meant an ontological screening. This was an analysis by a gawd in a laboratory, to decide the question with total objectivity.

Abbot Raze was now brought into the room. The procedure in ontological screening was that the subject had to dialogue for fixed periods of time with a control: someone of guaranteed Krischan sanity. The two were injectd with ecrephanerium (the same 'truth' drug Abbot NkDod had used for his 'confessions') and subjected to exactly the same neurograph analysis. At once the Abbot offered himself. He was desperate to find out what had happened to Jone. He was deeply distressed that he had not been able to prevent this happening. He was also fully aware of the threat posed to his mission by the prospect of a public trial, not for personal reasons, but because he could see protestantism in Embra would be set back years by it, and that would be a tragedy for Embra. The settlement in the hands of the Inquisitor's kind was not something any decent modern Krischan could contemplate even-mindedly. If he could guide the dialogue in any way to a sensible conclusion he would do it. And he had compassion for Jone too. Despite his anger, he would not have wanted anyone other than a satanist to be subjected to a public exposure of their whole life. She did not deserve to be destroyed in that way. The poor creature needed treatment in a Strylyan sanatorium and he would do his best to see that she got it. The Inquisitor readily agreed. If the Abbot thought he could manipulate the outcome of the screening he was in for a surprise. Jone was released on the Abbot's honour, pending the screening in three days' time.

All through the interview Jone had answered the questions with what seemed like a disembodied voice hovering in mid-air in front of her. Inside she was obsessed with her responsibility for Luner and what would happen to her. As she and the Abbot walked out she managed to ask him about her.

'She's being sent to a country monastery, we've seen to that, it'll be the best thing that's happened to her.'

At last Jone could lift her head above the pool of torment. If it was one of those liberal places, which most of them were, she could see Luner flourishing in it eventually. She raised her head for the first time to see Pallad coming towards her. It was like the sight of a mythomaniac angel. Jone almost fell and Pallad caught her. Jone went limp and Pallad put her arm tightly round Jone's back and walked her to the door. The Abbot strode round in front of them.

'Come home with me, Jone. You need looking after.' He was furious at the sight of a deviant saint, who was probably a major cause of Jone's problems, coming to whisk her away but he was also deeply concerned at the state she was in. Jone leaned her head on Pallad's shoulders and closed her eyes. Pallad looked firmly at the Abbot.

'She's coming with me,' and walked Jone out the door.

The ontological screening laboratory was one of the chapels of the cathedral. In it there was the gawd itself, the control room where the ontologist would observe the subjects through a one-way screen, refreshment area and the analysis room. A fine holomorph, furnished very sparely with Embra's best mathematics. It was geared to putting the subjects at their ease, by being both mathematical and bland.

When Jone and the Abbot walked in, neither of them felt at ease in the slightest. Both of them wanted the same result, for Jone to be labelled demoniac, but the sheer smooth professionalism of the place made both of them lose confidence in their hope of controlling what went on.

The ontologist followed them in. He was of medium height with a round face and squat features. A very down-to-earth appearance and manner for a man in charge of one of the most sophisticated pieces of equipment in the Kingdom. His homeliness was partly due to his complete faith in his gawd.

'As I'm sure you know by now, you're given an injection of Erph which opens you up. Unless you've some pathological blockage, you'll speak your mind, express your opinions and emotions freely, so I must start by emphasising that what goes on in this lab is totally confidential. As soon as the verdict is given the data is completely depersonalised and stored away. No one has direct access to it, not even me. Unless there's a spy hidden around somewhere, and I'm sure there isn't, there's no possibility of its getting out. Of course, you may think I'm a spy. On that point you'll have to trust me. Do you think you can?'

Both Jone and the Abbot nodded. They had no interest in complicating things and he seemed a man to be trusted.

'OK, well, the next point I want to make is about the gawd itself. I think there's a mistaken idea that we say the gawd is pure objectivity. Well that's nonsense. As a theologian I know there's no such thing as pure objectivity. But apart from that, the gawd is making a value judgement, not just observations. So the obvious question is what's its criteria in making the judgement? Now you may well have heard people say it serves the Kingdom as a whole, but even that's not true. It's not the Kingdom as such that it serves, but the ultimate goal of the Kingdom: the creation of Almyty Gawd. That's its standard, what serves the purpose best. Now all of us know the Kingdom is far from ideal, so what serves the Kingdom as it is now isn't necessarily identical to what serves Almyty Gawd. Do you understand? I hope that reassures you both. Because of that I think you will agree it's going to be more objective than any human judge could be.'

With that, neither of them could disagree, but neither of them felt comforted. Jone's reaction was: but I'm an atheist, I don't believe in the goal of Almyty Gawd, doesn't that make me obviously a heretic from the start? The Abbot's reaction was: what if Almyty Gawd requires this heresy to be publicly ridiculed. What do I know about the deep functioning of that awesome creation? What does its cosmic data store care about the interests of two small individuals? Neither Jone nor the Abbot spoke their thoughts.

'Well,' continued the ontologist, 'if you don't want to say what your thoughts are on this now, perhaps you'll want to take them into consideration when it's switched on. Remember your interests are served by feeding it as much data as you can. It will make estimates of your unconscious mind of course, but it has no complete access to it. Even with a deinhibitor you are still being what you want to be, because in a sense we always are.'

'What exactly does Erph do?' said the Abbot crisply. Neither he nor Jone were in the mood for philosophical contemplation on the nature of human consciousness.

'Well, it inhibits fear, that's the main thing. It's three different agents rolled into one. One to inhibit fear, one to heighten emotion, and one to increase your ability to articulate. So the emotion doesn't overwhelm logical thinking.'

The ontologist saw the worried look on Jone's face and understood it. If she had wanted to play things deliberately to get a verdict of demonia, the Erph would spoil that.

'It's really no use holding back,' he said sympathetically. 'The less you say, the more likely the gawd is to give an insufficient data verdict, and then send you back to the Inquisitor.'

Jone slumped back resentful of the ontologist's perceptiveness. 'Let's get on with it,' she said and the Abbot agreed.

The ontologist deactivated Jone's and the Abbot's souls, administered the drugs, and fitted on the electrode helmets. It took only a few minutes for the Erph to take effect. Not that either Jone or the Abbot were conscious of its happening. The emotions welled up and took over their minds, not blind emotion but with crystal-clear understanding of why it came up.

The Abbot was first off the mark.

'When I think that in one meaningless, thoughtless act of carnal indulgence you could destroy the best chance there is for spiritual renewal in this colony, I find it impossible to maintain the pity I should feel for a sick mind. If you had become a Babylonian heretic why didn't you come to me and say you no longer believed in our mission and wanted to resign? Instead you just go ahead and show your contempt for canon law, with this heroic act of sabotage, whose only possible effect will be the destruction of protestant mission, not orthodox reaction. You've been a protestant. I thought you were a protestant. You know as well as I do that orthodox reactionaries like the Inquisitor say, "Protestantism breeds heresy." And now he has a living example handed to him on a plate. Here we are, both of us, at the mercy of this machine, deciding the fate of protestantism at this time in Plotin, and all because one demoniac takes it into her head to be a Babylonian?'

'I didn't have carnal knowledge of Luner as an act of Babylonian-ism. I wasn't even sure what I believed at the time –'

'In that case, why do we need to carry on?' the Abbot turned to the blanked window into the control room. 'The subject is freely admitting a complete lack of control of her id circuits,' and he turned back to Jone, 'or are you trying to tell me you were completely innocent of the consequences of the action? Which frankly seems equally demonic?'

The stream of Jone's anger reversed inward to become guilt, 'I didn't think I would be reported.' Then she remembered Skwyer and those laughing women and the stream turned out again. 'I don't think I would have been if Reverend Skwyer hadn't been worried about protecting himself from being caught out in carnal activities.' The Abbot was phased for a moment. He had been angry at Reverend Skwyer for going straight to the Inquisition, though he hadn't said this, given that Skwyer was perfectly within his rights. Now he was suddenly faced with the possibility that Skwyer had a motive in not going to him.

'What do you mean? Are you saying he was worried you would report him for carnal sin? That's a dangerous accusation, what evidence do you have for it?'

'He was with two females. Luner said she'd seen the females at the moonpalace with saints. No, it's not evidence for a courtroom, but I believe Luner.'

The Abbot was relieved, 'You mean Reverend Skwyer was with an ethnic Krischan female. Oh, yes indeed. He has an amorade, a very nice young girl. I've seen him with her at the Hedonarea. I've no doubt that's where they were going, and in the unlikely event they were going to indulge in carnal knowledge, you just might remember that carnal knowledge of baptised ethnics may be ethically dubious, but it is not against canon law –'

'Oh yes, I see, the fact that Luner just happens to be unbaptised, though she's just as emotionally mature as anyone else I know, makes me a sinner, and Skwyer not.'

'I'm hardly going to accept that Ned Skwyer is a sinner on the testimony you've produced.'

'Luner's word may be of no value to you. But it's of as much value to me as yours or Ned Skwyer's.'

'Look, I see no point in getting bogged down in this. Luner even on your admission didn't say she knew Ned Skwyer had been at the palace, and that is the point, the details of these females' past is totally irrelevant.'

'I know perfectly well it isn't concrete evidence. I still believe it's true. I still believe that was his motive for contacting the Inquisition.'

'It seems you base most of your behaviour on instincts and feelings, quite uncorroborated by any facts or tempered at the very least by common sense.'

'I'm not going to win any war of words with you here. I know that. You're so much more experienced at domination than I am, I'm sure –'

'Oh Jone, Jone. I don't want to just wage a war.'

'No, you want to prove I'm demonic.'

'Yes, yes, of course that's true. I believe you are and I very much hope the gawd will believe it too, but I also want to understand you. I want the gawd to understand. After all it's not just making a verdict, it's also giving an analysis of where you are, how you are what you are –'

'How I'm to be treated as a demoniac.'

'Jone, forget the machine. I genuinely want to know. Why, why did you do it? Why do you think you did it?'

'It's strange when something happens, something quite simple, that changes your life. It's like you've crossed a river and the world looks different from the other side. When the Church says that it's a sin for two people, without harm to anyone else, to express affection for each other by physical contact, then I say the Church is wrong. I wasn't a Babylonian before, but I am now.'

'I think maybe you are innocent after all. It seems that preserving our elite from the reality of pagan life backfires on us. They take to it, like BA primitives took to alcohol, one taste and their will was destroyed. You really believe that what you did was as simple as that? "Expressing affection", that must be the oldest and still the silliest of self-delusions. Whatever it is that's infecting your brain, it's clearly burnt out sense. I don't deny you and Luner have affection for one another, but please don't try and tell me that in having carnal knowledge of her, you weren't also expressing lust, otherwise why on earth would you express affection through carnality? When you know perfectly well that transceiving expresses emotional affinity, without the ugly disfigurement of idism.'

'Yes, that's what I was indoctrinated to believe, but I don't believe it any more. I don't see that there's any real spiritual difference between transceiving and expressing affection through sex.'

195

'I find it difficult to believe what I'm hearing, I really do. With one flick of the hand, you dismiss the whole accumulated wisdom of the Church, and you assert that sex – sex of all things! – is no different from transceiving. I'm having real problems taking this seriously and I don't mean to be patronising about it. Let me try and get this clear. Are you saying that you reject the Church's teaching on idism? Are you saying that what the Church says about the Kayos of the world coming from the Kayos of lust and aggressions within is completely wrong?'

'I – I suppose so.'

'You suppose so! For fusion's sake, Jone, I'm trying to understand your thinking and you don't even know what it is yourself! Look, if you believe in sex, then I presume you don't believe idism is the source of evil?'

'No, I don't think so –'

'Then what is the source of evil?'

'I don't know. I'm not setting myself up as the Archangel Michael with the answers to the origin of everything. I just don't happen to think he found the answer either.'

'If you haven't got an answer and he hasn't got the answer, who on earth has?'

'I don't think having "the answer" is the point. I just believe the Babylonians are going on the right path and the Church is going on a wrong one, and I believe that because of my own experience not because I set myself up as an Archangel surveying the whole of human history –'

'All right, tell me. Tell me what this right path is, that the Babylonians are going on?'

'It's the path for some of us. It's a heresy, and heresy means choosing your own path. Freely choosing your own path in alliance with others who want to reach the same goal. Babylonians and Neronians are in alliance, because they're federations of small communities of people trying to live in equality. I suppose if I have to say what the source of evil is, I believe it's inequality and I don't know where it came from in the first place. All I know is that only those who are genuinely struggling against it in their lives are the ones who are on the right path.'

'Jone, what is the whole Church about but the struggle for equality? What is Almyty Gawd but absolute equality, through the unity of all minds in one universal mind?'

'I don't believe the Church is struggling for equality, that's exactly what I don't believe and that's exactly what I've been finding out ever since I came to Plotin, I've been finding out what a gigantic lie the Church's commitment to the oneness of all is. The real aim of the Church is to maintain its hierarchy, with the male imperialists at the top and everyone else perfectly graded all the way to the very bottom: and who's at the very bottom? The females of Fairmead, and that's the way the Church aims to keep it forever and forever. And the cleverest way they've found of achieving their aims is all this fancy garbage about brain circuits.

'I don't believe in all the Church labels of what is idist and rational anymore. Because I don't believe in the Church's motives for using those labels anymore. The Church calls what ethnics do idist so that it can excuse itself for not letting ethnics have equality. If it didn't use what it calls idism it would be something else. You ask me if I've now decided I'm in favour of idism and I can't answer it because I don't know what idism is any longer. They say it's lust and aggression, but I don't see those as being evil in themselves. I don't see that either of them inevitably leads to violence and cruelty. Oh yes, I've seen violent and cruel ethnics, but the worst and most terrible violence and cruelty is the violence and cruelty of the Church. The violence that keeps the ethnics in the habitats, keeps them deprived of all the luxuries we take for granted, and deprived of the right to have power or rationality or whatever other excuses they can find. In the BA days their excuse was scarcity of resources, now we have fusion and a full supply of energy that'll last as long as the planet earth. So what do they do? Replace that excuse with something else, so now it's rationality instead of resources that's scarce, because the philosophy hasn't changed one particle. Keep some people with some of the power, the rest with less and less, grade by grade, and that is what the Church is all about.'

The Abbot sat back, thoughtful at last, now she had made a point, a real point. At last, he felt challenged. Now he had something he had to answer.

'I don't deny that I'm part of a hierarchy. I don't deny I'm one of the people with a bit more power than a lot of other people, but I do categorically deny that that is my goal and aim in life, to keep things that way forever. Yes, the Church is very corrupt, why else am I a protestant? But I'm struggling for equality and I use the structure of the Church I struggle within, because I don't believe there is an alternative outside it. Oh you can, I'm sure, get very eloquent on the sins of the Church. They are many, I know.

'But you talk about Babylon and Rome trying to achieve equality as if they were the only places it was being tried. What rubbish. Haven't you been to one of the protestant monasteries? That's exactly what they try to do and they do it remarkably well. I know that from personal experience. But what's your personal experience of Babylon and Rome? Propaganda chapters? Oh Jone, what cloud has your brain floated off on? What on earth do you want us to do? Bring down the whole structure of the Church and replace it with millions of little encampments? Haven't we heard of that somewhere before? Haven't you heard of something called the Kayos? Haven't you heard the world was made up of small communities then and look what happened? The sexualism of the matriarchies and the machophrenia of the Barbarian Hordes.

'What reason could there be for that not to happen again? Look at all the conditioning the Church tries to give to wean males from machophrenia and yet still there are deep gender inequalities. So how are you going to change it? Why do you think we do look on sex with such deep suspicion? Because sex was the norm in the Kayos: sex and rape. And the only thing that keeps us all from going back there is the hierarchy that you so revile and seek to destroy. You can't make people equal by throwing them into an anarchy and saying right, get on with it. It doesn't work, it's been tried and the only people it's ever worked with are small groups of highly developed spiritual people. It doesn't work in a world-wide society. At the present level of development, without hierarchy you have Kayos. We have to develop people beyond that state and that's what I've dedicated my life to, giving those deprived of grace every opportunity to acquire it, and that's what protestant mission is trying to do.

'Oh, I know the ideal is a long way off. I don't believe anyone denies that, but I don't believe there's any alternative, certainly not yours. Certainly not through committing an act of sin like this, the only likely result of which will be the destruction of the only real force for change in Embra and a victory for the forces of orthodoxy.'

'Sin? Sin? You still talk about sin. It's not my fault this has happened, stop blaming me. I can understand your concern that what you believe in is threatened, but I refuse to take the blame for it. If I was allowed to do what I want to do, what I don't believe harms anyone, I would never have been arrested and there wouldn't have been any scandal. When I think of what happened when I was arrested and I hear you go on about my sin, that's when my blood boils. You talk about the corruption of the Church as if it was some small cancer that just needs removing to make it healthy again, but I don't believe it, and not because I've got some grand historical theory about the causes of the Kayos, but because of the evidence of my own eyes. Three nights ago I spent a night in the arms of a friend, being close and loving, and in the morning. I woke up to find my mansion desecrated by the invasion of malevolent strangers. Our bodies treated like carcasses, our minds raped by savage verbal abuse, yes rape, that's exactly what it was, and it still makes me scream with pain when I think about it. In truth I believe he would have carnally violated us if he could. The only thing that stopped him was probably the thought that I might be smart enough to demand a medical examination. Not that I believe that would be much worse, the verbal rape was horrific enough –'

The Abbot coloured, he was shocked. He found it difficult to believe, but he could not disbelieve her. The depth of her feeling was too convincing.

'Jone, if you really were abused in this way, you should have told me –'

'And what could you do? Go and tell the Inquisitor and he would parade his sergeant in front of you who'd deny it all? Then who would you believe? After all who's going to take the word of a demoniac sex-freaker?'

'Jone, I do believe what you say happened but don't you see, this is what I've been talking about, how sex and rape are found together. Sex provokes that kind of hatred in spiritually underdeveloped males.'

'Spiritually underdeveloped? Does that include your ministers, your protestant ministers? This isn't the first rape I've experienced. A few weeks ago I was raped in a visional by one of your favourite protestant ministers.'

The Abbot groaned, 'Raped? Oh, Jone, Jone. I know as well as anyone that the muddy pools of carnality are around everywhere, even in the best of us. But I'm sorry, in this case I don't believe you. In a visional? You would have as much control over what went on. You reacted against it? Aren't I right? Yes, I think so. So it brought you face to face with your own sexualism. Isn't that what happened? You talk about the Church using labels. Aren't you using labels to project malevolence on others because you can't face your own illness?'

He could have caught her in his net if she hadn't been prepared. Oh, how grateful she was to Pallad for all the talking she'd done in the last forty-eight hours.

'Illness, sin, it always comes back to the same thing, sex. Tiamat, Kayos, rape, Luner's misbehaviour in the Abbey, my sin, sex is the root of all evil. Kayos barbarians or Church archbishops, the one thing they all hate is sex. Blame it on us, and you keep your power forever.'

'This useless argument is going on for ever, round in circles, that I can believe.' The Abbot slumped back wearily, and Jone put her head in her hands. A light appeared in the screen. The ontologist's voice came through the speaker.

'I can ask the gawd for an interim verdict.' The two subjects looked at one another, feeling, despite everything, instantly allied in their trap, and nodded. The ontologist came back: 'Actually it has a final verdict.'

Up in the hills of the wilderness, the night after Jone's ontological screening, a photoplane sat waiting for its final load of passengers before it took off. It sat there in complete darkness, for its presence wasn't known to the Kingdom authorities. It was a 'pirate ship', one of Sewer City's planes whose main function was to transport Sewer City's criminal bosses (the 'economists') to and fro on their business. A few places were always reserved for heretics in trouble, the economists' form of home charity.

Syny was always a pirate ship port of call, and this night there were quite a few passengers bound there. Among these were Rannan, Lazel and Luner. At about 24.00 hours, two hours before take-off, these three were sitting rigidly and silently in a state of fearful anticipation. The last passengers would soon be walking up the path. Had Pallad and the others succeeded in their plan to smuggle Jone to the plane in secret? If Jone had been judged demoniac, it would be fairly easy (assuming she'd agreed to come). If she had been judged a heretic, she would only be coming if she'd been put on honour. But would the Abbot have agreed to that? If he hadn't, who else would have taken it on?

Everyone, including Jone, had been hoping (or rather assuming, since the alternative was too grim to contemplate) that she would be judged a demoniac. Rannan's and Lazel's anxiety was by no means due to uncomplicated sympathy for Jone. The Yalida concert débâcle had made Rannan and Lazel's minds up. Babylon was the only choice. They were terrified of the Inquisitor's proposed clampdown on heresy. A future of endless compromise as minor servants of the Kingdom, without any chance of at least feeling they could struggle against it, was a tunnel with no light at the end.

As for Jone, they were happy to have her along with them, if she was prepared to take a stand alongside them as a sexualist saint. But then how would it be in Babylon? They had all seen the chapter on the ethnic saint splits among the Babylonians. It wouldn't be up to them to support her if she wasn't tough enough to take it. Sure, they had sympathy for her. But they weren't prepared to sacrifice their lives for hers. If she was judged a heretic and escaped, they risked getting arrested. And however hard the trial was for Jone, they would fare far worse at the hands of the Inquisition than she ever would. Someone would make a fuss about her, but nobody would make a fuss about them.

Still, they wanted her to come, for Luner's sake. But even that was ambiguous. Pallad, at Jone's request, had already told Luner how Jone had felt, that morning before the arrest. If she was to come to Babylon it was only fair to make it clear to Luner she could not come as her amoradon. It was fair to tell her, but it was them, not Jone, who had had to cope with Luner's feelings of rejection. Yet Luner still wanted Jone to come, despite the rejection. She still believed in Jone. Luner hadn't said it, but they were very frightened that, if Jone didn't appear in that last passenger load, Luner would rush off the plane.

And their fear was not unreasonable. Luner was refusing to say how she felt, because she was confused too. She knew the romantophilia was dead, but she loved Jone and she had, in truth, no idea what she would do if Jone didn't turn up. She shut her mind to the possibility and clung to the belief that the verdict would be demonia.

There was a sound of people outside, the last passenger load had arrived. Everyone crowded to the window, but it was pointless, the sky was clouded over. They would have to wait till the hatch opened. It opened. One, two, three people. Luner jumped and grabbed Rannan's arm.

'It's NkCroom!'

Rannan gasped, 'A don't believe it.'

'A do,' said Luner, remembering vividly his tale of the visit to Ur. He was with a young man, someone both Rannan and Luner recognised as one of last year's baptisms. If they hadn't been so agitated they would have roared with laughter. But a strange non-logical optimism seized Luner, if he was here, she would be here, because she had to be. It was a mythomaniac sense of providence.

She was about the last one to come on. But she was there. She saw them almost at once and walked across to them. No one rushed to hug her. Not just because they knew her mental state but because they could not understand the odd smile on her face. Everyone sat down and waited. At last she spoke.

'Well, you don't have to worry about the Inquo chasing us. I've been sent here officially, in secret of course.'

Rannan and Lazel grabbed each other in panic. What did she mean? They were all going to a sanatorium? Jone smiled reassuringly, understanding their look.

'Don't worry, you're going to Babylon, and so am I.'

She waited for them to settle. 'You see, the ontologist did explain to us that the gawd was acting in the interest of Almyty Gawd, not the Kingdom. I didn't think there was any difference, but it seems there is, or again maybe there isn't. At any rate, the gawd judged I was a heretic, but I must be free, to quote, "live out my heretical ideal without endangering the present stability of the Kingdom, while still being able to make a contribution, through filtering its ideas into protestantism, to the Data Store of Almyty Gawd". So here I am, bundled off without even the Inquisitor knowing, free to be a heretic, in the desert.'

'Almyty Gawd!' said Lazel, 'The grutij clever soggert. Keepin' us ootae harm's way, filin' our little chips intae his data bank. He's got the whole grutij world in his hands.'

She had said it all. Jone smiled in empathy, 'Takes the excitement out of getting away from it all, doesn't it?'

For Rannan and Lazel it felt like a kick in the face. All their wonderful dreams of the new frontier of atheism crumbled into a little spot on the dub of Almyty Gawd. Luner could see the irony in her head, but her heart was doing cartwheels that she couldn't stop, but she did her best not to show it in her face. Who cared about religion! She was going to be with Grif and Rannan.

They sat in gloomy silence for a while until the faint strains of 'Astral Travelling' percolated through from the studio at the other end of the plane. Rannan turned to Lazel and said with bitter humour, 'Let's go an' get launched an hae a dance, looks like that's all we're good for, eh?' They turned and smiled at the others. Jone said, 'I'd like to talk to Luner.' They nodded and went off.

Jone and Luner looked at one another, and Almyty Gawd and his Kingdom faded into the background. All the complexity of feeling that had been hidden under her Krischan conditioning: the longing for simple intimate physical love, the carnal desire, and the disgust, which she knew was hatred of herself, all of it began to stir in the darkness of Jone's melting iron core. She was becoming giddy, nauseous. She had to say something.

'I've got a lot of things in myself to work out, I feel like everything that's happened in this past week's been like the descent into Venus, burned and compressed by gasses into a pile of ash inside. D'you know what I mean?'

'A think so, Grif. Dinny worry aboot sex an' that, as far as A'm concerned.' She turned away embarrassed and changed the subject. 'A'm gontae miss Geever an' the gang, but A'd've no had them in the monastery either. In Babylon A'll still have Rannan an' you, as a pal, ken –'

'I hope so, but you know what the chapter said about ethnic/saint splits. That's something else the gawd said, "Desert communities are harmless because they tear themselves apart."'

Luner was suddenly filled with the angry inspiration, 'Grutag over this Almyty Gawd drid, keepin' us in the desert. A'm goin' back tae Plotin, A promised Geever as soon as A've done a bit more growin' up and got masel a few indoctrinations, A'm goin' back. A'm no stayin' in the desert the restae ma life. A'm goin' back. A'm no gontae be a chip in anybody's data store. The only gawd A'm gontae be part of is one that's made up ae people wi legs an' arms an' muscle an' blood and minds of their own an' Am gontae fight fur it till ma coronary organ stops circulatin'.'

Jone laughed and wanted to reach out and hug Luner but she was still too desperately frightened of her instincts. She turned to a window. 'The plane's moving, look up there, it's Venus.' The planet twinkled momentarily in all the spectrum of colours and they imagined the snakes of the winds.

Someone was singing behind them, a weird BA kind of song. They turned. Luner groaned good-humouredly, 'It's Mary, the auld Krischan mythomaniac, she's always wanderin' aboot the streets. She's no comin' tae Babylon, surely.'

The old woman was staggering straight towards them, grinning a toothless grin. Her eyes were shining with the fanatic gleam of the mythomaniac. As she came up, her foul smell filled Jone's nostrils, making her retch. But there was a hypnotic power in her looks that stopped Jone telling the old woman to go away. She leaned over them. 'Gie us a bit money, hen, and A'll gie ya a prophecy.' It was ridiculous. Jone giggled, embarrassed and a little frightened. As the woman bent down, the grease on her thick, matted hair glinted in the colours of the spectrum in the ceiling light.

Jone whispered to Luner, 'I haven't got any money.' Luner giggled and said, 'Maybe she'll like these,' and she took out a syringe and a tube of canethol. The old woman snatched it up and put it in one of the many pockets in one of the many torn jackets that haphazardly covered her. 'Now pit oot a hand in front of ye.' The two obeyed, stifling their ambivalent laughter. She seized Jone's arm, put a piece of paper on her palm and closed the hand down on Luner's hand. A strange shockwave vibrated through Jone. It was as if she was transported back to the night of the concert. Her negativity vanished and love, not romantophilia, but something else without a name of its own, was pouring into her from the clasped hands. Jone and Luner looked at one another and Jone said, 'I've got a feeling we'll both go back to Embra.' They stared at one another, sharing the mystery of what was happening. Both of them simultaneously looked back out of the window at Venus. This time they were convinced they could see the serpents. After a moment or two, they unclasped their hands. There no longer seemed to be any desperate need to touch. Jone saw the piece of paper and she realised they'd forgotten the old woman and turned round. She had disappeared. There was writing on the paper. It said:

Though the seed is tiny and trampled underfoot
It will grow to be the greatest of trees
Blessed are the poor, for theirs is the kingdom of God.